GIRL IN THE GRAVE

C.J. CROSS

LIQUID MIND PUBLISHING

Copyright © 2022 by C.J. Cross.
All rights reserved. No part of this publication may be copied, reproduced in any format, by any means, electronic or otherwise, without prior consent from the copyright owner and publisher of this book.

Liquid Mind Publishing
This is a work of fiction. All characters, names, places and events are the product of the author's imagination or used fictitiously.

ALSO BY C.J. CROSS

<u>Dana Gray Mysteries</u>

Girl Left Behind

Girl on the Hill

Girl in the Grave

Stay up to date with C.J. Cross's new releases and download her **free** Dana Gray Prequel, *Girl Awakened* by heading to the link:

PROLOGUE

Vega

She walked through the busy terminal toward her gate. He continued to watch. He had to be sure she boarded the plane. He'd stacked the deck perfectly. Soon the game would begin. She was the catalyst he'd been waiting for.

1

Despite the frigid November air, Dana Gray was glad to be back in D.C.

Five months on the road was grueling, though she still stood by her decision to publish. Sharing the Priory of Bones manuscript was the right thing to do; for her, for her profession, for the world. Knowledge was meant to be shared—something she and her publisher actually agreed on.

One lecture turned into two and before she knew it, a few speaking engagements snowballed into a full-fledged book tour. Thirty-six lectures in ten countries in five months.

She'd never been so happy to return to the comforts of her own home. The orderly quiet of her office three stories below the Smithsonian was calling to her, but oddly it wasn't her first stop.

Dana strode across the icy parking lot toward the J. Edgar Hoover Building. It'd been almost six months since she'd last seen Jake Shepard. They hadn't left things on the best of terms, but he'd been right to tell her to figure out what she wanted.

All her time away had given her ample opportunity to think. The conclusion she'd come to: being alone was overrated. Working with Jake and the FBI had proven it was nice to have backup from time to time. Perhaps there was room in her life to let someone in. The right someone. She couldn't say with absolute certainty Jake was that someone, but it was worth finding out.

Her work would always be important to her. Shining light on the mysteries of the occult was a calling she believed in. The last few months demonstrated how vital her research was. Publishing her findings on the world's most secret society was not only noteworthy, but it would hopefully save others from being manipulated by them. Others like Meredith Kincaid.

That was another stop Dana planned to make now that she was back in D.C.

Meredith was still at St. Elizabeth's. Even with the best attorneys money could buy, she'd spend the rest of her life in a padded cell. That didn't mean Dana would forget about the girl she'd once called her best friend.

Meredith was part of the reason Dana decided to publish. She didn't want the Priory of Bones to steal anyone else's future. Absently, Dana's finger found the ladybug charm on her keychain, rubbing it for luck. She kept it as a reminder of what she was fighting for.

The elevator dinged, and Dana exited onto Jake's floor. Right away her eyes landed on Margot. It seemed the last few months had changed the receptionist's life as well.

"Dr. Gray!" Margot put down her yogurt cup and blinked at Dana in surprise. "Is Jake expecting you?"

The glittering wedding rings on Margot's finger caught Dana's eye, but it was the receptionist's very pregnant stomach that left Dana speechless as she tried to do the math. "How far along are you?"

Margot grinned, resting her bejeweled hand on her swollen belly. "Almost six months. Can you believe it?" She took Dana's stunned silence as an invitation to continue babbling. "It came as a shock to me, too. But it's true what they say; sometimes you find the thing you've been looking for was right under your nose all along."

Dana felt like she'd just done three tequila shots on an empty stomach. She was too late. It'd taken her analytical mind too long to come to the conclusion that she wanted Jake in her life.

This was her fault. He'd told her he wouldn't wait, and she'd practically pushed Jake into Margot's arms before she left. She had no one to blame but herself.

The cell phone on Margot's desk rang, and she answered. "Hey, baby. Can you hang on a sec? Jake's got a guest I need to take care of."

Blood whooshed in Dana's ears, as realization tore through her like a bullet. The baby wasn't Jake's. Margot and Jake weren't together!

Margot pressed the phone to her chest, grinning as she reached for the desk phone to call Jake. Dana caught her hand. "Actually, I think I'll surprise him."

2

"So what do you think?"

Agent Jake Shepard looked across his desk at Jo Walsh. He hadn't been expecting his dumplings to come with a side of bombshell. Jo picked up on that.

"I know it's a big decision, but this is a once in a lifetime opportunity for me. I mean, it's HRT. Not many people get that call."

"I know. But it's on the other side of the country."

"It's Colorado, Jake. Not Siberia. Besides, the FBI has a field office in Denver. They'd be happy to have you."

He put down his water bottle. "You already looked into it?"

Jo's cheeks flushed, betraying the cool demeanor she always exuded. "Look, I know this is new, but we're good together, right?"

He nodded slowly.

"So this just feels like the next step."

In his mind, the next step was letting her leave a toothbrush at his place. Moving to Denver with a woman he'd been seeing for a few months? That was a fucking cliff jump.

"Nothing needs to be decided right away."

He swallowed. "When do you need an answer?"

"HRT knows I'm tied up with this case."

"It could take a while."

"I can be patient." She leaned across his desk, her long blonde ponytail swaying like a pendulum. "But Jake, I know what I want, and I'm ready to go after it. You need to take a look in the mirror and ask yourself the same question." Her fingers caressed his jawline, nails scraping across his scruff. "And maybe invest in a better razor," she teased, her thumb tracing his lower lip before she kissed him.

She wasn't playing fair. That mouth of hers could get her anything she wanted, and she knew it. She grabbed his collar, deepening the kiss. Her tongue swept his, erasing all his objections to her plan.

The sound of his door opening pulled them apart. Seeing who was standing there was like plunging into an ice bath.

"Dana?" Jake stood abruptly, tie askew, heart pounding. Even though she was the one who'd shown up unannounced she seemed as shocked as he was to be standing face-to-face. Walking in on him groping another FBI agent probably hadn't helped.

"No way!" Jo was standing, too. "You're Dr. Dana Gray."

Dana finally broke their staring contest and turned to look at Jo. "You know who I am?"

"You're sort of a legend around here. Librarian-detective who took down a serial killer and a secret society." Jo walked toward Dana, hand outstretched. "I'm Agent Joanna Walsh, but everyone calls me Jo. I really enjoyed your book, by the way."

Dana blinked. "You read it?"

"Figured it'd help me get some insight on my new partner here." Jo thumbed at Jake over her shoulder. "Speaking of, if you could not mention you walked in on us sharing more than lunch, that'd be great. The FBI hasn't joined the twenty-first century when it comes to workplace romance."

Dana's eyes were on Jake again. He felt like he'd just been caught cheating. He reminded himself he wasn't doing anything wrong. She'd had her chance. "What are you doing here, Dana?"

"I just wanted to let you know I was back and see if …" she trailed off, looking at Jo again.

Jo's pale green eyes sparked with excitement. "Wait! Did you come to help us with the Card Killer?"

"Jo." Warning laced Jake's voice.

"What? I'm not telling her anything the media hasn't shared. Vultures," Jo muttered.

"Anyway, I would be honored to have you assist, Dr. Gray."

Dana frowned. "I'm not sure Agent Holt would sign off on that."

"Then it's a good thing he doesn't have to." Jo smirked. "Holt retired."

Dana's warm brown eyes filled with questions. "Who took his spot?"

"I did," Jenkins answered, walking into Jake's office. "And I'd love to have you on board considering forensics just identified a significant change in pattern that puts this case in your wheelhouse."

Assistant Director Remi Jenkins held out a folder. Jo grabbed it, flipping it open as Jake joined the three women standing in the middle of his office with trepidation. "What kind of change?"

"The last victim wasn't left with an ordinary playing card stuffed down his throat." Jenkins pointed a manicured finger to a photo inside the folder.

Dana moved in closer, the scent of her perfume taking Jake back to the last time she'd been in his office. He shut down the memory, focusing on the evidence in front of him.

He stared at the photograph of the badly decomposed card. At first glance, it was easy to see it was larger than the others, but that wasn't a major change. "Playing cards come in all different shapes and sizes, Jenks."

"True, but this isn't a playing card."

Jake squinted, angling his neck to try to make out the design. "Then what is it?"

Dana sucked in a breath, her eyes widening. "The Tower." She looked at the group. "It's a tarot card."

Jenkins snapped the folder shut, grinning at Dana. "Exactly. Looks like you came back to D.C. just in time."

3

"Shepard, Walsh, get Dr. Gray up to speed on the case while I'll get her consulting status reinstated."

Dana tried to argue, but Jenkins breezed out of the room, her cell phone already to her ear.

The sound of moving furniture drew Dana's attention back to the office. Jo was dragging another chair over to Jake's desk. She marched around to the other side and keyed something into his laptop. A moment later she was spinning the screen toward them.

Dana did her best to ignore how comfortable Jo seemed in Jake's office. The beautiful female agent exuded confidence. If Dana hadn't walked in on her practically climbing over Jake's desk to kiss him, she might even admire the woman's bravado. But thanks to her unfortunate timing, Dana was now preoccupied imagining the other pieces of office furniture Jo's long legs might've straddled.

Jake took one of the chairs, but Dana chose to remain standing.

"This is our first vic," Jo announced. She sat on the edge of Jake's desk so she could point at the image on the laptop screen. It was a close up of a severed head. "Keller Kent. Professional execution. Single bullet to the brain."

Jo switched to a new image. Another gruesome decapitation. "This is victim number two. Azi Udo. Same cause of death. Both known members of Nigerian TOC."

Jake spoke up when he saw Dana's confusion. "Transnational Organized Crime."

"Right, pardon my acronyms," Jo added.

Dana's shoulders tensed. "Organized crime? Like the mob?"

"Yes, but we're not talking Sopranos," Jo answered. "This is the dawn of a new mafia. Drugs, arms, human trafficking. On an international level."

Dana's gaze landed on Jake. "I don't understand. You don't work mob cases."

"I do," Jo replied. "My experience with the FBI's organized crime division landed this case in my lap, literally."

"The head was mailed to Jo's office," Jake explained. His brow furrowed with concern as he looked at Jo. "I still think someone's trying to get your attention."

She gave a shrug. "Well, they got it. Along with a hefty cleaning bill. I'm still not sure I'll ever get rid of the smell of decomp. Thankfully, Jake's been kind enough to let me work out of his office while mine gets re-carpeted."

"I was already helping with ballistics," he added, as though Dana would believe that was the only reason he was assisting the gorgeous blonde agent.

Dana's gaze bounced between Jake and Jo as they rattled off details about the case. It was like watching tennis. They were an even match; a thought which stung. Dana was beginning to see how easily she'd been replaced.

"We didn't discover the playing cards until the second body. Coroner's short staffed," Jo added.

Jake chimed in. "After the third body turned up with the same MO, I officially joined the case."

"So you think this is serial?" Dana asked, her stomach churning at the thought of hunting another serial killer.

"We did," Jake said. "But if the third victim swallowed a tarot card, it changes things."

"It's definitely a tarot card," Dana confirmed.

Her doubts weren't about the card. What she really wanted to know was if she could go down this road again? And without Jake? She was a librarian, not a cop. The only reason she'd had success on the last two cases was because Jake was on her team.

They'd always had an unspoken bond, but with Jo in the room, Dana felt nothing but an icy chill from Jake. In her absence he'd turned back into the brooding agent she'd first thought him to be.

"The media has sensationalized this thing. Could be a copycat," Jo suggested. "Any theories right off the bat, Dr. Gray?"

No theories, but questions were already skimming through her mind. However, asking them would only ensnare her further. Something she wasn't sure she wanted.

She didn't come back to D.C. to get dragged back into solving crimes with the FBI. She came back because she missed her life and the people in it. She came back for Jake and Claire and Meredith. She came back because she cared about them, and she finally felt strong enough to show them. But there was one major flaw in her logic. She'd neglected to consider that the world hadn't stood still while she was away figuring out what she wanted.

She was back, but the world she came back to wasn't the one she left.

A wave of panic hit her so hard she had the urge to run. She needed to breathe air that wasn't charged with tension and regret. "I just got back today," Dana said, starting to back away.

"No better time than the present to catch a killer," Agent Jenkins replied. She'd reappeared at the office door as silently as a cat, blocking Dana's escape. There was a laptop tucked under her arm and a take no prisoners look on her face. "You're good at this, Gray, whether you like it or not. And we could use your help navigating the occult angle now that the Card Killer has jumped into the realm of tarot."

"Can I have some time to think about it?"

Jake snorted. "Typical."

Dana turned to address the rude comment but was silenced by the anger she saw simmering beneath the steel blue storm clouds in his eyes. There was nothing left to say. Whatever she'd thought they'd built had turned to rot like an untended garden.

She faced Jenkins. "I'm sorry, I don't think it's a good idea for me to come on board. If you need help deciphering the tarot cards, I can refer you to someone else."

Jenkins stepped in front of Dana, her voice calm and low. "I understand. Get me a name, but it will take time to get anyone you refer the proper clearance." She offered Dana the laptop she'd been carrying. "Take this. Just in case we need help with the tarot angle in the meantime." She fished a jump drive from her blazer pocket. "Your login codes."

Arguing with Jenkins was useless. Dana took the laptop and jump drive if only to escape Jake's office. "I'll send you a referral first thing in the morning."

4

Cursing, Jake took the steps two at a time. He'd known he'd crossed a line the moment he'd seen the hurt in Dana's eyes. Even so, his stubbornness made him wait five minutes before making an excuse to chase after her.

In the Army, his iron will had served him well. Stateside, not so much. He heard his uncle Wade's voice in his head. *Stubborn and hot-headed; it'll leave you perpetually single. Take it from me.*

But Jake wasn't single. His secret FBI girlfriend was sitting in his office while he chased down another woman. Again, Jake cursed himself for letting his temper get the best of him. There was just something about Dana Gray that brought it out in him. But he needed to fix this. She'd saved his life. He owed her.

When it came to life debts he had a lot to atone for, and that wasn't going to happen without Dana. She was the best damn partner he'd ever had, and now that these mob hits had taken a turn for the witchy, he had a feeling he'd need her more than ever.

Rushing through the lobby, he pushed open the double doors scanning the parking lot. Dana must've been on a mission to get through security so quickly. He prayed she wasn't already in her car. His chest eased when he caught sight of her, brown hair swirling in the wind. Jogging to catch up he called out her name. "Dana!"

She turned, crossing her arms when she saw it was him, but at least she didn't keep walking.

"I'm sorry," he said, lungs burning from the cold. "I didn't mean what I said back there, and that's not how I wanted you to find out about Jo."

"It's not my business."

"It is if that's why you're turning this case down."

"It's not."

"I didn't plan this, Dana. Jo and I connected three months ago on a case and—"

"I don't need the details, Jake. You said you weren't going to wait, and you didn't. I think the best thing we can do is move on."

"I don't."

"Do you really want me as a partner again?"

"No." He could see that stung, but he needed to be honest. "But I do want to solve this case before it escalates into an international war in our capital, and I think you're the best chance we've got."

"I already told Jenkins I'd refer another specialist."

"And she told you getting FBI clearance for someone new will take time. Time we don't have. I have three dead and a media frenzy that's turning this into a Hoffa hunt. A bunch of yahoos were arrested digging up graves at Glenwood last night." Dana's eyes widened, and he knew she was thinking of Cramer. "Security got to them before they could do any real damage. Luckily the ground's frozen solid this time of year."

Dismay filled her brown eyes. "Why would people do something like that?"

"There's a reward for the bodies that go with these heads."

"What? From who?"

He nodded to the laptop she was clutching across her chest. "It's all in the reports."

"Jake, I want to help, but this isn't a good idea."

"Just sleep on it," he urged, turning her back the way she'd been heading, ready to walk her to her car. "Where'd you park?"

"I didn't. I told you, I came straight here."

"From the airport?"

"Yeah, I flew into Regan and took the train."

His chest tightened. She'd come to see him first. "You haven't seen Claire yet?"

"No."

Jake frowned, rocking back on his heels as he pulled a stick of cinnamon gum from his pocket and popped it in his mouth. He rubbed his hands together, wishing he'd thought to grab his jacket. It was freezing out.

Dana's eyes narrowed. "What's wrong with Claire?"

Jake looked up, momentarily forgetting Dana knew him so well. He only chewed gum when he was stressed. And the Claire situation was, well ... stressful.

"Jake, what is it? Is she okay?"

"She's ..." he trailed off. "You'll see for yourself when you go to the library."

"I'm heading there now."

"Just go easy on her, okay?"

"What's that supposed to mean?"

"It means I'm not the only one you abandoned."

"Abandoned?" Color filled her cheeks, and it wasn't from the cold. "I went on a book tour! I was doing my job. I didn't abandon anyone."

"Yeah, well that's not what it felt like," he muttered.

"Jake, you told me to figure out what I wanted."

"And did you?"

Her eyes shone like liquid amber in the fading sunlight as her anger drained. "It doesn't matter."

It did matter. Standing there staring into her eyes, it felt like the only thing in the world that mattered, and that's why he looked away. He couldn't go down that road again. He'd been burned one too many times. He needed to focus on things that had a fighting chance, like solving this case. "You're right. I suppose it doesn't."

5

By the time Dana reached the Smithsonian the sun had fully slipped behind a blanket of thick clouds, calling it a day. Something she wished she could do. It'd been a long journey home.

Dana started the day in Milan. 6810 kilometers later, she was so jetlagged she didn't even know what time zone she was in, let alone what day it was.

She should've gone home and gotten a good night of sleep, so her head was on straight before going to speak to Jake. That was the smart play. But for once Dana didn't want to make decisions with her head. It was her heart that led her back to D.C.

Little good it did her.

The truth of it was, she'd come back for Jake, but he wasn't where she'd left him. He'd moved on and so should she. Telling him would only make working together that much harder. Not that she'd decided to get involved with another FBI case. The stress of the last two made her need time away. But she was the only occult specialist with FBI clearance in the city. It was inevitable their paths would cross again. The best thing to do was forget about her heart and remain professional.

As she pushed through the doors into the Smithsonian's lobby,

Dana went through her mental checklist. She'd reordered it in her time away. Family, friends, work. She was convinced she finally had her priorities in the correct order, even if Jake no longer fell into any of those categories. The balancing act was never easy, but Dana had been ready to let her career take a backseat after spending the last few months lecturing. Maybe she still would.

She still had Claire and Meredith. Without Jake, it just meant Dana would have more time for her friends. She let that thought soothe the sting of Jake's rejection.

Dana's footsteps echoed off the marble floor. The employee lobby was quiet at this hour. Everyone was most likely at home readying dinner or doing the other normal domestic activities she'd never been good at. Despite her well-intended priorities, here she was, back at work.

Pressing the elevator button to sublevel three, Dana contemplated the downside of her safety net. She had a sanctuary to retreat to when things didn't go right. But maybe having a place to avoid life wasn't a good thing.

Books had always been her escape. As curator of the Smithsonian's Occult History and Ritualistic Artifacts department it was easy to disappear into the stacks of rare cultural phenomena waiting to be deciphered.

If the last few months taught her anything, it was that her time at the Smithsonian was well spent. The things she'd uncovered were important. Her most recent case was so relevant that it had almost cost her a best friend. *More than that,* her subconscious reminded her, serving up the memory of Meredith wielding a gun at Jake.

As the elevator descended, her conscience began to nag her. *All those relevant, life-saving discoveries never would've happened without him.*

The last two cases she'd worked with Jake Shepard and the FBI had cataclysmic results. It's why she'd needed a break from it all. Now that she was back, she wanted to punch a clock like everyone else in this building and go home to a life outside of work, but somehow she kept getting sucked in.

With the FBI laptop heavy in her arms, she could admit she was intrigued by the subject matter. She'd done extensive research into tarot when she thought it might tie to her parents' deaths. It hadn't, but it was still a fascinating topic. Tarot dated back to the 1400s, with a variety of different decks and cultural relevance. Maybe she'd take a look at the files so she could direct Jenkins to the best specialist on the matter.

The doors whooshed open, and Dana stilled. She blinked, willing her eyes to adjust to the utter darkness. With the lights off, staring into her subterranean library was like staring into an abyss. For a terrifying moment she worried the power had gone out, but she could tell the air was still on. The Smithsonian had installed multiple backup generators to her library as a precaution to keep her rare books and artifacts in the optimal humidity-free environment to prevent further decay. But that didn't explain why the lights were off.

A key card was necessary to access them. A key card only she and Claire were authorized to have. Even when they left for the day, the lights stayed on. Changing the light level was destructive to the already fragile books her library housed. That's why they'd built it underground and kept the lights dim at all times. Her office and the lab were the only areas where lights could be manually adjusted to normal levels.

Dana stepped into the darkness, reminding herself she didn't need her sight. She knew this library like the back of her hand. Even after being away so long, muscle memory kicked in, guiding her easily toward her office. Her mind raced ahead to what would have to be done. Looking up access codes, resetting the lights, raising them gradually so as not to cause further damage.

Her shin struck something solid. Yelping in pain, Dana bit her lip to keep her anger from boiling over. She could be mad later. Her first priority was fixing the lights. Gingerly reaching around, she discerned the object she struck was a chair. One that should've been in its rightful place tucked neatly beneath a research table.

What was going on? Claire was as meticulous as Dana when it came to putting things where they belonged. Her conversation with Jake came back to her, flooding her with worry. If something had happened to Claire, he would've come right out and told her. At least she hoped he would. But from the disarray of the library it was evident that something was most definitely wrong.

Dana's intern was a creature of habit, peculiar and particular in her own way. She was often misunderstood by the rest of the world, but to Dana she was family. There was no one else she would've entrusted the care of her library to while she was away. But if Claire had let things get this far off kilter, there was no telling what was wrong.

Worry quickened Dana's pace. She struck another chair in the darkness before finally making her way to her office door. She turned the knob and the door opened soundlessly. Her hand automatically sought out the light switch.

Light flooded the room and something shrieked! The blur of movement charging forward caught Dana off guard. Before she knew it, she was on her ass. Rolling to her side, she untangled her purse strap and reached inside, pulling out the taser she kept on her at all times since her encounter in the catacombs.

The light in the adjoining lab flipped on giving Dana a clear line to her assailant. She aimed, ready to fire, when Claire leapt in the way. "Stop!"

6

Shock twisted to rage as Dana climbed to her feet. Thanks to Claire, the intruder had time to flee. The assailant turned back just long enough for Dana to make out her face: a frightened teen with long purple hair and a lip ring. Not someone who belonged in her library, but she'd seen enough to give a description to the police. She grabbed her phone, ready to make the call, when Claire spoke. "What are you doing?"

"Calling the police."

"Don't."

Dana turned her seething gaze to her intern. "Why not?"

Claire fidgeted, wringing her hands like she did when she was anxious. "I didn't know you were back."

Dana's anger boiled over. "That much is obvious, Claire! What on earth is going on here?"

"It's not what it looks like."

"Really? Because it looks like you forgot the rules."

All at once, Claire's fretting vanished. Her soft voice filled with venom. "You mean *your* rules? You left me in charge, remember?"

"Yes, because I trusted you to understand the importance of protecting these archives."

"The books are perfectly fine."

"You turned the lights off, Claire. You know how damaging that can be."

Claire's ice-blue eyes narrowed with anger. "That's all that matters to you, isn't it? You're precious work. I don't know why I even bother."

"Bother with what?"

Claire stalked away, all long black hair and fury, but Dana wasn't finished with their conversation. Rushing after her, she grabbed Claire's thin shoulder. The girl shrieked like a cornered cat, whirling on Dana. "Don't touch me!"

Claire had rigid physical boundaries, always keeping most of her skin covered with garish black clothing. Dana knew it was a defense mechanism meant to keep people at bay, but right now she was too pissed to care. "Claire, I need you to tell me exactly what's going on here."

"Nothing. I got kicked out of my campus apartment, so I've been crashing here until I find something else."

"Kicked out? Why?"

"It's not important."

"I say it is."

Again, bitterness overtook Claire. "And whatever you say goes."

"Actually yes. As your boss, mentor and dissertation committee member, I'm making the decisions regarding your future here. I trusted you could handle the responsibility while I was gone, but it appears I was mistaken. Unless you can tell me exactly what's going on and who that girl was, I'm calling the police to report her."

Claire's paperwhite skin paled to nearly translucent. "You wouldn't."

Dana crossed her arms. "I most certainly would. She was trespassing."

Anger crackled behind Claire's black cat-eye frames. "Her name is Sadie. She's a friend who needed a place to stay. I'm not like you. I couldn't just abandon her. But I wouldn't expect you to understand."

"I didn't abandon you."

"Whatever," Claire muttered.

Dana threw her hands up as she stalked after Claire. The girl was acting like a moody teenager, not the well-educated doctoral candidate Dana knew her to be. "No, not whatever. You let an unauthorized guest into a restricted area of the Smithsonian, and from the look of it, more than once." Dana gestured to the stacks of takeout piled on a table in the lab. "This is serious. It's grounds for termination unless you can promise me it will never happen again."

Claire blinked up at Dana, seemingly stunned for a moment. Then she huffed a laugh and dug into the pocket of her black cardigan. "Don't worry. It won't." She slapped her key card and ID badge against Dana's chest before storming out.

Watching Claire's thin figure walk away, Dana clutched the key card and badge to her chest. It felt like Claire had punched a hole straight to her heart. Jake was right, something was wrong. And the worst part was, he was the only person she wanted to talk to about it.

It was becoming painfully clear to Dana that she'd been foolish to assume she could slip back into her old life. Before she could pick up where she left off, she needed to pick up the tattered pieces she'd left in her wake. Which was precisely why getting involved in another FBI case was a terrible idea. She needed to focus on repairing broken bonds. But first she needed to repair her library.

7

Jo followed Jake into his kitchen, making herself at home as she opened the fridge and grabbed a bottle of water to quench her post-workout thirst. Jake went straight for his wet bar, pouring himself a bourbon. It was a habit she was trying to break him of, but the more she nagged, the more he resisted.

There was a lot to like about Joanna Walsh. But her alcohol-free lifestyle was one of Jake's least favorite traits.

"I was really hoping to work with her," Jo grumped between gulps of water. "Do you think she'll change her mind?"

Jake huffed a laugh, shaking his head as he walked to the window, rocks glass in hand. "Nope. The woman's more stubborn than a two-headed mule."

"Ha! How on earth did you two work together?"

Jake turned around. "I'm not stubborn."

"Sure, and I'm not ambitious." Jo sauntered over, wrapping her arms around him so she could steal a kiss. Her lips were salty and greedy, mixing perfectly with the bourbon stinging his tongue. Jo deepened the kiss, and Jake felt his control slipping. He wanted to let go, to let Jo ease his burdens, but thoughts of Dana kept pulling him back.

Despite her being gone these past few months, he'd never really been able to shake his thoughts of her. And after she'd walked back into his office today, he wasn't sure he'd ever be able to rid himself of the strangled feeling that crowded his chest when the occult librarian was near. Even now, it was like she was still here in the room with him.

What he and Dana had endured together connected them. He sensed her as if a part of her lived under his skin. When she was near, he felt comfort, if only for the fact that he knew she was safe and not off running headlong into danger. But right now, knowing she was near, but still so far out of reach ... it was killing him.

What the hell is wrong with me? Jake was ignoring the sexy, confident woman in front of him to pine after one who played head games. Jo was straightforward and, more importantly, here.

Pushing all thoughts of Dana from his mind, Jake drained his bourbon, ready to give Jo the attention she deserved. He let himself get lost in the feel of her. She set his glass down, pulled his shirt off and started to kiss a path down his neck. He stopped her before she got to his chest. His patchwork of scars was a turn off. He didn't let anyone touch them. *Except Dana.* But that was a lesson learned. He'd let her in, and now she was buried under his skin.

Shit, he was thinking of her again. Tearing off Jo's sports bra remedied the situation. Sweat still glistened between her breasts from the rigorous workout they'd just completed. But it seemed she had energy for more. Jo grabbed the waistband of his shorts and tugged him toward her, kissing him hard. He moaned into her mouth when her hand slipped into his shorts, teasing him the way he liked.

"Come on. Let's shower," she whispered, towing him behind her.

Though Jake preferred to be the one in charge, it was hard not to give in to Jo's wicked ways. The woman knew how to get what she wanted, but he couldn't make it too easy for her. "What, you just expect me to follow you? That shit might work over in TOC, but I'm Army. I don't follow, I lead."

Jo grinned. "Don't I know it."

She had her own 101st Infantry tattoo to prove it. Her service record was what drew him to her in the first place. The woman was a badass in her own right. An equal. Someone who could be a true partner—if he'd let her.

"Come on," she grinned. "I'll make it worth your while."

That much he knew. He looked longingly at his bourbon collection, but decided to follow her to his bathroom instead.

Steam swirled around them both in the shower as Jo lathered him with soap, her hands gliding over him until he ached. "You know, if you come to Colorado, we could do this every day."

His eyes snapped open. He didn't want to talk about Colorado right now. He didn't want to talk, period. His blood was busy elsewhere, leaving his brain to make poor decisions if he opened his mouth. Something Jo was aware of. They were both seasoned interrogators, which sometimes complicated things. Other times it led to great sex. Jake was willing to roll the dice.

Jo was torturing him in the best way, her lips lingering in all the right places. She knew the precise type of pressure to apply to get exactly what she wanted from him, and at the moment, he just wanted relief. Anything to let him shut out the chaos crowding his head. He pushed Jo against the shower wall, ready to take what he wanted when the sharp ring of his phone interrupted.

"Ignore it," she ordered, but then her phone began to ring next to his on the bathroom counter.

Their eyes met, both of them knowing gratification would have to wait. Postponing pleasure was something Jake was used to in his line of work. He'd learned death took joy in making sure the living had none.

Opening his shower door, he grabbed a towel to dry his hands and face before answering. "Shepard."

He was greeted by Jenkins' voice. "We got another one."

"Christ. Already?" The killer was escalating, which meant he was desperate. Desperate equaled sloppy. Sloppy meant Jake had a better chance of catching him. "Where?"

"Ninth and T."

"Roger that. Walsh and I will meet you there."

"Jake, I'm gonna need you to bring Dr. Gray in on this one."

"She made it pretty clear she's not interested, Jenks."

"No, not for consulting. We need to question her about the vic."

Panic hit him so swiftly he grabbed the counter for support. Dana had already lost too many people in her life. "Who's the vic?"

"Jane Doe for now, but we've got a witness who can place Dr. Gray with the body less than an hour before TOD."

"Is this a credible witness?"

The pause in Jenkins' voice filled Jake with dread. "Dr. Gray's former assistant, Claire Townsend."

Former? The word snagged his thoughts like a splinter. What the hell was going on? His questions would have to wait. "Claire's at the scene?"

"Yes. I'm here with her now."

"Tell her I'm on my way."

8

"Heroin?" Dana scrolled through the toxicology results on the laptop screen. Jenkins had left out some major details about this case. It was more than rival mobs and tarot cards. This was drugs, gangs, and executions. It was a few prostitutes short of a Scorsese film, and way out of her league. Even if it weren't, there was little expertise she could lend to the case with one tarot card.

At least that's what she told herself as she shut the files and closed the laptop.

She'd looked at the case like she'd promised, she owed Jake and Jenkins that much, but her mind was made up. She needed to distance herself from the FBI and the chaos it brought into her life. And with the Nigerian cartel bankrolling a ransom for the bodies of their fallen enforcers, Dana wanted to keep her distance. She had enough problems of her own at the moment.

With the lights back up and running and the library restored to order, Dana was ready to focus on repairing emotional bonds. She hated how she'd left things with Claire. She needed to talk to her, but she wasn't sure how. Did she need space? Time? Tough love?

They'd never fought before. It was one of the many things Dana adored about her quirky intern. The girl was rational with an analytical mind. She was much like Dana in that way.

This was uncharted territory. Did she call or was this a face-to-face situation? Once again, she wished she could call Jake for some insight. He'd alluded to something being off with Claire. It would've been nice if he'd warned her just how bad things were. If Jake knew Claire was homeless, he should've stepped in to help or at the very least let Dana know.

Grumbling under her breath, she closed up her office and got on the elevator, vowing to find a way to fix things. She pulled up Claire's campus address, hoping her roommate might shed some light on things. Her phone rang as she stepped off the elevator. The shrill sound pierced the silent lobby. Seeing Jake's name on the caller ID sent a wave of heat rushing through Dana. She didn't know if she was happy or angry that he was calling, but she knew what he wanted.

Answering, she began speaking to cut off his bargaining. "Jake, I haven't changed my mind about the case. I don't—"

He interrupted, his voice clipped with anger. "Dana, it's Claire."

Everything stopped. Her feet. Her heart. Her world. "What's wrong?"

"I'm sending you the address. I need you to come. Now."

"On my way."

DANA ARRIVED AT THE SCENE, her heart pounding as she swallowed back the bile assaulting her throat. It started the moment she saw the blue and red lights. Each flash brought with it a crime scene memory she wished she could forget.

Too soon. Too much. Not ready.

She fought to silence her fears. "You're here for Claire," she reminded herself. "She needs you."

Dana didn't ask Jake what was wrong. She didn't have to. She knew him well enough to know he only used that tone when things were dire. His anger came through when he couldn't protect the people he loved. Hearing it when he'd referenced Claire threatened to steal the steadiness Dana gained in those months away.

She'd thought leaving was the right thing. She wanted to get her head right so she could be her best self when she came back, but maybe leaving was a mistake. Or maybe returning was. She didn't know, but either way, she'd never considered that her absence would hurt others. She'd spent a lifetime teaching herself not to need people and that sometimes made her forget not everyone felt the same.

It was natural to need companionship. Healthy, even. But after she lost her parents, Dana existed in a fortress of solitude. There was only room for research and vengeance. She allowed very few people to breach her walls: Meredith, Claire, Jake. After Meredith burned her, Dana shut down. It wasn't until this exact moment she saw the true aftermath of that decision.

Claire stood in the middle of the crime scene, blood smeared across her pale cheeks. She looked as fragile as an eggshell as Jake held her, sheltering her from the gruesome scene.

A body lay draped in the street, dark smears of blood staining the sidewalk where the assault must've started. A frigid breeze ripped through the scene, lifting the sheet enough for Dana to catch a glimpse beneath. Purple hair, a nose ring. Her stomach dropped. It was the girl from her office. The one Claire had been trying to help.

Was this Dana's fault, too?

Out of the corner of her eye, a flickering of color caught Dana's attention. She watched something dancing in the wind: purple, yellow, black. The whirl of color stopped at an officer's feet. He bent down with gloved hands and picked up the tattered rectangle, a perplexed look on his face before he placed it in an evidence bag.

Another tarot card!

Dana couldn't tell which one it was from this distance, but she couldn't stop the tingle of intrigue. Someone was trying to send a message. The question was to whom?

Claire's sob broke through the pounding in Dana's temples. Time stood still as she looked in on a life she no longer belonged to. The sharp ache in her chest told her she should be standing there with Claire and Jake, not on the safe side of the yellow tape.

She wasn't sure when exactly she'd adopted the lifestyle of protect and serve, but it stung to be pushed out. But what could she do?

Standing with the crowd of onlookers, she watched the bizarre display of affection between agent and witness. Claire hated to be touched and Jake, well, touching him wasn't an option. Dana closed her eyes, trying not to remember the feel of his skin when he'd made a rare exception to his rule. Electricity dwelled inside his veins. Six months ago, he'd almost kissed her, but she'd stopped him. Being that close to Jake Shepard was like grabbing a live wire. And that terrified her.

It was the first time Dana had truly run from her fears. She always preferred fight over flight. It's why she'd come back. She wanted to fight to put things right. Starting with Claire and Jake.

Even from here Dana could see the way he was holding himself back. It wasn't often that he let his professional persona slip on the job. But Claire had a way about her. She could worm herself into even the stoniest of hearts. Dana longed to cross the police tape and join them, but she stayed put. She was on the outside now. She'd have to earn back their trust.

9

"Dr. Gray. We need to speak."

Dana jumped at the sound of Jenkins' voice. She forgot how stealthily the keen-eyed agent moved. One nod from her and the police officer holding the line lifted it to let Dana pass beneath the yellow tape. She walked toward Jenkins. "I came as soon as I heard. What happened? How is Claire involved?"

"What exactly did you hear?"

"Jake called. All he said was Claire needed me."

"Good." She waved a man in a suit over. "We're going to need a statement."

"A statement. About what?"

"Your last conversation with Claire Townsend and your whereabouts for the last few hours."

"I was at my office. Going over the files you gave me."

"You used the access codes I gave you?"

"Yes."

"Good. That will help corroborate your story."

"It's not a story. I was looking at the case like you asked, which is a lot more involved than you initially shared."

Jenkins lowered her voice. "Yeah, I'm gonna need you to keep that to yourself. There are too many agencies involved already." The man she'd summoned arrived. "Dr. Gray, this is Agent Fuller of the CIA. He's going to take your official statement. He does NOT have clearance to our active investigation. The CIA has *temporary* jurisdiction over this crime scene. Understood?"

"We'll see how temporary it is," Fuller muttered.

Dana looked between Jenkins and Fuller, panic making it impossible to speak. Agent Fuller focused on her, a greasy smile spreading across his face like a virus. "Well, if it isn't the infamous Dr. Gray. I knew we'd see each other again."

"You two know each other?" Jenkins asked.

Fuller grinned. "We go way back."

Dana did her best to block out the unpleasant memories of her first interaction with Agent Mike Fuller, one he'd made as hostile as possible. Ignoring him, she looked at Jenkins. "I don't understand. Am I a suspect?"

"You tell me?" Fuller quipped.

Baffled, Dana sputtered. "I-I have no idea what this is about."

"Try again, Dr. Gray. The vic was found dead hours after trespassing in your office, something you were outraged by, according to your former employee."

"And you think I came here and killed her?"

Fuller crowded her personal space. "Nah, that's not your style, is it? You like to lure people in, earn their trust first. Say how are those friends of yours, Grant, Rickman and Cramer? All dead? And the Kincaid girl, she might as well be from what I hear." The smell of stale coffee and cologne assaulted Dana as Fuller leaned in closer, his voice a harsh whisper. "Why is it people who get close to you always turn up dead?"

Rage and fear quarreled inside, filling her with the same slithering anxiety she'd tried to outrun when she left D.C. Her hands balled into fists while she took a few steps back, torn between hitting the arrogant prick and running away. The worst part was, he wasn't wrong.

"Dana!" Claire's shrill voice cut through the chaos in her mind. Dana turned in time to see her intern sprinting toward her. A moment later she was in her arms. Dana barely had a chance to embrace her before Claire was yanked away again.

Fuller hauled Dana backwards, wrenching her arm painfully behind her back while another officer restrained Claire.

Claire screamed, going feral at the touch of a stranger. The panic on her face had Dana trying to shake Fuller's grasp, but it was unnecessary. The officer manhandling Claire managed to get one cuff on her wrist before Jake was there. He looked ready to breathe fire. "You have two seconds to get your hands off my witness," he snarled.

"My scene. My witness," the cop snapped.

"Gentleman ..." Warning edged Jenkins' voice as she tried to diffuse the situation, but it was useless. Dana could sense the calm before the storm, and she was ready.

Jake struck the officer holding Claire. The jab was swift and true. One second the guy was sneering, the next he was on his ass clutching his windpipe. Dana made her move in the moment between, driving her elbow into Fuller's solar plexus. He sucked in a startled breath, wheezing with the wind knocked out of him. It gave Dana the time she needed to get to Claire.

Once again, she had her intern in her arms, pulling her behind Jake for cover as a dozen officers and agents drew their weapons.

10

WEAPON TRAINED ON THE JACKASS IN FRONT OF HIM, JAKE TOOK A STEP back until he felt Dana's form against the back of his leg. Her warmth seeped into him, spreading a false sense of security. This powder keg was one hair trigger away from exploding. He shouldn't feel comfortable. But he did. He lived his life balanced on the edge of a blade. This was his element.

With both women behind him he searched out all viable exit strategies even while Jenkins tried to talk down the officers wielding weapons. Jake caught Jo out of the corner of his eye. For a moment she'd faded into the background. He didn't have time to worry about what that meant or that if he hadn't been well-trained, he might've registered her as a threat when she moved up to cover him.

She approached from his left flank. Her subtle nod told him they were good to move, but he shook his head. He'd spotted the easiest way out too, but Jenkins was their best bet to end this thing safely.

"Fuller, put it down and everyone will follow," Jenkins ordered.

"Why should I? Your man assaulted a police officer."

"We're all on the same team," Jenkins replied. "We have enough mourners here today, don't you think?" Jake watched her eyes sweep over the crowd of onlookers who were foolishly standing by, phones out, ready to capture the latest headline.

The public's fascination with gore and tragedy baffled him. Here they were standing around risking catching a stray bullet for a glimpse of what he was trying to forget. Maybe if they knew death's stain couldn't be washed away, they wouldn't be so quick to pull out their phones, but some things had to be experienced to be understood.

The only good thing about the mob of people standing by was that it made Fuller think twice about how far he was willing to take this power struggle. Working joint cases was never easy. The FBI had a big footprint. Toes were bound to get stepped on and the CIA was notoriously sensitive. That's why having Jenkins here was crucial. The woman was a negotiating savant.

Jake remembered a time when he was about seven and she'd talked him out of the last popsicle in the icebox. He still didn't know how she'd done it. *She could talk the devil into an ice bath.* Or at least that's what Wade always said.

Jenkins was working her skills on Fuller now. "It's your scene. I'm just trying to help you get everyone through it in one piece. We'll follow your lead."

Realizing there was no win in sight, Fuller made the smart call and lowered his weapon, giving the call for his team to follow. With the tension defused, Jake felt Dana sag against him. He holstered his Sig Sauer and turned around to offer her a hand. His blood ignited with her palm pressed against his. Thankfully Jo was there, front and center, to remind him where his loyalties belonged.

Jo reached down to help Claire, but the girl yelped away from her. Jake reacted, pulling her reflexively to his side. She reached for Dana, burying her head in her mentor's chest, with one hand still clutching his arm. Dana's brown eyes burned with questions as they met Jake's. He could do nothing but stand there, holding Claire, entangled in Dana once more while Jo, Jenkins and the others looked on disapprovingly.

There was nothing he could say. Actions spoke louder than words.

And once again, his actions had drawn a line in the sand. From the look on Fuller's face they'd also painted a target on the backs of the people he cared about most.

11

"Start from the beginning," Fuller demanded.

Dana gripped the edge of her metal folding chair as she stared through the reflective glass. By now it was clear that the body under the draped sheet at the crime scene was that of Sadie Azeez; the purple-haired girl who'd been sleeping in Dana's office.

From what Fuller said, the girl was a known addict. It was still beyond Dana how Claire befriended her, but after filling out a police report about Sadie's trespassing, Dana was brought here to listen in on the interview.

Dana did her best not to chew her nails while she sat quietly in the precinct viewing room. Claire was on the other side of the dingy glass, trembling across from Agent Fuller, who was taking pleasure in terrifying her while she recounted her story.

It seemed his tactics hadn't changed much since Dana's encounter with him. The only difference was his hair was thinner and he was with the CIA now instead of the FBI. She didn't know if that was better or worse. It just meant another agency to deal with. At least with the FBI she had Jake and Jenkins in her corner. At least she thought she did.

Dana glanced at Jake who alternated between pacing and scowling, his jaws working the cinnamon gum harder than the saltwater taffy machines at the boardwalk. Jo was in the viewing room with them, doling out coffee and calming antidotes every time Jake took his frustration out on a folding chair. Jenkins was on the other side of the glass with Fuller and Claire.

Assistant Director Remi Jenkins was an ally, but Claire didn't know that. From her point of view, she'd just witnessed a friend murdered and was now being isolated from the only people who could comfort her.

"Take me through the assault again," Fuller demanded.

"Sadie was standing with her back to me. S-she kept looking down the road like she was waiting for someone. Then a black SUV pulled up, and she walked over. It happened so fast. The window rolled down and ... s-she screamed. There was so much blood."

"Then what?"

"I ran toward her, but I-I was too late. She stumbled into the street and ..." Claire's words dissolved into sobs. She looked so small under the bright interrogation lights. The forensic team had taken her clothes and belongings for analysis. The pale blue DOC uniform she wore made her look like she'd already been convicted of whatever Fuller was accusing, which was still unclear to Dana.

Sadie had obviously been assaulted by someone in the black SUV Claire described, then stumbled into traffic. Dana had overheard the first responders at the scene saying the body was badly damaged. She knew what that meant. It would make the coroner's job harder to discern what damage was from the vehicle that hit her and what was from the murder weapon.

It didn't help that the case was in no-man's land.

The FBI wanted it because a tarot card had been found at the scene. Metro Police had a claim since they'd been first on the scene and there was a traffic accident, but Dana still hadn't figured out what piece of the pie caught Agent Fuller and the CIA's interest.

"How do you know Sadie Azeez?" Fuller demanded.

"I-I told you, we're friends. We met at a club."

"What club?"

"I-I don't know."

"Like to party, do ya?"

Claire's eyes widened. "No, I-I mean I ... what does that have to do with what happened to her?"

"I'm the one asking the questions," Fuller barked. "Why was she trespassing at your place of employment, or should I say former employment?"

"She needed a place to stay. I-I was trying to help her."

"Yeah, help her get murdered."

"Fuller." Jenkins' tone was clipped.

Fuller changed tactics. "You one of her little junkie pals?"

Claire shook her head.

"You sure?" He reached for her arm, but Claire yanked it back.

"How is your boss involved in this?"

Claire's wide eyes focused on the glass, and Dana felt her fear.

Fuller snapped rudely in front of Claire's face. "Don't look at them. They can't help you. Look at me. I want to know how you knew where to find my informant."

Claire blinked up at Fuller, her clear blue eyes suddenly devoid of fear. "Informant? You! You're the reason she's dead. She wanted out! But you made her go back in. Do you have any idea what they did to her in there?"

Fuller stood up, slamming his fist into the table. "It'll seem like nothing when I'm through with you, you little bitch! Now tell me what you know!"

Jake burst into the interview room before anyone could stop him. Dana followed right behind.. Every instinct told her she needed to get Claire out of there before the girl's fragile coping mechanisms failed and shock took over completely.

"Time's up, Fuller," Jake snarled.

"It's up when I say it's up, hotshot."

Dana caught Claire's eye. "Are you feeling unwell? Too unwell to continue?"

Catching on quickly, Claire nodded. It was all Jenkins needed. "The witness has had enough for today. Fuller, you can set up another time to interview her after she's had a chance to rest and recover."

"She hasn't answered my questions!"

"Then you can refer to the police report she gave at the scene."

"That's bull and you know it!"

"Actually, it's not," Jo interjected. "Research shows witnesses give the most accurate statements immediately following trauma, followed secondly by accounts given once their memory has had time to recover. Furthermore, you know as well as I do any eyewitness testimony obtained under duress holds no credibility."

Fuller scowled. "She's not under duress."

Jo pointed to the cameras in the room. "They might show a different story."

Fuller's expression soured as he took in the scene. Claire cowered, still seated and shaking while Dana and three FBI agents crowded into the small room in her defense. "Fine, but she's spending the night in custody."

"Not unless you charge her," Jenkins countered.

"We can get lawyers involved if you'd like," Jo pressed.

Finally, Fuller relented. Shoving past Jake, he paused in front of Dana. "And don't think I've forgot about you, Princess. This time Cramer's not around to protect you."

Dana hated that she flinched. Hearing Cramer's name still made her physically ill. Jake hadn't missed it. "What was that about?"

"It's not important," she muttered. "I'm more concerned about Claire."

Jenkins spoke up. "Give me a few minutes, and I'll get us out of here."

12

An hour later Dana found herself back in Jake's apartment. She still couldn't quite wrap her head around the fact that Claire wanted to come here rather than her place. She'd spent the night at Dana's dozens of times before—another reason it was strange she'd chosen to hole up in the library rather than ask to stay at Dana's. Her home was warm and inviting. Jake's was the complete opposite, not to mention a one bedroom.

But when she'd offered her home as a refuge, Claire immediately turned it down. "I'd rather just go back to Jake's." *Back to,* like it was comfortable, routine. Which begged the question, if Claire and Jake had been spending so much time together, how had he let things get so out of hand?

Dana pushed the thought aside. It'd been over twenty-four hours since she'd slept. And judging from how today was going, she wouldn't be climbing into her bed anytime soon. She needed to save her criticisms for when her critical thinking was less impaired.

Dana followed Jo, Claire and Jake into his living room. Once again she was reminded she was an outsider as everyone else moved around the sparsely decorated space with ease. Jo started a pot of coffee, while Claire curled up on the couch, taking the heavy blanket Jake offered.

"Who wants coffee?" Jo called.

"Make it strong," Jake grumbled.

Dana raised her hand.

Claire said nothing. Jake sat next to her, speaking softly. "You need to eat something, Claire."

"I'm not hungry."

"You sure you don't want some coffee?" Jo asked. "Sugar will help with the shock."

"I'm not in shock," Claire snapped. "I'm pissed." A tear spilled down her cheek, and she angrily wiped it away. "I'm pissed that after everything I tried to do for her, it didn't matter."

Dana perched on the armchair near to the couch. "What did you do for Sadie?"

"Are you really going to make me relive her murder for the hundredth time?"

"I'm not talking about what happened today," Dana said. "Why do you blame Fuller for what happened to Sadie? You said she wanted out, and he made her go back in."

Claire wiped the errant tears from her cheeks. "I didn't know she was an informant. I knew someone was threatening her, but I just thought it was one of them."

"Who?" Jake asked.

Claire slouched further into the couch, tightening the blanket around her until only her shaking hands were visible. Claire's knuckles were raw, her cuticles red and cracked around her chipped black nail polish. It was unlike her. Claire was neat and orderly, bordering on obsessive-compulsive. Seeing her so disheveled, even after what she'd been through, had Dana on edge. "You need to tell us what's going on."

The icy look Claire shot at her stung. "Oh, now you care what's going on in my life?"

"Claire," Jake warned, but she turned her glare on him.

"Don't defend her. She left you behind, too."

"Yeah, but if you want justice for your friend, we need her on our side."

Dana cringed. Did they really believe she wasn't on their side?

Claire bit her lip, her eyes watering as she glanced back at Dana, then the floor. "You're right," she whispered. "That's all that matters." Finally, Claire looked up, meeting Dana's gaze. "You'll help, right?"

Dana knew she couldn't say no. Not with Claire looking at her like that, but she hesitated, not sure what to say. She hated when her emotions surfaced. Everything about this felt too close to home. Young, vulnerable women being preyed upon. She'd almost lost Meredith to a monster with the same tastes. She couldn't lose Claire, too.

The similarities between Claire and Sadie were too much to ignore. If Claire's raven hair had been purple the two might've been mistaken for sisters. One was a PhD candidate, the other a junkie, but still they'd both started out in this world the same way before fate altered their paths.

Dana knew what it was like to have the ground torn out from beneath her, swallowing the best laid plans and paths. She easily could've ended up like Sadie if she hadn't channeled her grief into revenge. Still, the jury was out on whether or not she'd truly survived. Losing her parents at such a young age had forever scarred her. Some days survival just felt like trading one nightmare for another.

But this wasn't about her.

Everyone deserved justice, not just those with the privilege to afford it. This was her chance to even the score. "I'll do everything I can to help find who did this to Sadie."

"Thank you!" Claire threw her arms around Dana, sobbing wildly into her hair. The uncharacteristic display of affection was over almost as quickly as it had begun. Claire untangled herself and stood, wiping her cheeks with trembling hands. "I'm sorry, I-I just need a minute."

Dana watched Claire walk down the hall toward Jake's bathroom, baffled by her mood swings.

Jo ambled over, passing out coffee. "I don't know how you take yours," she said, offering Dana a mug.

"Black is fine."

"Just like Jake," she quipped, making a show of pouring a heinous amount of creamer into her own cup.

Dana was surprised Jake even had creamer in his fridge. *Or maybe she keeps it here.*

Pushing the stinging image of their domestic bliss from her mind, Dana gratefully sipped the piping hot beverage. She preferred tea, but she wasn't picky. She needed the caffeine. Wrapping her long fingers around the mug she tried to shake off the cobwebs of drowsiness clouding her mind. She needed to stay sharp. For Claire. For Sadie. For all the other victims out there who never got the justice they deserved.

"I hate to say it," Jo mused, "but I think Fuller might be right."

Jake's eyebrows knitted together. "About what?"

"Claire being a junkie."

He put his coffee mug down so hard some of it spilled over onto the table. Dana hated that the oozing pattern reminded her of blood. But she couldn't blame that on Jake or today's crime scene. Her morbid mind was triggered long ago.

Shutting out the images of her parents' crime scene, she pulled in a steadying breath to keep herself in the present.

Jake was on his feet. "She's not on drugs, Jo!"

"How can you be sure?"

"Because I know her."

"She's displaying all the signs. Mood swings, agitation, tremors, and her pupils look like bullseyes."

"Cut her some slack. She just watched her friend get murdered. There's no play book for that."

"Actually, there is," Jo argued. "And we're trained to know the signs."

Again, Dana felt she was watching a tennis match, or perhaps a battle of wills. Joanna Walsh was not to be trifled with. She'd gone toe-to-toe with Fuller today, and now she was skillfully taking on Jake. She looked cool as a cucumber while doing it too, which was more than Dana could say for Jake. The deep red coloring of his ears said he was two seconds away from flipping the coffee table as Jo rattled off the signs of shock like she was reciting the FBI handbook.

By the sounds of it, Jo was even more of a stickler for protocol than Jake. But all the humor Dana might've found in Jake having met his match drained away the more she realized Jo might be right.

13

Jake was doing his best to remember every technique he'd been taught to keep his cool as Jo threw the rule book at him; like he didn't know the signs of addiction. He had enough firsthand experience battling demons to write the Bureau's procedures and protocols. But right now, that didn't matter because they were talking about Claire. He knew her. Hell, she was like a little sister to him.

These past few months he'd been worried about her and doing his best to look out for her. He wouldn't have missed something so critical. "You don't know her like I do. She's not on drugs, Jo."

Jo was about to argue, but Dana cut her off. "Jake, I think she's right."

"Excuse me?" He whirled on her, the veins in his neck bulging. "You've been back all of a minute, Dana. Maybe you should consider how well you understand the situation before you start throwing around accusations."

She pointed toward the bathroom. "I understand that isn't the same Claire I left."

"Yeah, no shit! You haven't spoken to her for six months."

"That's not true."

"Emails about extending your lectures don't count," he countered, cutting off her argument.

He stormed to the bar. Hell with coffee. He needed something stronger. The irony of the situation was not lost on him. Long ago he'd beaten one addiction by trading it for another. His love of a good bourbon was acceptable, but he knew he teetered on the edge of what was healthy. Right now though, for the sake of everyone in the room, he poured himself enough to take the edge off.

Gulping it down, he took a moment to relish the pleasant burn followed by the even more pleasing calm. Collecting himself, Jake turned back to face Dana. "Did you see any tracks on her arms?"

"She's too smart for that, and you know it."

He did. There were lots of ways to disguise pain and the remedies people used to mask it. Taking another drink, Jake fought the sinking feeling in his gut. The bourbon was already doing its job, dulling his temper enough to let him think clearly. What Jo said made sense, and he couldn't deny that Claire had been acting irrationally. It was more than just what she'd witnessed with Sadie today. There'd been a sadness about her over the past few months, like she was carrying the weight of the world. He'd blamed it on Dana, but maybe he was just projecting.

Had he missed it? Had he failed Claire, too?

Resigned to at least listen, he walked back to the living room. "So what do we do?"

Jo spoke up first. "This isn't a halfway house, Jake. We're not equipped to deal with something like this, let alone the withdrawal. She needs to go to a methadone clinic."

"We don't even know what she's on," he argued.

"After Fuller said the vic was a junkie, I did some digging. Sadie Azeez has a rap sheet a mile long. All drug charges. The last six, heroin."

"I might have something." Dana stood up and walked to the kitchen counter. She dug through her purse, pulling out a small round tin that looked like shoe polish.

Jake followed her. "What is that?"

"Something to help her sleep off the withdrawal. I just need to boil water to make tea."

"I think she's gonna need something a little stronger than tea," Jo interjected.

"Trust me, it'll work. Even in micro-doses it's powerful stuff."

"Why do you have it?" Jake asked

Dana's gaze met his. "Insomnia."

"Still?"

She shrugged, and he fought the urge to pry. He wanted to ask her what else she had in her purse, his eyes straining, as if he could see through the leather. Did she still carry the prescription bottle in case Cramer came to haunt her dreams? He wanted to ask, but that wasn't his business. Not anymore.

"What's in it?" Jo asked, curious now.

"Mostly valerian root and a few other herbs. It's from a shaman in the Philippines. He's the only one who knows the true ingredients."

Jo blanched. "That's a little too trusting for me."

"Many are the afflictions of the righteous," Dana replied.

"What cult came up with that beauty?" she teased.

Dana smirked. "It's from the Bible, so I guess it depends on your take."

Jo's cheeks colored with embarrassment while Jake tried not to be impressed. Dana had always floored him with that beautiful mind of hers. Now he just hoped she'd be able to put it to use on this case.

14

WHEN CLAIRE CAME OUT OF THE BATHROOM, THEY HAD THEIR STORIES straight. Jake would play "bad cop" and Jo "good cop," which left "concerned friend" for Dana. Staging an impromptu intervention wasn't in her plan for the evening, but at least she was comfortable with her role. She needed to regain Claire's trust, and this was as good a way as any.

Guilt gnawed at her as she watched Claire take up her spot on the couch again. She looked so brittle as she curled her legs beneath her. There was no denying Dana was to blame for Claire's downward spiral. If she'd been here, she would've spotted her struggling. Or maybe she wouldn't have gone down this path at all.

Dana should've stayed put and continued to mentor her. She hadn't meant to be gone for so long, but the book tour took on a life of its own. One lecture always led to another. Truthfully, Dana had craved the time away. She needed the distance to make sense of everything she'd been through, with Jake, the FBI, Cramer, Meredith. It was a lot to unpack. There was no doubt her sabbatical had been necessary, but she was learning there was a price for clarity, and Claire had paid it.

Dana pushed the mug of tea toward her. "Here, this will help."

Claire took it, wrapping her boney fingers around the warm ceramic. "Help with what?"

"The detox," Jake said.

Eyes wide, Claire stilled, the mug halfway to her lips.

"Yeah, we know you've been using." Jake's tone was sharp enough to cut.

Claire set the mug down. "No I'm not."

Jo spoke up. "Claire, we're all on the same team here. We want to help, but that only happens if we're completely honest with each other."

"Sadie was a known user," Jake accused, "and that SUV you saw, I'd put money on it belonging to her dealer."

"It's not like that."

"Then help us understand," Dana pleaded.

Claire looked frightened, her pale eyes darting between them like a cornered animal. "I can't."

Dana kept her voice soft. "Why not?"

"The people Sadie worked for … it's not safe to get involved."

Jake scoffed. "A little late for that."

"I've got a call in to one of my old TOC friends," Jo added. "They're looking into the SUV. It's only a matter of time before we find out who's behind this. The sooner you tell us, the better chance we have of apprehending them."

On cue, her phone rang. Jo held up a finger and excused herself, her voice trailing down the hall until she disappeared into Jake's bedroom.

Dana spoke. "Claire, I know I haven't been here for you, and for that I'm sorry, but I want to make it up to you. We all do. But you have to let us in."

Tears welled in Claire's ice blue eyes, but she made no move to wipe them. "It could've been me." She shook her head slowly. "Sadie was just looking for a way to fill the void, to take away the loneliness. I thought I was helping her. I thought we were helping each other."

The pain in Claire's voice reached inside of Dana and opened a door she'd locked the day her parents died. She knew what it felt like to have a gaping hole inside, one so cavernous it felt like it could swallow the universe. That's why Dana had locked her emotions away. It was the only self-preservation she understood. It meant she couldn't connect, it cost her friends and relationships, but it kept her upright.

Claire was different. She wore her pain like a badge of honor. Dressed in black clothes and gothic jewelry, there was no mistaking she'd been brushed by death's icy hand. But somehow, she'd used it to make her stronger. Dana wanted to help her find that version of herself again. "Claire, please let us help."

She picked up the mug of tea, her eyes meeting Dana's. "This will get me through the withdrawals?"

Jake's knuckles were white as he gripped the arms of his chair. Dana expected the wood to splinter, but she kept her focus on Claire. "It will."

She took a sip, then another. "I met Sadie outside the Grave. It's an underground club here in D.C."

"Where?" Jake ground out.

"It's somewhere new each time. Never the same place twice."

"What kind of club?"

Claire looked into her tea. "Whatever you want it to be."

Jake was standing now. "What the hell were you doing at a place like that?"

Claire shrugged. "Looking for something to fill the void."

"Did Sadie work there?"

Claire nodded. "But I didn't know that at first. She was fun. We'd get high and dance. That was it. She'd text me the next address, and we'd do it again, but then I started to get creeped out by the men who were there ... I could tell they were bad news. I tried to get Sadie to go to other places with me, but she refused, until one night, I showed up and she wasn't there. I asked around, and one of the other girls told me she'd OD'd. I'd seen what happened to people who partied too hard at the Grave."

"You found her?" Dana asked.

Claire nodded. "In a dumpster off 8th. She was still alive. That's when I took her back to the Smithsonian."

"Why didn't you call me?" Jake yelled.

"I wanted to, but Sadie begged me not to. That's when she told me what was really going on at the Grave."

"Which is?"

"Diablo, that's what they call the guy in charge, he brought Sadie here from Venezuela. He offered to give her a job and get her family refuge in Brazil. She just had to bring a package to him first."

Jake's hand gripped the back of his neck. "She was a drug mule."

"Worse. Diablo got her hooked on H and made her work at the Grave." Claire trembled. "She told me about the things the men did to her there. She told me he threatened to have her family killed if she tried to leave. That's why I didn't tell you. We thought if Diablo thought she was already dead she'd be safe to leave. I was just trying to help her get clean first."

"Except she forgot to mention she was a CIA informant," Jake muttered. "Do you have any idea what kind of danger she put you in?"

Claire flinched at his harsh tone. "I was just trying to help her."

"Then you should've come to me!"

"Jake," Dana warned. He was taking his "bad cop" role too far. Claire was opening up to them. If they were going to rebuild their trust, she needed to tell her side of the story without judgment.

Dana moved closer to Claire on the couch. She stroked her long black hair. It was tangled and limp. "You're telling us now. That's what matters."

"No, he's right. If I'd said something earlier, we could've saved her."

Dana took Claire's hand. "We can't change the past, but we can stop this guy from hurting anyone else."

She nodded. "I'll tell you anything you want to know."

Jake sat back down, pulling his notebook from his pocket. "This Diablo guy, what can you tell me about him?"

Claire shrugged. "Not much. I never saw him."

"Ever heard him called by any other names?"

"How 'bout Obasi Ikemba?" Jo asked, striding back into the room. "I just got off the phone with my TOC contact. He confirmed our SUV belongs to a dealer who goes by the name of Keke. He's part of Ikemba's crew."

Jake swore.

"What?" Dana asked, not following.

"The Ikemba Cartel is the largest narcotics organization in Africa." Jake explained. "They've been bankrolling the Nigerian mafia by using Venezuelan drug mules to move product from South Africa to Europe and now the states. And if they're running the Grave, you can add human trafficking to their resume."

"Yeah and it gets worse," Jo added. "I got CCTV footage of the same SUV doing a second look while Metro was on site."

Jake stood abruptly and kicked his chair, swearing again.

"I don't understand. What does that mean?" Claire asked.

"It means they saw you, Claire. It means you're on Ikemba's radar, and that is *not* a place you want to be."

15

THEY SPENT THE NEXT HOUR GOING OVER ALL THE LOCATIONS CLAIRE could remember for the Grave along with the type of clientele she saw there. That plus the dump site where she'd found Sadie painted a picture Jake didn't like. Drugs, arms, human trafficking; it was a criminal trifecta, which meant there was no way he'd be able to pry this case back from the CIA. Especially since Jo's contacts also revealed that Fuller and his team had been tracking Obasi Ikemba for more than a year.

Jake knew it was only a matter of time until Jenkins called Fuller, trying to spin the joint task force angle. It wasn't ideal, but at least it would mean the FBI wouldn't be shut out. There were far too many people involved in this case that he cared about for him to be left in the dark. Three of them sat in his living room.

Caught in the middle wasn't a place Jake liked to be. Working a case with his current flame and past flame was hard enough. Knowing Claire was a target made it worse. The pressure was seeping in, distracting him from doing his best work. Which was probably why he'd missed the connection between the Grave and Ikemba. But still, something didn't fit.

Jo was showing Claire photographs of D.C. dealers to see if she recognized any of them from the club. So far, of the three decapitated vics, Claire recognized the first two. Jake already pegged them as low-level organized crime thugs, so Claire putting them at the Grave wasn't news. They were probably bagmen for Ikemba. Blowing off steam at a sleazy underground club was par for the course.

The thing that bothered Jake was the third victim. He still hadn't been identified and Claire didn't recognize him which meant he probably wasn't on Ikemba's payroll. It was also where the pattern changed, playing cards to tarot cards. Then there was Sadie. Was she a part of this or were the Nigerians just tying up loose ends? A tarot card had been found at her scene too. Not jammed down her throat like the others. Another pattern change. Jake tried to get access to the card but Fuller refused.

If Ikemba was behind Sadie's murder, then it meant the tarot cards were his calling cards. It could mean the playing cards were the signature of Ikemba's rival, but without more to go on, it was barely a theory.

Jake hated this part of the hunt. He had more questions than answers.

Who'd left the playing cards? Was this as simple as a turf war between drug lords? And how the hell had he let Claire get tied up in it?

Again, his mind drew him back to the crime scene. From the blood spatter on the sidewalk, he'd guess the girl's jugular had been severed. It was consistent with Claire's account of the assault. Thanks to Sadie's unfortunate luck of stumbling into traffic, it would be a while before forensics could confirm cause of death. The car that hit her sent her up and over, only for her to be run over by the car behind.

The corpse had reminded Jake of a broken rag doll. Purple hair, vacant eyes, twisted limbs. He hated that Claire had to see that. For him, it was just another day on the job. He'd seen a lot worse. In a way he was grateful the Army desensitized him to such brutality. But for those who weren't, he imagined it would haunt them.

He watched Claire. She sat on the couch between Jo and Dana, her eyelids growing heavy. Dana's potion was finally kicking in. Jake studied the women, the way they interacted. As usual, Jo was all business, but

Dana looked strangely maternal as she stroked Claire's hair or squeezed her hand. Even stranger than that, Claire let her. Whatever was in that tea must be powerful stuff. Or maybe Claire's drug use was more than the brief recreational dabbling she was trying to brush under the rug.

Jake had seen just how deep a drug could penetrate, altering personalities until people he thought he knew became unrecognizable. A memory of his mother strapped to a hospital bed surfaced before he could stop it. He could still hear her screaming. It had been his father who'd broken her spirit, but the drugs had taken what was left. Jake refused to let that happen to anyone else he cared about.

He continued to watch the women, his eyes finding their way back to Dana as she mothered Claire. It wasn't that Jake thought Dana was cold. He knew she cared about Claire the same way he did. But he also knew she was damaged, just like him. Dana rarely let her emotions show. She had trouble letting people in. Claire was the same way, but at the moment, she didn't seem to mind being comforted by her mentor.

Maybe it was the tea, or maybe it was a step toward Dana and Claire reconciling. Either way he was glad to have both of them here. He always felt better when he knew they were safe. And right now, Claire needed protecting more than ever.

A moment later her head drooped onto Dana's shoulder. "She's out," Dana said.

"You sure?" Jake moved to get a closer look. Sure enough Claire's eyes were closed, her breath finding the steady rhythm of sleep.

"Now what?" Jo asked.

"We let her sleep." Dana said.

"How much did you give her?" Jake asked.

"Enough. She'll be out for at least eight hours."

He nodded. "I'll put her in my room." Stooping between Dana and Jo he scooped Claire into his arms. She was even lighter than she looked. His chest tightened. How had he let this happen right under his nose? He'd failed her.

Gently, he carried her down the hall to his bedroom, vowing to make it up to her.

16

Dana watched Jake disappear down the hall, Jo moving alongside him to help. Again, she was left with the nagging feeling of emptiness. Before Jake, she'd always been comfortable being invisible. If people didn't see her, they couldn't see her flaws, her pain, her secrets. But Jake had seen her, and he hadn't looked away.

Now, standing alone in his apartment, it was hard to feel unseen.

Feeling like an intruder, she went about gathering her things. Jake and Jo could take it from here. Claire would spend the next eight hours or so sleeping, which was what Dana needed to do if she was going to be of any use tomorrow.

She was halfway to the door when she heard Jake's voice behind her. "Where do you think you're going?"

She turned to face him. He looked as tired as she felt. "Home."

"The hell you are. You just drugged our only witness. You're not going anywhere until she wakes up, and I know that tea isn't worse than whatever she's already on."

"Do you really think I'd give her something if I wasn't certain it was safe?"

"I don't know what I'm certain of anymore."

And there it was. Jake laid it out for her as plain as day. He didn't trust her. Dana sucked in a breath, gutted. She'd saved Jake's life, twice. He'd told her about the soldiers he'd lost. She'd told him about her parents. Hell, she'd had enough faith in him that she'd let him shoot her to get to a serial killer. How had they fallen so far from that safe space?

But that was the thing about trust. It took a lifetime to gain and a moment to lose.

Jo walked into the tension filled room. A trained FBI agent, there was no way she missed the strain between them, but she was gracious enough to try to diffuse the situation. "I'm starving. Why don't we order some food? I'm sure Claire will be hungry when she wakes up. She likes Chinese, right?"

"Thai." Dana and Jake said the word in unison, their eyes still locked in a showdown.

"Right." Jo rifled through a pile of menus she pulled from one of Jake's kitchen drawers.

"We don't need a menu," Jake muttered. "I'll just order the usual."

"Oh. Okay." Jo shut the drawer. "Am I figured into the *usual*?"

Jake was still staring at Dana. When he didn't answer, Jo cleared her throat. "Okay, I guess you can just get me whatever you're having."

Jake finally turned away from Dana to look at his girlfriend. "You don't like spicy food."

"Then I'll have what Dana's having."

"It's vegetarian," Dana replied.

Jo gave a tight smile. "I can make that work."

Jake pulled his phone from his pocket and quickly called in the order. "It'll be here in twenty," he grumbled once he'd ended the call.

"Great." Jo stretched her hands above her head, her back popping loudly. "Mind if I take a quick shower? I'd love to get the smell of crime scene off me before we eat."

Jake gave a stiff nod. Undeterred, Jo crossed the kitchen and kissed him. Running her hand through his short brown hair, she grinned up at him. "Everything looks better after a shower and a hot meal." She gave him a smack on the ass. "Hooah, soldier."

"Hooah." Jake's reply was automatic but lacked enthusiasm, though

Jo didn't seem to notice. She padded down the hall and disappeared into the bathroom, taking her good-natured attitude with her.

Without Jo in the room the tension returned ten-fold. For Claire's sake, Dana knew she had to find a way to make things right. If anyone was going to break the ice, it would have to be her. "Jake, you know I'd never purposely endanger Claire."

"Neither would I."

"I know that." She took a step toward him, but he moved around the kitchen island into the living room, stopping in front of the bookcase. Dana watched his gaze settle on the folded American flag. Her mind pictured the dog tags she knew he wore beneath his shirt. Was he thinking about Ramirez? "We're going to protect her, Jake."

"What if we can't?"

"You can."

He turned to face her. "Not with the CIA involved. They only care about results. Anyone who gets in the way is collateral damage."

Dana's skin crawled as she thought of Fuller. It seemed the snake had finally found a place where he belonged. Was Jake right? Would the CIA look the other way if Fuller's aggression went too far?

"How do you know him, by the way?" Jake asked.

"Fuller?"

"Yeah. There's no way we shake him off this case, so I'd like to know what I'm up against. What's the story with you two?"

"There's no story."

"With you, there's always a story."

His words hit their mark, but Dana refused to show he'd wounded her. Jake had enough to deal with without knowing Fuller had harassed her years ago and possibly framed and murdered someone who'd been willing to help her when no one else would. Mentioning it now would do no good. Besides, it was a lifetime ago, though it seemed Fuller had staying power when it came to holding a grudge.

Let him, she thought. He may have found where he belongs, but so had she. She wasn't the same scared girl she'd been back then. She'd slayed demons worse than him. If he came at her again, she'd be ready.

"There's really nothing to tell," she said. "Our paths crossed a long time ago. He was a jerk then, he's a jerk now." Jake didn't look convinced, but Dana shifted the conversation back to what mattered. "Why didn't you tell me what was going on with Claire?"

"I didn't think you cared."

"That's not fair, Jake."

"Yeah, it didn't feel very fair when you left her behind either."

"I left to go on my book tour. To shed light on the Priory of Bones so their darkness wouldn't infect anyone else. Claire knew that."

"You're too smart to play dumb, Dana."

She threw her hands up. "And you're too blind to see what's right in front of you!"

"Just what the hell is that supposed to mean?"

"It means it doesn't matter why I left. I'm back now and I'm here to help Claire, so get over yourself so we can keep her safe."

Anger simmered off Jake in waves, his nostrils flaring. She watched him chew the inside of his cheek for a full five seconds before he muttered, "Fine."

He turned his back on her and walked over to his wet bar to pour another drink. Dana's mind immediately jumped to another time when she'd come here to share a drink with him. She shoved the memory back into her vault and locked it away. Changing gears, she asked, "How is she managing her course work in the middle of all of this?"

"She's not."

Dana stilled. "What do you mean, she's not?"

Jake corked his bourbon and faced her. "She took a break."

"Jake! PhD candidates don't get breaks! She's on an accelerated program."

"Considering I'm focused on trying to keep her alive, I'd say PhD's can wait."

"How could you let this happen?"

Jake crossed the room so quickly Dana barely had time to keep her balance. She backed into the wall. With nowhere else to go, Jake invaded her space. His breath was warm with a hint of bourbon as it caressed her skin. To an outsider, they might look intimate, but there was nothing inviting about the way he was looking at her. "Don't you dare blame this on me. We both let her down."

Dana swallowed hard. "You're right."

"We need to fix this." Jake stood there, glaring at her like he was waiting for her to tell him how. He was a man tormented by the guilt of past failings. She wouldn't add to them.

"We will," she promised, though she hadn't the slightest clue where they went from here.

The doorbell rang, breaking the spell that held them a breath apart. Jake stepped away first, leaving Dana feeling like she did before she'd left—unsteady.

17

Jenkins called the next morning. Just like Jake predicted, they'd been assigned to a joint task force with the CIA and a select few members of Metro police. Fuller was running point. So far, the only thing going Jake's way was the fact that he'd gotten some shut-eye.

He'd set up shifts to watch Claire through the night while still managing to give each of them some rest. Jake had strategically set the schedule, so he was never alone with Dana. He didn't trust himself. They needed to put the past behind them and find a way to work together for Claire's sake, but he didn't know how. And until he did, he planned to keep his distance when he could.

Currently, Dana was sitting at his kitchen island with Jo, pouring over the new evidence the CIA had sent over while Jake made eggs. It felt strangely domestic, despite the fact that both women were pouring over crime scene photos like it was a Sky Mall catalog.

Jake put a plate of eggs in front of Jo and she grinned. "Thanks, babe."

"Dana, what can I make for you?"

"Coffee's fine," she said, taking a sip from the mug in front of her.

"You've got to try Jake's eggs," Jo prodded. "They're the best."

Dana eyed the eggs distastefully. "I'm a vegetarian."

"That's right. Do you want some of your leftovers from last night? Oh, or I think I saw a waffle maker in the cabinet. Jake, why don't you whip her up some waffles?"

Dana's dark brown eyes met his. They filled with regret before she looked back into her coffee. "I don't really have much of an appetite for waffles these days."

Jake cleared his throat, trying not to read too much into her comment. *They're just waffles, Jake. Let it go.* He looked at Jo. "Anything new to go on?"

"Yeah, too much. This is like a year's worth of research."

"Did the CIA give us access to the tarot card from yesterday's scene yet?" Dana asked.

"No. They claim they're still processing evidence from yesterday." Jo pushed her laptop toward Dana, presumably showing her the BS chain of command email they'd received this morning.

Dana frowned. "How do they expect us to get anywhere without all the evidence?"

"They don't," Jake answered, his tone flat. "This evidence dump is the first of many roadblocks."

Jo explained when Dana blinked her big brown eyes in confusion. "It's basically a bureaucratic needle in a haystack situation. It's something other agencies do when they're told to cooperate but don't want to."

"Then what's the point of a joint task force?" Dana asked.

"Good question," Jake muttered.

"They *do* work," Jo defended. "Although I have to admit they work better when they're conceptualized and created from the ground up, not cobbled together at the eleventh hour."

"How do you know so much about this?"

Jo shrugged. "Lawyer's kid."

Jake huffed a laugh. "Modest."

"Okay," Jo conceded, "My father's the DA, but to me he's just Dad. He puts his pants on one leg at a time like everyone else."

Jake smirked. "Somehow I don't think anyone else can get away with saying that about Stonewall Walsh."

"He hates that nickname, by the way." Jo continued perusing the files. "I'm pretty sure my time could be better spent seeking out some of my old CIs."

"Not by yourself," Jake shot back.

Jo gave him her famous *don't patronize me* glare. "Yes, because I need you to hold my hand. Remind me, were you there on my first tour in Afghanistan or was it my third? Oh, that's right, neither."

"I'm not questioning your ability, Jo. I'm just suggesting teamwork."

"And I'm suggesting you sit this one out. My CIs will take one look at you and be in the wind."

"Fine, but you need backup. Call Fuller and get someone from the task force to go with you."

"I'll go," Dana offered.

Jake's temper spiked. He gripped the dishrag in his hand to keep from cracking his knuckles. "That's not the kind of backup I had in mind."

Now he had both women glaring at him.

"Why not?" Dana challenged. "You're the one who wanted me on this case."

Actually, no he wasn't. This clusterfuck was Jenkins' doing, but he couldn't very well say that.

"See, look at that," Jo boasted, testing his patience. "I have back up. And someone from the task force, no less."

"I meant take someone in law enforcement," Jake ground out.

Jo turned to Dana. "Was he always this hard to work with?"

Dana smirked. "You have no idea."

Jake conceded. "Fine, we'll all go."

"Someone needs to stay with Claire," Dana objected.

He scoffed. "And I'm the obvious choice for babysitter in this scenario?"

"Who needs a babysitter?" Claire asked.

She stood in the hallway, dwarfed in Jake's oversized ARMY sweatshirt. Her eyes were bloodshot, and her black hair stuck out in every direction. "Good morning," Jake greeted. "You hungry? We got Thaiphoon last night. I saved you some dumplings."

Claire shook her head.

Concern softened Jake's voice. "You need to eat something, Claire."

"What you need is more tea," Dana said, crossing the kitchen to turn the kettle on. She fetched her tin and scooped some of the powdered concoction into a mug. Setting it back inside her purse she felt Claire's forehead. "How do you feel?"

"Like I'm gonna be sick," she said before rushing from the kitchen.

Jake flinched when he heard the bathroom door slam. His eyes met Dana's, matching her unease. "How much longer will she be like this?"

"If she was truthful about the last time she used, I'd say the next twenty-four hours will be the worst of it."

"Are you sure we shouldn't take her to a clinic?" Jo asked.

Jake shook his head. "I'm not letting her out of my sight until I'm sure she's not on Ikemba's hit list."

"Then it's settled," Dana said, pouring the boiling water. "You'll stay here with Claire, while Jo and I go talk to her CI."

18

"That was like poetry back there," Jo said as she turned on 6th Street. "You just effortlessly spun Jake's argument back on him. You've got to teach me how to do that."

"I think you do well enough on your own."

"Well sure, being able to hold my own comes with the territory. I didn't make it this far in a career dominated by men with inflated egos without knowing how to play the game. But Jake's different."

Dana arched an eyebrow. "How so?"

"Well for one he's the most pig-headed man I've ever met. Don't get me wrong, he can be incredibly sweet too. But the moment we started dating he turned into this overprotective goon. It drives me nuts. Did you have to deal with that when you were partners?"

Dana cringed at the word, realizing she'd assumed they were more. "It can be frustrating, but it's natural to want to protect the people we care about."

"I get that. But he acts like this is my first rodeo. I've served as many tours as he has, *and* I've been with the Bureau longer."

Dana gripped the door as Jo took a screeching left onto O Street. "It's nice that you have so much in common."

"Tell me about it." Jo grinned. "Finding decent men to date in this city is impossible. Finding one that understands this job and the military ..." She laughed. "Jake Shepard is a goddamn unicorn. I can't tell you how great it is to be able to talk about Afghanistan with someone who gets it."

Dana swallowed something that tasted too close to jealousy. "He talks to you about that?"

"When he needs to."

"Good. I'm glad he found someone he can open up to."

Jo laughed. "I don't know if I'd use those exact words. I practically need a can opener to pry anything out of him. The man's like Fort Knox when it comes to emotions, but I get it. We went through some dark shit over there. It's not something that's easy to let out in front of anyone who hasn't lived it."

"Why not?"

She shrugged. "I don't know. I guess it feels like it might make people view us differently. It'd be like someone seeing your kill sheet, rather than seeing you. We were different people over there. We had to be. For me, I left that life behind when I started at the Bureau. But I think Jake still carries it with him."

Dana agreed. She wished he'd let it out before it ate him alive. She knew the burden of carrying a painful past. She hadn't exactly gotten closure with her parents' murders, but at least it wasn't something she had to hide anymore. Maybe now that Jake had Jo, he wouldn't have to hide either.

Uncomfortable with the heaviness settling over the car, Dana changed the subject. "So why'd you choose the FBI?"

"It sorta chose me."

"How do you mean?"

"When I was discharged, my dad was working this big mob case. I didn't have a job so he hired me on at his office. I helped dig up the dirt they needed to prosecute the scumbag. Next thing I know I get a call from the FBI to work organized crime. I jumped in with both feet."

It was hard not to like the woman. She was strong, funny, confident and gave Dana the respect most people in the Bureau didn't. "I haven't had a chance to thank you, Agent Walsh."

"Please, call me Jo. And what are you thanking me for?"

"For helping Claire."

"The way I see it, she's family. Like you said, we protect the people we care about. Claire's important to Jake, so she's important to me. Same goes for you."

Dana didn't know what to say, only that she wished she could hate the beautiful blonde agent next to her. But so far, Jo's only flaw seemed to be her driving skills. She veered onto 7th. "Ya know, I'm really glad we get to work this case together."

"You are?"

"Well, yeah. I wasn't kidding when I said you're a legend at the Bureau. Getting to work with the great Dr. Gray before I transfer to HRT is the perfect bookend to my career in D.C."

"You're leaving D.C.?"

Shock flashed across Jo's flawless complexion. "Jake didn't tell you?"

Dana shook her head, not wanting the excitement coursing through her to seep into her voice.

"I guess you two haven't had much time to catch up. Besides Jenkins, you're the only one who knows. As soon as this case is over, I'm heading to Denver to start training. I'm still pinching myself. HRT has been my dream since I was a kid." She laughed at herself. "I know, most little girls don't dream of joining the FBI's most elite tactical unit, but what can I say, I was an Army brat. This lifestyle is just in my blood."

"What about Jake?"

"He's been incredibly supportive. Honestly it was an easy choice to accept the position once I found a spot in the Denver field office for him. It's all falling into place. Now we just have to wrap up this Card Killer case."

Dana gripped the door handle, as Jo's words harpooned her hope. Jake was leaving. The news stunned her. She hadn't realized she still held hope that somehow, they'd get back to that place they'd been before she left. But this was the final blow. She'd taken him for granted, and now she had to deal with the repercussions.

That hollow space in Dana's heart pulsed with regret. Silencing it with thoughts of the case helped. Claire was someone else she'd taken for granted, but she wasn't lost yet, and Dana was determined to keep it that way.

19

Dana felt queasy as she exited Jo's SUV in the pay-to-park lot, unsure if it was from the agent's breakneck driving or the news she'd shared. Still reeling, Dana did her best to focus on the case as they walked the short distance to a tattoo parlor on 9th.

"I'll warn you," Jo said. "Needles is a sleaze ball, but he's harmless."

"All that matters is that he gives us a lead."

"If anyone knows what Ikemba is up to, it'll be Needles. He specializes in inking lowlifes. His shop is like a gossip hub for gangbangers and drug lords."

"So what's the plan?"

"The plan is to let me do the talking. If I can get Needles to ID our third vic, we can figure out if this is a cartel war or something else."

"What about Claire?"

"If you want to keep her safe, keep her name out of your mouth around Needles."

"But how will we know if Ikemba is coming after her?"

"We won't."

Dana stopped walking. "Then what are we doing here?"

"We're trying to gather dirt. With enough of it we might be able to bury Ikemba. Our best chance of protecting Claire is getting him off the streets."

"That's it? Just gather dirt? That's not good enough."

Jo exhaled. "I know. But right now, it's all we have." When Dana didn't reply, she pressed on. "Look, I know it's hard, but you need to trust me. I'm good at what I do. If Ikemba is behind these attacks like we think he is, Needles can help point us in the direction of the tools we need to bury him. It's a process, but it works."

Knowing she didn't have another option, Dana conceded. She hated relinquishing control, especially when it came to protecting those she loved. She and Jake were the same that way. But if Jake trusted Jo, then Dana could too, even if she didn't like it. "Does this Needles have a real name?"

"Why?"

"You can tell a lot by a name."

Jo grinned. "It's Vincent Dega Pinkerton."

"I see why he changed it."

It was surprisingly bright inside the tattoo parlor. Three of the walls were painted a cheerful red. The far wall was yellow with a giant mural of a purple needle piercing a screaming heart. Even though the image was violent, it was created with an almost cartoonish, childlike quality. Dana couldn't stop staring at it.

"See something you like, chica?"

She jumped at the whisper-soft voice behind her. Dana turned ready to strike, but Jo was faster. She was already facing the scrawny, ink-covered man. He had a shaved head and was covered in tattoos that started at his throat, disappearing beneath the collar of his black t-shirt only to reappear again on his arms to his fingertips. His affinity for jewelry was evident in the dozens of facial piercings and the large silver chain he wore around his neck. It unleashed a sudden image of the chains on Dana's childhood swing set in West Virginia, dingy and smelling of pennies.

"We're here on business, Needles," Jo said.

"All work and no play," he teased, his dark, beady eyes sparkling with mischief.

He had a long, thin nose that gave him weasel-like features that seemed to fit his persona. He was tall, but stooped, moving with a slink to his step, and when he smiled, it was part darkness, part juvenile.

But under all that ink and steel, Dana could tell Vincent Dega Pinkerton still existed; a scrawny boy who'd most likely been bullied. But he was a survivor, a chameleon. He'd found a way to camouflage his weakness and take the power back. Through needles and ink he could inflict pain and gain control while calling it art.

Had Pinkerton found the perfect career path or was it a gateway to something more?

He made to move closer, but in one swift move Jo had his arm painfully twisted behind his back.

His howl of pain turned into a laugh. Puckering his pierced lips, he made kissing noises. "Oh you know I like it rough, Jo-Jo."

She wrenched his arm up, sending him hissing to his knees. "I live to serve," she quipped.

His eyes traveled to Dana, glinting as he did his best to hide his pain, but his voice betrayed him. "Who's your friend?"

"Needles, meet Dr. Gray. Dr. Gray, this is Needles."

"Nah! You brought me the Witch Doctor?" Needles' dark eyes brightened. "Please tell me I get to ink that flawless skin, chica."

Jo winked at Dana. "Told you you're a legend." She dragged Needles back to his feet and released her grip on his arm. "Sorry to disappoint, Needles, but I told you we're here on official business."

Rubbing his shoulder, he clicked his tongue at Jo. "Word on the street is you're getting outta the game, Princesa?"

"I might be, but you know I always have time for my favorite informant."

"I knew you couldn't stay away."

"We're here about the Card Killer."

He sucked his teeth. "Took you long enough."

"What's that supposed to mean?" Dana asked.

Needles glared at her. "I don't answer to you." Leaning closer, he stroked a finger down her cheek. "Now it'd be a different story if you let me needle that virgin skin of yours."

It was Dana's turn to bring him to his knees. Without warning, she jammed her knee into his thigh, sweeping his opposite leg as he fell off balance. He hit the floor with a thud.

Grinning up at her, Needles laughed. "Mierda, Jo-Jo, this one's feistier than you, and that's saying something."

Jo reached down and helped him up. "Yeah, and she doesn't have a badge to answer to, so I'd cut the act and answer our questions before she messes up your pretty face."

The various rings and barbells adorning his face danced as he grinned. "Alright. Whatcha wanna know?"

Jo showed Needles the photos of the three decapitated victims. "You know them?"

"Sure."

"Names?"

Needles held out his hand.

Jo shook her head. "You'll get the usual fee once I get answers."

"This is gonna cost double."

"How do you figure?"

"'Cause we're talking about Ikemba."

Jo reached in her pocket and pulled out a wade of cash. Counting out half of it, she handed it over to Needles. "We already know the first two headless horsemen. Azi Udo and Keller Kent."

Needles nodded. "I seen their faces all over the news."

"And number three?" Dana asked.

Needles clicked his tongue. "That's not how this works, chica."

"We have to get there on our own," Jo explained, "Or Needles will be labeled a snitch." She gave him a cynical smile. "And we wouldn't want that, now would we?"

"Snitches get stitches," he sang, his voice almost giddy.

The man was clearly sadistic, but Jo had brought her here for a reason. Dana had just met her, but she could tell the agent had good instincts, so she did her best to be patient.

Needles moved behind a small glass display case and bowed. "Consider me your criminal oujia board."

Dana balked at the twisted game he was playing. He was taking pleasure in wasting their time. For all she knew Ikemba had people hunting Claire right now. "This isn't a game," she warned.

He mocked her. "Oh, is someone not having fun?"

Jo pulled out more cash, refocusing his attention. Dana hated that they were paying the little rat of a man, but she'd do whatever it took to ensure Claire's safety.

"This is the third victim," Jo said, holding up the photo. "Is he with Ikemba?"

Needles shook his head, his piercings dancing in the light.

Jo guessed again. "One of his rivals?"

Needles nodded.

Jo rattled off names like she was reciting the alphabet, but Needles just stooped lower, leaning his boney elbows on the glass countertop above an assortment of jewelry and piercing equipment. "Come on, Needles," Jo muttered. "You gotta give me something."

Needles shook his head, looking up at Dana through dark lashes, his voice a whisper. "You first."

A familiar chill swept through Dana as a name slammed into her mind like a freight train. "Vega?" she murmured.

Needles cackled. "Vega's history. But you already knew that, right, Witch Doctor? What you didn't know is that you left Deanwood for the taking."

Dana shuttered, remembering the last monster she hunted with Jake, the one who had a hand in brainwashing her best friend.

Jo spoke up. "If you mean she helped rid the city of a snake, then yes, you're correct."

Needles raised his shoulders to his ears, still smirking. "Cut the head off one snake and two more grow back."

Dana's breath caught. "What'd you say?"

"Ignore him," Jo ordered.

"No, that's it. With Vega out of the way his territory is up for grabs. That's what Ikemba is after. But he's not the only one."

"Ding! Ding! Ding! Ten points to Hufflepuff!" Needles sang.

Jo glared at him, holding up the photo of the third victim. "Who does he belong to?"

"How should I know?"

"Because once they get made, you're the only one these creeps let tag them."

"Well, I *am* very talented," he said, spider-walking his long fingers up the ink covering his arms.

"Who's he with?" Jo asked again.

His eyes gleamed with pleasure. "Guess."

"Do you know how many different gangs and dealers there are in this city?"

"Start with the ones closest to Deanwood," Dana suggested.

Jo's slender eyebrows arched. "That would narrow it down." She paused, lost in thought. "It'd have to be someone with enough cojones to go toe-to-toe with Ikemba." Her eyes brightened. "Santos?"

Needles grinned, nodding this time. "You're good at this game."

"Yeah, but I'm getting tired of playing. I need a name for my vic."

"Did you say you need a tattoo? I've got some beauties to show you." Needles pulled a black binder from beneath the counter and flipped to a page. There were photographs of people, but no faces, just the art he'd given them. "This piece has been very popular."

He pointed to an image of naked women locked inside a skull. Jo snapped a photo with her phone. "Thanks, Needles. It's been a pleasure as always." She threw the rest of the cash at him and grabbed Dana's hand.

On the street Dana pulled free of Jo's grasp. "Why'd we leave?"

"We got what we need. The tattoo database will do the rest. It'll give us a name and confirm the ID of our third vic. And if he's one of Santos' guys, we have a motive."

"For what?"

"For a drug war." Jo's green eyes sparkled in the pale winter sun. "Dana, you nailed it! This proves we're not dealing with a serial killer. This is two kingpins of organized crime going after Vega's piece of the pie. This is good news!"

It didn't feel like good news, but Dana's attention was already on something else. She stared at the shop across the street, the neon sign calling to her like, well ... a sign.

Jo was still babbling. "The city has funding for this. The mayor will issue all hands on deck. It'll give us the manpower we need to flush these guys out. I'll get my guys on the tattoo, but we should go back to Jake's and tell him the news. He's lead on our team, so he'll need to be the one to send it up the task force chain of command."

"Fine," Dana murmured, still staring at the glowing letters in the shop window: *Seeking Answers? Palm Readings. Tea Leaves. Tarot.* "I'll meet you back at the car. There's something I need to do."

20

"I've got news, too," Jake said after Jo filled him in on what they'd learned from her CI. "The CIA finally released the evidence from yesterday's scene." He spun his laptop around to show the two women seated at his kitchen island. The image of a tarot card filled the screen. "I looked it up. It's called the Wheel."

Jo gave it a once over and shrugged. "I don't know that it matters now that we have a name for our third vic. My guys ran the tattoo through the database on the way over. Meet Marcos Silva, lowlife-dealer extraordinaire for the Santos cartel."

It was hard to argue with Jo when she found a lead she liked. She was like a blonde bloodhound on a scent. He couldn't deny she was making progress. Her visit to her CI uncovered one more piece of the puzzle, but Jake couldn't help thinking the cards meant something.

Most people didn't have tarot cards lying around and even if they did, they wouldn't randomly choose one to shove down someone's throat after beheading them. He'd worked enough serials to know there was a method to most madness. The cards had to mean something. It was a message, a clue. Jake just didn't know how to decipher it.

His gaze moved to Dana. If anyone could figure it out it was her.

He'd watched her decode spell books in dead languages like she was doing a child's crossword puzzle. So why wasn't she offering any input?

She'd been quiet since they'd returned. At first, he chalked it up to Jo's enthusiasm. It could be hard to get a word in edgewise when she was excited about something, but now he sensed it was more.

Had something happened with the CI?

If that creep touched her ...

Jake forced his anger back down. Dana wasn't his to protect. Plus, he knew she was perfectly capable of taking care of herself. He didn't need to perform a repeat showing of how to patronize his partners. He'd had his fill of eating crow this morning.

Sitting at home twiddling his fingers nearly killed him. His only peace of mind was knowing that Claire was sleeping soundly in the next room; safe. Jo and Dana had returned safely, too. Jake had nothing immediate to worry about, and yet he still couldn't shake his unease.

"Dana, do you have any theories?" he asked, tapping his computer screen to gain her attention.

Her eyes met his, searing him with a flash of anger. It only lasted a moment before she looked away, but he hadn't missed it. He also hadn't missed the way she avoided looking at the screen completely.

Dana stood abruptly. "Jo's right. You should focus on drafting a statement to get the task force up to speed on Santos and Ikemba. The tarot cards are insignificant."

Dana Gray was turning down the opportunity to fight crime with the occult? Something was definitely wrong, and Jake was through ignoring his instincts. "They're not insignificant. These murders were well thought out. The decapitations were clean. That meant whoever did this is invested and precise. They had time to think it through. The fact that the cards were placed in the victims' mouths is a statement. Someone's trying to send a message."

"Maybe, but I don't know what it is, and that makes my expertise unnecessary."

"You're as necessary to this case as I am," Jake shot back, his temper slipping. "Claire would tell you the same thing."

Again, he caught a simmering rage behind Dana's normally warm brown eyes. "I don't know what you want me to tell you, Jake. It takes more than two cards to read tarot."

"Yeah, but you *can* read them, right?"

"I understand the basic principles."

"So take a stab at it."

"Is that how the Bureau does things now? Haphazardly?"

"It's better than walking away without trying." Jake realized his comment might be about more than the case, but he didn't regret saying it. Not when it was true on all accounts.

Dana's eyes narrowed, the gold flecks in her irises dancing like glowing embers. "You want me to try?" She marched back to the island and slammed her purse onto the counter, pulling out a deck of large purple cards.

Okay, so maybe some people did have tarot cards laying around.

Dana rifled through the deck, giving Jake glimpses of the delicate white artwork scrawled on the back. She placed two cards face up on his black granite countertop. "Here. The Tower was with Marcos Silva. It means intense and sudden change, release, painful loss, tragedy, revelation. Want me to take a *stab* at deciphering it? Maybe this card means someone was trying to tell him he was going to die."

"Having your head chopped off is definitely a painful loss," Jo snarked, but Dana wasn't done.

She jabbed a finger at the next card. "The Wheel, or Wheel of Fortune as it's more accurately known, was found with Sadie Azeez. What message do you think she was supposed to get? The card means chance, destiny, fate, karma, life cycles. Not so bad, unless you draw this card in reverse." Dana spun the card so it was upside down. "Now it means upheaval, lousy luck, setbacks from external forces like divine intervention and timing. Sounds like getting stabbed and falling into traffic to me."

"Wow, these are spot on," Jo remarked, intrigue pouring off her.

Jake bristled, his unease growing. He knew Dana was passionate about her work, but this went beyond passion. She was angry and not just about the deaths of these strangers. He knew pressing her for more might not be the best idea, but he'd never been one to shy away from a fight. "How do you explain the playing cards?"

"There's an explanation for everything if you look hard enough."

Jake had a feeling the comment was for him. He was busy trying to read between the lines when Jo spoke up. She tapped the counter in front of the tarot cards like she was at a blackjack table. "Do a card for me."

This was no time for games. Jake tried to object, but Dana was already shuffling. She pushed the cards closer to Jo. "Cut the deck."

Jo cut and Dana drew a card. "The Chariot. Upright, it means now is the time to go after what you want. This card is about overcoming obstacles and achieving goals through determination. It means you're motivated, ambitious and in control. Now if it'd been reversed it means lack of direction, wasted energy and self-doubt."

Jo grimaced. "That's worse than my horoscope."

Jake's brow furrowed as he tried to discern if she was being sarcastic or not. But in her next breath Jo was clamoring for more. "Do Jake's."

Dana shoved the deck in front of him, but he crossed his arms. "This is ridiculous."

"Oh, come on," Jo pleaded. "It's fun."

"Yeah, Jake, it's *fun*," Dana snipped, sarcasm dripped from her like venom. "Besides, it's not like you really believe in all this stuff."

He exhaled slowly trying to leash his temper. Dana was baiting him. "You've made your point. I get it, tarot cards aren't an exact science. Whatever the Card Killer's message is, we're not going to find it in the cards."

"I don't know," Jo argued. "We might not know what directions the cards were meant to be facing but think about the way Sadie and Marcos died. I'd say the interpretations are dead on."

Unable to resist, Jake asked "What about the playing cards?"

"They're another piece of the riddle," Jo answered. "I bet the answer's staring us right in the face. But I think you're right. The cards clearly make a statement. I mean, think about it. Of all the cards I could've gotten, the chariot came up. Overcoming obstacles? Going after what I want? It's obviously referencing HRT and our move to Denver."

Jake's heart skidded to a stop. His eyes met Dana's. That's when he saw it. It wasn't anger he'd seen simmering there. It was betrayal. Jo must've told her. They'd been together all day. He should've seen this coming. But even if he had, what could he have done? He was caught between his past and his future. He'd just gotten Dana back. He wasn't ready to tell her goodbye. But Jo had a one-way ticket to Denver. He couldn't ask her to give up HRT for him. She'd worked too hard for her spot, and it wasn't a tap she'd get twice.

Jake stared at the cards, wishing he believed they'd offer guidance. The only thing he knew for certain was a painful goodbye was in his future. He didn't need a tarot card to tell him that. He drew a breath, unsure of what to say, but Dana cut him off. "Cut the deck."

He shook his head. "Enough games."

"Jake, don't be a baby, just cut the deck already," Jo teased.

He held fast.

Jo rolled her eyes. "Fine. I'll cut it for you."

Dana slammed her hand down on the cards. "No. He has to do it for the reading to be accurate."

Jo raised her hands in surrender, leaning back. "Do what the woman says, Jake." Her tone was light, and Jake wanted to keep it that way, so he finally gave in, hoping to end this charade.

He cut the deck.

Dana flipped a card. "The Fool."

The room was silent for a moment while the three of them stared at it. The meaning seemed obvious, but he asked anyway. "What does it mean?"

"That you're on the verge of an unexpected new adventure. One that may require you to take a blind leap of faith." Dana's gaze locked on his. "You are on the precipice of change, but it'll require you to face your fears."

Jo's laughter broke through the tension, but still Jake didn't drop Dana's gaze. "Oh, come on!" Jo yelled. "Jake, you can't deny how perfect that is! Forget horoscopes. I'm gonna start getting tarot readings."

She stood up and began clearing the clutter of coffee cups and takeout containers from the counter. All the while Jake was still staring at Dana, words stuck in his throat. He felt precisely like the card he'd drawn. The Fool.

He was stupid to put stock in a bunch of brightly illustrated cards, but the readings were hard to ignore. Jake didn't usually believe in these sorts of things, but he hadn't believed in a lot of things before he'd met Dana.

Jo's phone rang, breaking the spell gripping Jake. He tore his gaze from Dana to Jo in time to watch her frown.

"What's wrong?" For Jake, the question was a reflex.

Jo shook her head. "Nothing. It's my dad. He only calls when it's important. I'm gonna take this," she said, heading to his front door.

As soon as Jo was gone Dana stood, collecting her things. Jake followed. "Are you leaving?"

"No, but I hear you are. Denver, huh? It'll be cold this time of year."

Panic made him block her path. "Dana, let me explain."

But she didn't. She shoved past him and walked out his front door, living a chill colder than anything Denver could ever offer.

21

DANA STEPPED INTO THE FRIGID D.C. AIR. SHE LEANED BACK AGAINST Jake's building, letting the cold stone seep into her bones, cooling the raging fire inside her. Jake was leaving, and he didn't even have the decency to warn her. It was petty of her to use their ignorance of tarot against them. But he and Jo had drawn the cards. Dana merely interpreted them the way she preferred. It was the only way she'd get the truth. And after what she'd learned in the tarot shop, she needed to be sure.

Her lungs burned as she shook her own reading from her thoughts. She should've known better than to reach into the realm of mystic sight. Futures, once glimpsed, often became self-fulfilling prophecies.

Dana tried to catch her breath. She felt like she couldn't pull enough air into her lungs. Ever since Jo dropped the bomb about Denver, Dana's world had been spinning out of control. She hadn't let herself fully believe it was true until Jake pinned her with that look. She'd seen the truth in his eyes, and it gutted her.

She hadn't waited for him to explain. She couldn't. Her emotions were too close to the surface. In the past twenty-four hours she'd been thrown into a blender of loss, fear and betrayal. The world she returned to was upside down; reversed like a bad tarot card.

Claire was broken and Jake had moved on. And Dana had no one to blame but herself.

A yellow cab sped by, slogging through the gray slush the snow left behind. Dana shivered, clutching her jacket tighter around herself. She wanted to go home and bury herself under her covers, not waking until the world set itself right. But she knew better. If she hid from her problems until they disappeared, she'd never seen the sun again.

As tempting as the idea of running home was, she couldn't do it. Home was a myth anyway. Since the moment her parents died, Dana had been a girl adrift, shuffled from her grandparents, to private schools, to universities.

The Smithsonian had been the closest thing she'd ever had to a home. Her carefully curated library was a consistency in a world of chaos, a safe place in the storm that raged around her. Even in her own life she'd always felt like a bystander, watching from the outside.

It was Meredith who pulled Dana off the sidelines, who made her feel and laugh and love. Meredith opened the door for Claire and Jake. All three of them had made Dana dare to dream of more. More than living in books. More than studying death. They made Dana want to build a life. A home.

When Dana pulled the trigger that night at the lake, she'd thought she'd lost everything. All the scraps of her fledgling hopes and dreams. The bullet meant for Meredith had spawned a tornado that tore Dana's world apart. Running had felt like the only option. But distance allowed her to see through the wreckage, to the foundation that remained.

Running was easy. It was staying that was hard. But Dana was ready to do the work.

She was wrong to let Meredith's betrayal erase everything else. She still had people in her life worth fighting for. That's why she'd come home. Home didn't have to be a myth. A home was built brick by brick. And Dana was ready to carve one out for herself.

She closed her eyes, squeezing out the last of her pain as she inhaled deeply. She prayed for the strength to drag herself back through Jake's marble lobby, to the elevator that would take her back to his door. He might be leaving, but she was done running.

The question was, if she told him the truth, would it make a difference?

22

At war with himself Jake paced a path to his front door and back. He wanted to go after Dana and explain, but what would he say? He squeezed his temples, his head feeling like it was splitting. This case was tearing him apart.

This was only the preliminary investigation. Thanks to the bureaucratic bullshit of the task force, they were getting nowhere. Sharing information in theory was great but having to wait for each agency to put their stamp on every last detail so they felt important was an infuriating waste of time and resources.

He checked his phone again. No messages. No emails. Nothing. He'd shared the third victim's identity along with his affiliation with the Santos cartel the moment Jo confirmed it. It was time to take action before another head showed up.

He exhaled, muttering profanities under his breath. Patience was not his strong suit. And his current situation wasn't helping. He could do without the emotional turmoil of being personally involved with two of the investigators and a victim.

One investigator, he reminded himself.

Dana was in his rearview. Or at least that was the plan. He also reminded himself that Claire was only a *potential* victim. She was still sound asleep in his bedroom thanks to whatever the hell was in Dana's knockout tea.

Jake briefly wondered if the shaman knew he could make a fortune selling the stuff to politicians looking for a discrete way to clean up their dalliances. Many a D.C. career had been cut short by Paparazzi on rehab recon.

In the hall beyond his front door, Jo's voice floated back to him. He wasn't intending to eavesdrop, but every time his pacing brought him closer to the door, he caught bits and pieces of her conversation. Tension sharpened her tone as she spoke with her father. It didn't sound like they were merely catching up.

At last the door opened. Jake turned to catch Jo's shock of blonde hair tearing into the room. "Turn on the news!"

Jake grabbed the remote and enabled the projection function. A moment later his living room glowed to life. Flashbulbs sparked, illuminating Fuller's ruddy face on the screen.

"You've got to be kidding me," Jake muttered.

He and Jo stared at the press conference like it was a car wreck.

"Yes, that's right," Fuller was saying, "Ikemba has full immunity in exchange for his cooperation."

Jo growled. "I didn't want to believe it was true."

"Your dad?" Jake asked.

She nodded. "He called to give me a heads up that Ikemba turned himself in."

Shit. That's why Jake had heard crickets from the task force. So much for teamwork.

He was so absorbed in the BS Fuller was shoveling he hadn't heard Dana return, but he sensed her before she uttered a word. She came up behind them, stopping next to Jo. "What's going on?"

"Fuller burned us," Jo muttered.

Dana's deep brown eyes focused on the screen, her eyebrows knitting together as she read the banner scrolling across the bottom. "I don't understand. Ikemba turned himself in?"

"Thanks to Fuller." Jo shook her head in disgust. "The dipshit offered him immunity."

"So even if we prove he's responsible for Sadie and Santos' guy, he walks," Jake clarified.

"We need to get down there," Jo ordered.

Jake shook his head. "We can't leave Claire."

"Ikemba's off the street. The threat's over."

"She witnessed a murder, Jo. I'm not taking any chances."

"I can stay with her," Dana offered.

23

DANA SAT AT JAKE'S KITCHEN ISLAND, THE CARDS SPREAD ON THE counter in front of her. *Two roads converge, a path to be chosen. Heartbreak or happiness.* She tried to tuck Madame Blanche's words into the deep recesses of her mind, where she kept all the other fears she chose not to face, but like a bad cold, they kept resurfacing.

It didn't help that Dana felt the need to recreate the spread the old woman had dealt her. She stared at the Three of Swords. The image haunted her: three blue swords thrust through a swollen red heart. The card bisected the Lovers card, representing a crossroad on Dana's mystical life journey. Three paths lay before her. She touched each card hearing Madame Blanche's words. *Strength. The Fool. The Chariot.* She knew who each were meant to represent. Fate proved it when they'd drawn the exact cards themselves. One was the object of her desire. One was her obstacle. One was her hopes and fears.

Dana. Jake. Joanna. Staring at the representation of each of them spread out before her made Dana's stomach knot. She hadn't shared her reading with the others. She didn't intend to. At least not until she made up her mind.

Her gaze fell upon the Strength card where a woman subdued a savage lion. The card represented persistence and strength. It was the card Dana had drawn to represent herself, and it indicated she possessed the power and persuasion necessary to achieve her goals. But at what cost? The lion in the illustration looked broken, its eyes rolled back in pain as the woman wrenched its jaws apart.

It was impossible not to make the comparison to her and Jake, the FBI agent with a lion's heart. Would Dana's inability to let go of what might've been destroy him?

Her fingers traced the noble sphinxes on the Chariot card. It just so happened to be the card most opposite to Strength in the deck. *Fitting,* Dana thought. She and Joanna Walsh were opposites in every way. Well, except one. Her eyes traveled back to the Fool. The card sat between the two women. Dana on the left. Jo on the right.

Dana's chest tightened, and she tried to ignore the significance of her position. The card on the left always represented the past. She reminded herself the reading was hers, not Jake's. Besides, she knew the cards weren't absolutes, merely interpretations of possible outcomes. The future was never set in stone. Not when she still had the ability to alter her choices.

The sound of bare feet padding toward her was a welcome distraction.

Claire poked her head into the kitchen. Though she still resembled the walking dead, her eyes were clearer, and she seemed steadier.

"Welcome back," Dana greeted, abandoning the cards. "How are you feeling?"

"Starving and sticky."

Dana fought a grin, grateful to see Claire's signature quirkiness returning. "It's a good sign that your appetite's back. Why don't you shower, and I'll order some takeout?"

"Thaiphoon?"

"Where else?" she teased.

Claire looked around the room as if just noticing its emptiness. "Where's Jake?"

"He and Jo went to meet with Agent Fuller."

"Did something happen?"

"There's been a development."

"Good or bad?"

"Ikemba turned himself in."

"That's good, isn't it?"

Dana nodded, but she could feel Claire's scrutiny. The frail girl took a step closer. "You're reading tarot cards. Has there been another murder?"

"No."

Claire's pale blue eyes studied the spread. "What do the cards say?"

The reading from Madame Blanche echoed through Dana's mind before she could stop it. *Heartbreak or happiness. You must look inward for the answers you seek.* Shaking the prophecy away, she shrugged. "Nothing. Everything." She shrugged. "That's tarot."

But Claire wasn't buying it. "If Ikemeba is off the street, why are you still looking for answers?"

Dana hadn't realized she was, but as soon as Claire said it, she felt as though she'd put her finger on something she'd been searching for. "I guess something's still bothering me."

"What?"

"When I figure it out, you'll be the first to know. Now go shower so we can eat."

Claire hesitated, her fingers twisting anxiously. "I'm sorry."

"For what?"

"What I did ... letting Sadie into the library ..."

"It's water under the bridge."

"No, it's not. I'd do it again if it meant I could save her. But I'm sorry I violated your trust. Working for you ..." she trailed off, swallowing back emotion. "It's been an honor."

"Then I hope you'll continue."

"But I ... I don't work for you anymore."

Dana's lips quirked up. "Says who?"

"But you said—"

"I know what I said." Dana interrupted. She exhaled deeply. "Let's leave the past where it belongs. Your future is at the Smithsonian. Your job will be waiting for you when you're ready to return."

Claire grinned, her pale hands trembling as she gripped the counter. "Really?"

"Really."

Unable to contain her excitement, Claire rushed across the kitchen and threw her arms around Dana. The rare display of affection was touching. It made Dana realize that not all the changes in her absence had been for the worst. "Now go shower. I mean it. You stink."

Claire padded away, looking almost giddy. They were a pair. Who else would be so delighted to devote their lives to death?

24

"Face it," Fuller sneered. "We were called in to do your job. And we did it better."

"This case isn't over," Jake growled, stepping up to Fuller's arrogant posturing.

"I say it is. Deal with it and move on, boy scout. Or don't. I don't give a rat's ass."

"You only cleaned up half a mess, Fuller. Santos is responsible for at least two deaths in this case."

"So what? It's dealers killing dealers. For all I care they can keep at it. Makes my job easier." With a final smirk, he turned his back on Jake and walked away content to do nothing now that his stake in the game was done. Ikemba was off the street. With immunity to wash away all his sins.

Fuller's cocky smile taunted Jake, his knuckles popping as he tightened his fists, watching the prick shake hands with agents and officers as he strutted down the precinct hall to undeserved praise.

By the time Jake and Jo arrived, the press conference was over. They sat in on the post conference briefing where Jake did his best to plead his case, but it fell on deaf ears.

"It's too simple," Jake argued, trailing Jenkins down the busy hall of the police precinct.

Her short blonde hair bobbed in agreement. "Yeah, but that's how the CIA likes it. All the loose ends tied up into a tidy little bow."

"That oxygen thief probably expects a medal for getting Ikemba off the street," Jo grumbled.

Jake huffed a bitter laugh. "Yeah and all it cost was immunity."

Jo walked beside Jake, throwing a heavy dose of side-eye his way. He was just as pissed as she was, but if Jenkins and the police chief had already signed off on Ikemba's deal, there was nothing they could do. The drug lord was going to retire somewhere cushy and live out his days collecting dirty money he'd generated breaking the backs of others.

He wasn't the head of the Nigerian mob, but he was the highest rung on the stateside ladder. The state department would pat themselves on the back for a while over this coup, which was the last thing D.C. needed. Complacency was crime's best friend. Content with this win, Jake could only imagine how many minor busts would go unimpeded. Not to mention the immunity clause made it impossible to prosecute Ikemba on anything he admitted to. "This is a fucking soup sandwich."

"Roger that," Jo grumbled.

Jake wanted to punch something. He couldn't believe he was back here again. Six months ago, he'd run Vega out of town and Metro PD let their presence in Deanwood lax. Now the neighborhood was even more dangerous as gangs made a grab for Vega's old territory. And with Ikemba off the streets, there would be no one to stop the sharks from gobbling up the minnows.

And Rafael Santos was a damned Great White.

Jake had shared his theory about Santos' involvement with the rest of the task force, but no one wanted to hear it. They had a win, and they weren't about to lose it by admitting Ikemba wasn't the only cog in the Card Killer machine.

With Ikemba in CIA custody there was little chance Jake would get closure on the four open murder investigations on his desk. Ikemba could fully admit to them, and it wouldn't matter. He had immunity. But that didn't mean he was untouchable. Jake could petition for a chance to question him. But he had another idea that might yield quicker results. "Jenks, I'm not ready to close this case. Give us a little longer."

Shock washed across Jo's face, and she wasn't quick enough to conceal it from Jenkins.

"Are you sure you speak for your partner?" Jenkins asked.

"What I'm sure of is Ikemba is scared. He wouldn't be cooperating if he wasn't. That means there's a bigger threat on our streets right now."

"I'm aware Ikemba's only asking his men to stand down to save his own ass."

"So give us a chance to figure out who he's running from."

"You said it yourself in the post brief. Santos is the obvious choice."

"Yes, so let us connect him to the card killings, and we'll have two major players off the street."

Jenkins sighed. "It'll take some time to officially close out this case. I suppose I can drag my feet with our end of the paperwork."

"That's all I'm asking for." Jake squeezed Jenkins' shoulders, forgetting as he often did, that she wasn't just the woman who helped his uncle raise him, but a high-ranking superior in the FBI.

"Don't make me regret this," Jenkins called after him, but Jake was already moving toward the exit, Jo by his side.

"Are you sure about this?" Jo asked, as Jake drove back toward home.

"No, but right now it's the only idea I have."

"Still, the dump? Do you how much manpower it'll take to search an area like that?" Jo frowned, obviously unimpressed with his plan. He knew he was grasping at straws, but he'd bought himself time and he didn't intent to waste it, even if that meant digging through the dump himself. Every instinct was telling him that this case didn't add up. Fuller knew it too, which was why he was rushing to close it.

"Jake, just promise me this isn't a pissing contest."

"This isn't about Fuller."

"Then what's it about?"

"Justice."

"I thought that's what we just got."

Jake glanced at her while keeping one eye on the road. Was Jenkins right? Was Jo not on board with seeing this through? They were normally on the same page, justice above all else. But something was clearly bothering her. "What's wrong?"

"For starters, I'd rather be popping a bottle of champagne and packing for Denver, but clearly you have other ideas. If I didn't know better, I'd say you're dragging your feet."

"I'm not. I just don't want to leave wondering if I missed something, or if I could've done more."

"Jake, there's always going to be more to do. The job is doing the best we can and taking wins when we get them. We make a difference one day at a time."

He knew she was right, but that didn't mean he liked it. He'd taken this job as a means to an end. The Army had left him with much to atone for. Leaving loose ends didn't feel like making progress. But explaining that wasn't simple. Jake knew if anyone would understand it'd be Jo. She'd served too, seen the same darkness he had and emerged on the other side.

The problem was, sometimes Jake felt like he was still there, stuck in that hell, fighting a war that had stopped making sense a long time ago. Maybe that's what bothered him about this case. About all the cases that crossed his desk. Death shouldn't be senseless.

If he didn't take the time to make sense of it, who would?

"Jo, I just need to see this one through. It's the only way I'll be able to leave with a clear conscience. I need to know Claire is safe."

Tension eased from Jo's shoulders and she leaned back against the headrest. "It's a good thing you're hot."

Jake huffed a surprised laugh. "What?"

"It makes up for how annoying it is when you're right," Jo replied, her easy grin returning.

"So you'll help?"

"You know I will. But I'm not going to the dump."

"Why not? Claire said whoever's behind the Grave was fond of taking out the trash. If he was tossing users in dumpsters, there's a good chance he did the same with the bodies belonging to our vics."

"Then let's go to the source." Jo scrolled through her contacts and tapped out a message, looking satisfied after pushing send. "Ikemba's not the only one who doesn't want to end up with a card in his mouth."

"Are you talking about your CI again? Jo, the guy gave you nothing. Especially considering he probably knew Ikemba was gonna roll over."

"He might not have. Besides, I paid him for information. I'm gonna get my money's worth."

"Meaning what?"

"I told him to text me the address to the Grave's next location."

"If Ikemba is Diablo, there might not be another Grave location."

Jo crossed her arms. "One way to find out."

"And you think your CI will come through?"

"Sure, unless he wants me to spread word that he's a snitch."

Jake's brows rose. "You'd give up an informant?"

"You're not the only one who doesn't like loose ends. This is my last case. I want to go to HRT knowing I did my best here. Besides, we're doing this for Claire, right?"

Reminders of everything Jake loved about the woman sitting next to him flooded him. Reaching across the seats, he took her hand and squeezed. "Thank you."

25

"It looks good," Claire mused, checking her reflection in her cell phone again.

When Dana saw her carrying scissors to the bathroom, she insisted she help with the new look the girl wanted. She had to admit, the shoulder length cut looked nice, and it hadn't taken very long. They'd finished right as their food arrived.

On good terms with Claire again, Dana found she was able to enjoy her meal. She'd truly missed the incredible takeout from their favorite Thai restaurant, and that was saying something considering she'd been to Thailand to study rituals of the Sak Yant.

She briefly thought of Needles, wondering how he'd measure up to the Sak Yant Ajarn, who spent a lifetime mastering the phenomenon of tattooing talismans into the skin using primitive methods and ink said to be blessed with magical properties.

Her fleeting thoughts were interrupted by Claire's girlish giggle. Dana looked up to see her thumbing through a stack of Jake's mail piled in a corner of his barren kitchen. She popped a dumpling in her mouth and held up a *Florida Sportsman* magazine with a large fish on the cover, turquoise water sparkling around it. The title jumped out at Dana. *Angling in the Florida Keys.*

A memory crashed into her so swiftly she gasped to catch her breath, but it didn't break her free of the sensation. Jake and her at the shooting range, the feel of his hands on her hips, the warmth of his tan skin.

"So you enjoyed Key West?"

"Everyone enjoys Key West. Palm trees, sunshine, piña coladas. It's paradise. I'd move there in a heartbeat."

"Why don't you?"

"'Cause I still have work to do here. Like teaching you how to shoot. Come on, you have to hit the target at least once before we call it a day."

Coughing, Dana drew herself back to reality. "You okay?" Claire asked.

Dana cleared her throat, coughing again. "Yeah, just went down the wrong way." She held up the water bottle she was clutching and took another sip, trying to ignore the spark the memory sent through her. She swore she could almost smell the metallic sulfur of gunpowder from the shooting range. That day had felt like the beginning of something. Perhaps it was merely the beginning of the end.

Claire prattled on. "It's weird, right? Jake doesn't fish. He doesn't even take vacation."

"That's not true. He went to the Keys last year." She didn't know why she felt the need to defend him. Perhaps she wanted to prove that she knew him. Or maybe it just made her feel better about her own recent absence. A guilty conscience was a powerful thing.

Her appetite gone, she carried her plate to the sink, Madame Blanche's prophecy weighing on her. *You must look inward for the answers you seek.*

Right now, she didn't want to look anywhere. Finished with her dishes, her attention snapped to Claire with irritation. She was still flippantly perusing Jake's mail. "You shouldn't go through people's mail."

Claire looked up. "I'm not opening it."

"Still," Dana marched over, removing the stack of envelopes and magazines from Claire's inquisition. "Jake's entitled to his privacy. It's bad enough we've set up camp in his one-bedroom apartment. Speaking of, are you sure you wouldn't be more comfortable staying at my place?" Dana would certainly be more comfortable there. She walked toward the bookshelf, ready to place the mail away from prying eyes when something fell out of the pile and hit her foot. She bent down to pick it up, and her breath caught.

"What's wrong?" Claire came to her side, both speechless as they looked at what stared up at them.

"Is it yours?" Claire whispered.

Dana shook her head slowly.

"Then how did it get here?"

"I don't know. It fell out of Jake's mail."

"What does it mean?"

Dana didn't know how to respond. She knew what the card meant and finding it here wasn't good. "Do you know where Jake keeps his kit?"

"Yes."

"Get me gloves and an evidence bag."

Dana kept her eyes on the tarot card like she expected the illustrated horse to gallop away. She stared at the cherub-faced beggars, her mind desperately trying to spin the meaning. But when Death stared back at you, it was hard to think.

Claire returned, handing Dana the gloves. She photographed the card with her phone and slipped on the gloves, careful to lift the card by the edges so she wouldn't damage any prints that might've been left behind. She slipped the tarot card into the evidence bag Claire held open, then sealed it shut.

"Now what?" Claire asked. But Dana's heart was pounding so hard she barely heard the question. She was no longer staring at the front of the card, but what was written on the back.

Your turn.

Dana grabbed her phone, dialing Jake's number. As soon as the line connected, she was speaking. "Jake, we have a problem."

26

"Where did you find it?" Officer Hartwell stood in front of Dana, his pen tapping against his clipboard.

"She's been over this already," Jake snapped, stepping between them. He knew Hartwell was just doing his job, but they were wasting time. Time someone didn't have if the message on the tarot card was to be believed.

Jake didn't take being threatened lightly. Especially in his own home. It didn't help that the officer asking the redundant questions was the same one he'd decked a few days ago. His place was crawling with Metro police and forensics.

As soon as Jake received Dana's frantic phone call, he'd called it in. He wasn't taking any chances when it came to keeping Claire and Dana safe. Once he'd been assured a unit was dispatched to his address, he made another call to Jenkins. She showed up a few minutes after he and Jo arrived at his place. She'd asked all the same questions Jake did, and now they were going over them again for what felt like the millionth time.

"We're wasting time!" Jake yelled. "You read the threat. Whoever sent this is out there plotting their next move."

"We have no idea when this threat was sent. For all I know it's from Ikemba, in which case the threat's been neutralized."

"And I'm saying it's not!" Jake jabbed a finger into Hartwell's chest. "You need to wrap it up here so we can get out there and do something about it."

"Shepard, why don't we let them do their job," Jenkins suggested, her voice full of warning.

"I'd love it if they did their jobs. If they did their jobs, I wouldn't be getting death threats in my home."

"Doubtful," Hartwell muttered.

Jake bowed up, getting in the much shorter officer's face. "What was that?"

To the runt's credit, he didn't back down. "I said, doubtful. I'm sure you got a line of people just waiting to knock you down a peg. I'm one of them."

Jenkins grabbed Jake by the arm, dragging him away from causing another interagency showdown. "Let it go, Shepard."

"Let it go? That jackoff just threatened me in my own home."

"From where I'm standing you threatened him first."

Wanting to punch something, Jake settled for a string of swears. Feeling marginally better, he faced Jenkins. "There's no way I'm trusting that incompetent grunt to handle this."

"I'm not saying you have to, but you also can't impede the investigation."

"At least this means we won't be closing the case," he muttered, trying to find the silver lining. "I want to put together a search party to help canvass the surrounding landfills."

"Jake ..."

"I know it'll take a lot of manpower, but a few K 9 units would speed things up. Hell, we can enlist volunteers for all I care. The damn press might as well be useful for once. They've given the Card Killer so much airtime people will jump at the chance to be part of the action. Plus, it's not like we're going in blind. Thanks to Claire, we have the Grave's addresses for the last few months. We can cross reference them with the dumpsters in those areas, find out who services them and get a starting point."

"It's not that, Jake." Jenkins' gaze darted to where Claire sat, speaking to another officer, while Jo stood by, her stance protective. "I think you're too close to this."

"What are you talking about?"

"You have a witness living with you. You need to take a step back."

"I appreciate the concern, Jenks, but I've dealt with worse." Something she was aware of, so why the apprehension?

Jenkins knew Jake better than most. She was partly to blame for his loyal nature. He'd grown up watching the way she and his Uncle Wade had each other's backs. She had to know he'd do the same for his friends. He protected the people he cared about and right now, one of them was a target. He was about to say so when his front door swung open and Fuller barged in.

"Late to the party as usual," Jake muttered under his breath.

Jenkins elbowed Jake in the side.

The surly CIA agent surveyed the scene with an arrogant superiority that made Jake want to slug him. When his gaze landed on Jake and Jenkins, he scowled. "What the hell is going on here?"

Fuller's flabby jowls jiggled as he marched toward them. How he passed the CIA's physical requirements was beyond Jake.

The out of shape agent's gut reached Jake before the rest of him. Gone was his triumphant expression from the press conference. Now his face had returned to its usual sour scowl.

"Shepard called in a threat related to the Card Killer case an hour ago," Jenkins explained. "We've got a team processing the scene."

"Guess we're not done working together," Jake added, unable to resist taking the jab.

Fuller shot him a glare before letting his eyes roam over Jake's home with unfiltered judgement. "Nice place, Shepard. I see the FBI's still underpaying." His eyes pinned Jake. "No wonder you can't get anything done."

Jake refused to take the bait. His place was fine, more than fine actually. But he couldn't care less about where he lived. For years he slept on the ground, picking off sand fleas to a lullaby of gunfire. The quiet comforts of being stateside had been one of the most difficult things to get used to. But Jake didn't expect someone like Fuller to understand that.

Jake looked into him the moment Dana indicated they'd had a less than pleasant encounter. Mike Fuller had served a short stint in the Marines, but much of his combat record was classified. He had a subpar record with the FBI, flagged with enough misconduct to make Jake wonder how he'd managed to secure his current gig with the spooks. The bottom line: Fuller was just another bulldog who thought his title gave him the authority to be an asshole.

Jake had nothing against the CIA. He knew there were good people working there, people who'd dedicated their lives to protecting this country. Fuller just wasn't one of them.

"Never trust anyone whose sole purpose is a paycheck." Jake replied.

Fuller smirked. "Let me guess, you're in it for the glory of true patriotism."

He shrugged. "I prefer to put my resources into making a difference."

Fuller's gaze landed on Jake's collection of whiskey, and he stifled a grunt. "Clearly."

Finished answering questions, Dana joined them. "I'm going to take Claire back to my place. It doesn't feel safe to stay here after ..." she trailed off, glancing at Fuller.

The man's lips curled back into a menacing smile. "Ah, Dr. Gray. I knew our time together wasn't up."

Her face remained impassive. "Does that mean you're reopening the case?"

"It means we'll be spending more time together," Fuller amended.

Jake stepped in front of Dana, cutting off Fuller's view. He didn't like the way the creep was staring at her, or the way she seemed to shrink under his gaze.

Just what the hell had happened between them?

"You're right, Dana, it's not safe here. I'll meet you back at your place as soon as I can shake free here. Take Jo with you."

Her cheeks flushed with anger. "I wasn't asking for a babysitter. I can take care of myself."

"I know you can." He pinched the bridge of his nose. "It's not that."

Dana's brown eyes bore into his. "Then what?" When Jake didn't respond she moved closer, her hand grasping his arm in realization. She lowered her voice to a near whisper, fear widening her eyes. "You don't think the threat was meant for you."

Grateful for how well she knew him, he placed a hand over hers and squeezed as Dana's gaze moved to Claire. Jake didn't want to say it out loud. Partly because putting it out into the universe was counterproductive and partly because he didn't know who he could trust.

His home was crawling with strangers. All of whom had access to pertinent information about the Card Killer, which made staging a threat like this plausible. Plus, he had to face the facts. Hartwell was right. Jake had a long list of people who'd enjoy seeing him suffer.

He wished he could tell them he already was.

Jake's eyes darted from Claire, to Jo, to Dana, to Jenkins. He wanted to protect them all. But it was his fault they were in danger. The message was sent to his home. He couldn't be sure who the target was, but he was certain of one thing. Jake had drawn them all to the eye of the storm.

"I hate to break up this Hallmark moment." Fuller slapped a meaty hand on Jake's shoulder. "But I'm the one calling the shots here, and no one's leaving until I get answers."

"Great," Jake responded, shaking free of Fuller's grasp. "Jenkins and I were just discussing the best way to do that. We need to canvass the area landfills. I'd suggest starting at Fort Totten, then expand into the surrounding areas."

Fuller's eyebrows danced in amusement. "You'd suggest?" The man's laughter made Jake's blood boil. "That's rich considering you no longer get to weigh in on this investigation."

"What are you talking about?"

"Ever heard of conflict of interest?"

Jake's head jerked back. "Conflict of interest? Are you joking? I'm the one who's being threatened. I have every reason to be interested."

Fuller grinned, clearly enjoying getting under Jake's skin. "Here's how I figure, boy scout. Based on the evidence found at your home, the inside knowledge you have on this case and your persistence to keep it on-going, I'd say you're now a prime suspect, or at the very least a person of interest. Either way, you're personally involved in the case, which means you can no longer be trusted to be objective. The only place you're going is to county."

Fuller nodded to Hartwell, who eagerly strode toward them, his hand reaching for his cuffs.

"Whoa." Jenkins intercepted him. "I can understand wanting Shepard off the case but there's nothing to warrant holding him and you know it."

"How 'bout obstruction of justice?"

Jenkins laughed. "That's a crock, Fuller."

"Why don't we let the lawyers decide?"

"Sounds good to me," Jo said, joining the conversation. She held up her phone, her finger hovering over a familiar name. "I have the DA on speed dial. Chances are you'll be the one in cuffs if I press this button."

Fuller's face reddened, but he waved Hartwell off. Clicking his tongue, he glared at Jake. "You're gonna let her play the daddy card? How emasculating."

Jake hated to agree. He hadn't asked Jo to do that. He was perfectly capable of standing up for himself, but his mind was still reeling over Jenkins' agreement to have him sidelined.

"Enough of this pissing match," Jenkins interrupted. "We have work to do."

"Some of us do," Fuller amended, his taunt aimed at Jake.

"Shepard will remain here," Jenkins confirmed, her tone full of authority. "Agent Walsh and I are at your disposal if you need further assistance."

"And Dr. Gray, of course," Fuller added, wearing his sleazy grin again.

"Of course," Jenkins agreed.

Satisfied, Fuller nodded and gave the signal for his team to wrap it up. But before he turned away, he stepped close to Jake, his voice low and full of malice. "If I catch a whiff of your cheap cologne anywhere near this, I'll have you locked up for obstruction of justice, and I know how to make it stick."

Jake was about to unleash a few choice threats of his own, but Fuller cut him off. "Just give me a reason, boy scout. With you out of the way, she's all mine." Jake followed Fuller's gaze to where Dana stood, consoling Claire. "You should ask her what happened the last time I locked up one of her friends."

27

It felt like ages before the apartment was quiet again. The last of the forensics team had left a few minutes ago. Jenkins followed them out, grumbling about paperwork. At least with her filing a report there would be one accurate account of the clue Dana found.

She'd been grilled by the Metro police and CIA about the tarot card she'd found at Jake's. She'd expected to give a statement, but she couldn't help feeling like their questions were purposely leading her in circles. She couldn't fathom why they'd try to trip her up or skew her account of events. Everyone was supposed to be on the same side. The side of truth and justice.

The trouble was truth and justice were proving impossible to find at the moment. There were no prints on the tarot card and the deck was generic, making it difficult to trace back to a source. Then there was the deviation from pattern. No other cards had been left with a handwritten message on them. Something that could be helpful if they had a suspect to match a writing sample to. Dana had been assured Ikemba's handwriting would be referenced, but she held little hope.

Like Jake, she believed there was something more complex at play. She just hoped they could prove it before whoever left the tarot card made good on their threat.

The only place left that might hold answers for them seemed to be the city dump.

Searching such a massive area was an insurmountable task, but Dana had faced overwhelming odds before. If she had to wade through a mountain of D.C.'s waste to stop a killer, she'd do it. Especially if Claire was the next target.

Jo left the apartment, her voice clipped as she spoke to someone on the phone. Claire was in Jake's room, packing the few items she had to relocate to Dana's. That left her alone with Jake, something she was trying to avoid. Her stomach coiled with tension as he approached. The air around him sparked with intensity.

She hated the look he wore. She knew it well, having seen it in her own reflection. It was the look of someone desperate for answers.

"Are you sure about this, Dana?"

"You know I'll keep her safe. Besides, we'll be surrounded by law enforcement. The landfill is the safest place for us."

"You don't have to do this. You and Claire can just go back to your place and stay put. I can stake out your block."

"Jake, you said yourself finding the bodies might help us figure out who's behind this."

"I know. I just don't like you going without me."

Dana tried to be sympathetic, but death wasn't exactly foreign territory for her. In fact, she considered her insight a gift. She'd made her peace with death long ago. They'd come to an understanding. Her research into the occult had allowed her to pierce the many veiled secrets death held. She did her best to shed light on the often-misunderstood darkness but there'd been a price for her knowledge. The cost was time.

Death had already stolen so much of Dana's life that she no longer feared it. How could she when she had so little left to lose?

She looked up at Jake, aching with regret. She wished she could say something to calm the storm clouds building in his blue eyes. "We'll be careful, Jake."

"That's not what I'm afraid of." His gaze pinned Dana. "What happened between you and Fuller?"

"I told you, it was a long time ago. It's not worth mentioning."

"Then why did he bring it up?"

Her heart slipped in her chest as her mind flashed back to another pair of piercing blue eyes. Dana did her best not to think about Dante but seeing Fuller again brought it all rushing back. "What did Fuller tell you?"

"He mentioned he has a history of locking up your friends."

Dana fought the goose bumps that tore across her skin. "He does."

"What kind of friends?"

"Ones with a mutual interest in what happened to my parents." When Jake's eyes narrowed Dana knew it was no use keeping it from him. He'd been by her side when Cramer was lowered into the ground. He knew the toll solving her parents' murders had taken. "His name was Dante Grant. We met at an auction. We were both bidding on the same amulet."

"Amulets? Like the ones the Romeo and Juliet Killer used?"

She nodded. "Dante told me he had information that might help me understand my parents' deaths."

"And you believed him?"

"I did."

"So what was it?"

"I don't know. Fuller never gave me a chance to find out. Dante's collection of occult artifacts might've been less above board than mine. Anyway, Fuller ambushed him before I could find out what Dante was going to show me. I still don't know how he knew where we were meeting. I think he tapped my phone when he interrogated me."

Jake rubbed his brow, exhaling slowly. "Dana ..."

"I know," she said, cutting off his lecture. If he thought what she'd just shared was bad, he really wasn't going to like this next part, but she needed to get it out. She'd kept it bottled up for far too long. And now that Fuller was back in her life, she couldn't ignore it. Not when she might finally get justice for Dante. "It's not something I'm proud of, but you know how important finding out what happened to my parents was to me. I wouldn't have trusted Dante if he hadn't given me every reason to believe he had credible information."

"Dana, I know you. You wouldn't have let his arrest stop you from getting answers."

"You're right."

"So what aren't you telling me?"

"I tried to visit Dante in jail, but Fuller made sure I hit a dead end."

"What do you mean?"

"Dante Grant died in jail. He supposedly had a heart attack, despite being in perfect health and having no preexisting conditions."

"Are you saying Fuller had him killed?"

"I can't prove it, but you know as well as I do how easy it is to force a heart attack with drugs that don't leave a trace."

"Dana, this is more than ancient history. If Fuller did what you're saying, there's no telling what he'll do now. He had a big win, and we just blew it apart. His reputation is at stake. If it turns out he gave Ikemba immunity for nothing, he's done. I know guys like him. He'll do anything to make sure he ends up on top."

"I know, but we have the advantage of knowing who he is. If he tries anything, we'll see him coming."

Jake scrubbed a hand over the tense expression on his face. "I don't like it. This changes things."

"How?"

"He's dirty. For all we know, Fuller could be in on this with Ikemba for some big payoff. I need to fill Jenkins in on what you just told me."

"I don't think that's a good idea, Jake. It was a long time ago and I can't prove anything."

"Yeah but it could be enough to discredit him and get me back on the case."

"Or it could backfire and get us all kicked off. Right now, at least a few of us are on the inside. Let's not kick the hornets' nest."

Dana knew he saw truth in her logic, but she could also see how much it was killing him to stand on the sidelines. Frustration and worry creased his brow as his lips tugged into a frown. He looked like he was going to say something but thought better of it. Instead, he took an impulsive step toward her, his cologne suddenly wrapping her in memories as his hand cupped her cheek. "Dana, if anything happens to you ..."

The emotion behind his words made her heart fall into her stomach. His deep blue gaze tore her in two, making her pulse race. She knew he could feel it as his thumb slipped beneath her jaw to catch the rapid beating at the base of her throat.

All of her awakened to his touch, which made everything hurt that much more. Jake might be standing right in front of her, but whatever they might've been was in the past.

The sound of his front door opening was the perfect reminder.

Jo walked back into Jake's apartment, shattering the moment and forcing Dana to take a step back. Jake's hand fell away from her, but the words unsaid remained in his eyes. Jo looked at them both without an ounce of suspicion which only made Dana feel worse about the heat still coursing through her.

"You ready to go?" Jo asked.

Dana nodded, crossing the room to where Jo stood to grab her things. "Claire, we're leaving."

Claire's head poked out from Jake's bedroom, a small duffle bag slung over her shoulder. "I'm ready."

Jake followed them to the door, concern etched across his features. "Be careful," he warned as Dana opened the door. She turned back to promise him she would, but his attention was elsewhere. His lips locked with Jo's in a passionate kiss, leaving Dana wondering if she'd imagined the last ten seconds.

28

Knee-deep in waste, Dana began to think Jake was right about Fuller. She hadn't been assigned to this section of the waste management center by chance. Fuller took pleasure in making her suffer at every opportunity.

At least she'd been given waders. The waterproof booted overalls protected her from the contaminants of the leachate pond but did nothing to disguise the feeling of cold, wet waste brushing up against her with every step. Then there was the smell. The N95 respirator mask was no match for the smell of runoff water from the landfill.

Dana surveyed the leachate pond she occupied with a dozen other law enforcement officials. Their job was to collect water samples from each of the massive drainage ponds.

The man-made pools were meant to collect excess rain and wastewater after it percolated through the landfill like a toxic cold brew, filling the leachate ponds with contaminants. Organic and inorganic chemicals, metals, and biological waste products in all levels of decomposition filled the ponds. The latter was what they were interested in.

Normally, this water was tested, treated and sent to wastewater treatment plants for recirculation. Today forensic specialists were testing the refuse water samples Dana and the others collected for evidence of human remains. If the Card Killer had been dumping his headless bodies here, this was how they'd find them. Each pond was fed by drainage pipes from specific areas of the landfill. If they found evidence of remains in one of the ponds it would narrow their search area. Something of vast importance considering the colossal size of the landfill.

The K9 units were already onsite when Dana arrived, but Jo had dashed Dana's hopes of the dogs speeding up the process. "They're not reliable with so much waste. The ammonia levels alone can send their highly trained noses haywire."

"Then why are they here?" Claire had asked.

"They're cadaver dogs. If we find a body part, they'll do the rest. But in a place like this, they need an exact bouquet of decay to go on."

Dana hadn't missed the way Claire shivered at Jo's words. Even now she looked like a shell of her former self. Maybe Dana had been wrong to bring Claire here. Sometimes her intern reminded her so much of herself that she forgot, despite her old soul, Claire was only in her twenties. She might share her life with death much in the way Dana did, but Claire's mind was still young and malleable. Perhaps she wasn't equipped to deal with their current situation as well as Dana.

Both of them understood death. But brushing up against it and knowing how to access the strength to survive was something that came from age and experience, both of which Claire lacked.

Dana waded deeper into the water, moving closer to Claire. From this angle she could see the girl's pinched expression. Her trembling hands gripped her safety pole tightly. That's when Dana noticed her water collection samples were empty. This was too much for her.

Ready to call the whole thing off, Dana called Claire's name, but the sound of a whistle drowned out her words.

"I'LL BE DAMNED," Officer Hartwell murmured as another of the dogs returned with a body part. This one was an arm.

It'd been hours since the whistle blew signaling the evidence of human remains in the water samples. It came from the very pond Dana and Claire had been wading through. *Knee-deep in death.* Dana pushed the thought away. Chilling thoughts weren't productive. She wrapped her arm around Claire's slender shoulders, trying to rub some warmth back into her.

Dana offered to take her home, but Claire was adamant that she stay, wanting to help identify the remains. She knew there was a good chance the dogs were bringing back more than just the bodies that belonged to the severed heads.

As they stood by the landfill turned mass grave, Claire admitted that Sadie wasn't the only one of Diablo's girls afraid for their lives. "I should've said something after that first night. I knew what the Grave was. But I turned away." Claire's jaw tightened. "I won't turn away again."

Jo stood with them, shaking her head as she cataloged the newest body part. So far, they'd recovered enough remains to indicate six bodies had been dumped, all headless at the moment. The forensic team was busy piecing them back together like a bad puzzle on top of the blue tarps covering the ground. Two of the bodies were female.

"Do you recognize them?" Jo asked.

"How could I recognize them?" Claire whispered. "They don't have heads."

Jo pointed to the tattoo running the length of a slender feminine forearm. "Did any of Diablo's prostitutes have tattoos?"

"I don't know. Possibly. I wasn't really there to check out their ink, and they weren't just prostitutes," Claire insisted, her voice clipped with injustice. "They were women, just like us."

Dana was glad to hear Claire's usual bite in her voice again. It meant she was still in there, still fighting her way back after all she'd endured, and Dana wanted to do everything in her power to help her get there. "Come on, Claire. Let's go home. Jo will let us know what they find."

Dana tried to steer Claire away from the crime scene, but she resisted with a surprising amount of strength. That's when Dana recognized the pain in the girl's strange, clear eyes. "They don't get to go home," Claire said, her voice strained with emotion. "So why should we?"

Understanding the sentiment, Dana wrapped her arm around Claire's shoulder once more. She couldn't very well fault the girl for asking the same question Dana asked herself when she lay awake at night. Death was fickle. Who knew why some were spared while others were not?

While perhaps the depth of such understanding might never be known, she knew one thing that helped lessen the pain. Squeezing Claire's shoulder, Dana stood proudly next to her intern, her friend, letting her know she wasn't alone.

29

THE PREDAWN LIGHT FILTERING INTO DANA'S BEDROOM MADE IT EASIER TO find her cellphone. After scrubbing her skin repeatedly under water that was just a shade hotter than she could stand, she'd collapsed into her bed for the first time since returning home.

Sleep had been waiting for her, a welcome distraction from the chaos she'd returned to. But with the incessant buzzing of her phone, reality rushed back at her much too soon. When Dana saw Joanna's name on her caller ID she was even more inclined to crawl back under her fluffy white duvet, but then another thought swept the cobwebs of sleep from her mind. *Jake.*

She answered the phone, her voice breathless with worry. "Jo? Is everything okay?"

"That depends. Do you have anything slutty to wear?"

Dana blinked, wondering if maybe she was still asleep, and this was some strange, twisted dream. "Excuse me?"

"Needles came through with the address for the Grave tonight. We need to put a game plan together. How soon can you be at Jake's?"

Dana looked at her watch and grimaced. She should still be asleep. "Give me an hour."

"Fuller's not going to do anything about this," Jake argued.

Dana hated to admit it, but she was on Jo's side. "Jake, if you get anywhere near this, it's only going to make things worse with Fuller."

Jake hit her with a stormy glare. "I can't sit here and do nothing."

She could see the toll yesterday had taken on him. Being sidelined had only amplified his short temper. His frown lines had deepened overnight, and he was chewing his cinnamon gum so fiercely she could hear his jaw creaking.

Dana made her peace with pretending she didn't see the bottle of bourbon in the trashcan when she threw away her fast food breakfast wrappers, but she wasn't about to overlook something that would ruin Jake's career. She knew how vindictive Fuller could be. Crossing him was not an option.

Jo placed a hand on Jake's shoulder. "I know it feels like we're doing nothing, but right now the medical examiner could be discovering evidence that will point to our killer."

"Or they could find nothing. With that level of decomp, I'm not optimistic."

He wasn't wrong. The body parts had been in bad shape. Just trying to figure out which pieces belonged to whom would be a challenge. According to Jo they'd found remains for almost a dozen bodies. They were still confirming cause of death. It was too early to tell if they were all victims of the Card Killer, but at least one of them was. A tattoo of naked women locked inside a skull had been identified on one of the remains. They'd found Marcus Silva's body. It was likely Keller Kent and Azi Udo were there as well.

Jake shook his head. "The ME's going to be swimming in body parts for days. We have a lead. I'm not willing to waste it. Not when it might finally end this."

"There's no guarantee we'll find anything at the Grave," Dana pointed out.

"There's no guarantee we won't," he shot back.

"Fuller was clear about not wanting you involved," Jo insisted, her tone more patient than Dana's.

Jake's temper slipped. "Yeah, well maybe I don't care."

"You should," Dana warned.

"How are you not getting this?" Jake yelled. "Fuller still thinks Ikemba is behind this. He's got his guy, he's not worried about the collateral damage. He's content to watch rival cartels take each other out."

"He sort of has a point," Jo answered. "Less scum on our streets is a good thing."

Dana balked at the similarity between Jake and Jo. Not long ago, he'd argued that same point on another case. It was something they would never agree on. To Dana, unnecessary death wasn't an acceptable outcome.

As if reading her mind, Claire spoke up. "If all you saw were dealers and junkies in that landfill yesterday, you're missing the point."

The sorrow in Claire's voice brought Jake out of his rampage. He no longer looked like he was going to put his fist through a wall. Instead, he ran a hand through his unkempt hair and squeezed the back of his neck, regret shadowing his voice. "I'm sorry, Claire. You're right. No one deserves to die like that." Anger flickered like blue flames in his eyes. "I hate not having any control in this."

"Then let's take the control back," Claire insisted, her voice steady, deadly. "We go to the Grave tonight and get answers."

Jake circled back to his original argument. "Fuller will never send a team to the Grave if the tip comes from me."

Dana spoke up. "Then let it come from me."

He shook his head adamantly. "No way. He's already looking for any excuse to get to you."

Jo frowned. "Something I should know?"

"We have a history," Dana said, unwilling to elaborate.

"What's the address for tonight?" Claire asked, steering the conversation back on track.

Jo passed her phone to Claire. She pulled up the street view of a nondescript building in Shaw. "Looks like a place they'd use."

"How reliable is your CI?" Jake asked.

Jo shrugged. "He hasn't wronged me yet."

"There's a first time for everything," Jake muttered.

Crossing her arms, Jo cocked her head to the side. "Hey, you're preaching to the choir, babe. You're the one who wants to do this off-book."

"Because we don't have another option."

"That's not true," she argued. "We should just follow procedure and send this tip up the chain of command."

"Procedures be damned!" Jake snapped. "If we don't act on this tonight, we miss out. There's no time to do this by the book."

"Fine," Jo conceded, "But you're not coming with us."

"The hell I'm not."

"Enough!" Unable to take more useless arguing, Dana pushed her way into the conversation. "The way I see it there's only one way we do this. Together."

He huffed a laugh in her face. "Well you're not in charge here."

"Neither are you. Actually, you're the last one who should be going to an underground club. You ooze law enforcement."

"The same way you ooze librarian," he tossed back.

"Is that a bad thing?" she challenged, seeming to remember him not having any qualms with her charms.

"Oh my god! You're both sexy!" Claire yelled. "Can we stop wasting time, please? We're all going."

"You're not," Dana and Jake said in unison.

Their eyes met. *Finally, something they agreed on.*

30

Glowing red light poured out onto the frozen asphalt as Jake watched the heavy steel door swung shut. "What are we waiting for?" Dana grumbled. But he didn't have an answer for her, just a gut instinct to wait.

He'd found a spot in a parking garage with a view to the back door of the dilapidated building that supposedly hosted the Grave tonight. It's not that he didn't trust Jo's intel, but he didn't know her informant and the soldier in him wanted to make sure this wasn't a trap.

He'd had enough time to do a basic stakeout of the building, counting exit points, potential hazards, but he still had no idea what was inside. The building was in Shaw, an eclectic D.C. neighborhood commonly referred to as Little Ethiopia thanks to the recent boom of African cuisine. The popular restaurants had breathed new life into the once poor area. The result was a mix of thriving bars and bistros, next to rundown businesses and gentrified row homes.

Research of the address showed it was a failed commercial laundry facility. Jake didn't like the idea of going in blind. It was something he'd done many times with his Special Forces team with mixed results. He refused to take chances with the two women accompanying him.

Dana and Jo sat in the backseat of his SUV, looking cold despite the long jackets they wore over their scandalous outfits. Jake pursed his lips, trying to ignore the glimpses of pale flesh he saw whenever he glanced in his rearview. He couldn't afford distractions.

So far, he'd counted six people go inside the Grave. None came out. He didn't like those odds. But they'd been watching for less than an hour. Whatever awaited inside was most likely an all-night kind of affair.

"Jake …" Jo prodded. "We can't sit here all night."

"I know."

"So, let's get this over with."

"Just a little bit longer," he ordered, watching the bouncer open the door for a couple who approached. The girl leaned in, speaking to the doorman. He gave a brief nod and let them in; the red glow swallowing them whole.

Even with the password Claire had given them, Jake still couldn't shake his feelings of unease. He didn't know if it was the fact that they were doing this without backup, or something more. No matter what waited for him on the other side of the door, Jake was confident in his ability to take care of himself. It was Dana and Jo he worried about.

He'd prefer to go in alone, but he'd lost that argument. The only battle he'd won was that Claire would stay out of harm's way. She was their fail-safe, waiting at Dana's for confirmation that everything had gone according to plan. If she didn't hear from them, she had instructions to contact Jenkins.

Thinking about the disapproving look the Assistant Director would give him when she found out about this made Jake want to call the whole thing off. But they'd come this far. And he needed the answers behind that door. It was the only way to keep Claire safe.

IT WAS DECEIVINGLY dark inside the Grave. The dull red light of the door faded quickly behind them as they walked through the narrow corridor. The bouncer had barely looked at him after he recited the password. *Reckoning*.

The foreboding word put Jake more on edge.

Dressed in worn jeans and a black hooded jacket, he'd done his best not to "scream law enforcement." Having not shaved in almost forty-eight hours, his scruff added to his unkempt look. But the bouncer didn't take any notice. His gaze was solely fixed on the women on Jake's arms.

And when they entered the main chamber of the club, so was everyone else's.

Jo and Dana turned heads, which was saying something in a place like this.

"Claire could've warned us we were walking into fifty shades of freaks," Jake grumbled under his breath.

His stomach clenched as he kept his expression neutral while surveying the garish scene. Cages, poles and thrones perched on pedestals. A single dim light shone above the figures bound to each in the dark room. Despite the bondage, they did their best to dance, writhing in a slow trance, out of sync to the jarring music.

This is where Claire found refuge?

Jake felt sick. Around him, people conversed, watched, or actively participated in the sadistic show.

"Did I miss something?" Jo asked, moving closer, "Or did Claire forget to mention that this was a kink club?"

Dana's eyes sparked with intrigue as she took in the room. "Sado-masochism is simply a hierarchical exploration of societal ranking. It's a tool that's existed for centuries to help give power to the powerless."

Jake frowned. "The only powerless people I see here are the ones chained to the stages." He didn't care what the blow-back was for being here against orders, it was going to give him immense satisfaction to shut this place down.

"Are we still going through with this?" Jo asked.

"We're here," Dana answered. "If we split up, we'll be more effective."

Dana was already on the move. She was right. They'd cover more ground that way, and people would be more likely to open up to them one on one. But it also meant he'd be splitting his focus, making sure he never lost sight of Jo or Dana.

Following Dana's lead, he and Jo separately made their ways to the makeshift bar. From the way the patrons moved around him, Jake had a feeling they were enjoying more than just alcohol. The clear plastic shot glass shoved his way confirmed it.

He stared at the little pill, a quote from *The Matrix* popping into his mind. *You take the blue pill, the story ends, you wake up in your bed and believe whatever you want to believe. You take the red pill, you stay in wonderland, and I show you how deep the rabbit hole goes.*

But this pill was yellow, and he certainly wasn't standing in wonderland.

This was a test. And if he didn't pass, he'd be back out on the street in an instant.

The bartender stared at him. Jake stared back, glancing at the hellscape one last time before bringing the cup to his lips.

31

It was clever, handing out Rohypnol to guests. It would make it harder for them to remember what they saw here and even if they did report this place, it would be gone the next day, discrediting their story further.

Claire may have left out some major details about what went on at the Grave, but she'd at least warned them about the little yellow pills that flowed freely. The favor Jake had called in with the Alchemist was well worth it. He felt no effects of the drug in his system, but he had to be careful not to let it show.

For the past hour he'd endured his own personal hell watching women be exploited. He doubted any of them were here by choice. He'd seen enough human trafficking to know how the sex trade worked. It was just one more cog in the machinery that funded these cartels. They were the modern-day mob, funding terrorism here and abroad through drugs, arms and prostitution.

He'd seen desperate people take irrational risks for the promise of salvation. A job opportunity in a foreign land. The offer of drugs to ease homesickness seemed like a kindness. That was all it took. Before they knew it, they owed more than they could ever pay off. Then voila, they became property. Owned by people with the means and ammunition to keep them that way.

It was amazing how easy it was to control someone when their worth was stripped away and replaced with shame. Jake cracked his knuckles as he thought of his mother. Suddenly itching for a fight, he wished someone would give him a reason.

Bumped from behind, Jake turned to catch a woman by her elbow. The dark hair that hung in her eyes made him think of Claire. Reminded why he was here, he spoke. "Sorry about that. I keep bumping into people."

She giggled and raised her plastic cup. "That's sort of the point."

Still holding onto her, he asked, "How come I've never seen you here before?"

Slinking her way against his chest she gazed up at him. "Maybe you haven't been looking hard enough."

"Are you one of Diablo's girls?"

She stiffened. "I'm no one's property, creep!" Shoving away from him, she disappeared back into the crowd.

Discouraged, Jake moved back to the edge of the crowd to continue his rounds. He hoped Jo and Dana were having better luck. So far, most of his interactions had gone like the last one, resulting in zero information about Diablo.

The more time he spent in the Grave, the less he was convinced it was run by some low-level thug. Even Ikemba didn't seem capable of something this well-organized. And the fact that the Grave was still operating despite Ikemba's arrest made it less likely that Ikemba and Diablo were one and the same.

His inner demon stirred. He felt like he was missing something. If they didn't get intel on who was in charge, this whole operation would be a bust.

Keeping his movements slow and slightly off-balance Jake made his way around the shell of the laundromat-turned-nightmare. The old laundry equipment still remained, pushed to the perimeter to make way for the pop-up fetish club. Curtains hung from the dry-clean carousels to cordon off private areas. Watching Dana wander into one made it hard for Jake to breathe.

Teetering on high heels, she was doing her job too well. He found Jo, perched safely at the bar chatting with two men. She gave him the slightest nod, letting him know she was fine. That made Jake's decision to follow Dana easier.

He ducked into the curtained area where a dominatrix was doling out punishments with a riding crop. A burly guy with black hair, greased into a man bun at the base of his wide neck stopped Jake. He pressed a scarred hand to his chest and grunted. "One to watch, two to play."

Frowning, Jake reached for his wallet. As if this wasn't unpleasant enough, now he was parting with his cash. He pulled out two fifties and handed them over only to be met with laughter. The guy tossed the cash back at Jake. "Get out."

Leaning into his role of belligerent intoxication, Jake got in the guy's face. "What's wrong with my money? You said one to watch, I gave you one."

"One grand, moron. Now get out. This ain't a charity."

"He's good for it." Jake stilled at the sound of Dana's voice. He hadn't let himself look at her since entering the curtained area. She stood next to the man she'd walked in with, his arm possessively gripping her waist.

"Unless you're paying for him, I say he's leaving," the bouncer threatened.

"You should tell him who you are," Dana said to Jake.

He didn't know what she was playing at, but he wished she'd stop. They were supposed to get intel and get out, not adlib as they went. But Dana had garnered the thug's interest. "Who are you?"

Jake shrugged. "Someone Diablo won't be happy you threw out."

"You know Diablo?" The guy's man bun bobbed as he laughed. "Yeah right."

"I know he's looking for girls." Jake answered. "And I brought him some."

This wasn't the plan, but Dana hadn't left him much choice. The big man's head swiveled from Jake to Dana and back again. "Shit, she's with you?"

Dana nodded. The guy who'd been attached to her suddenly released his grip, backing off, hands up. "Hey. I didn't know."

"It's alright," Jake said. "I don't mind letting you sample the goods."

"She never said she was working." Stammering, he looked at Dana. "I-I thought you just wanted to have a good time."

"Who says I don't?" she answered.

Shaking, the spineless pervert skirted around Jake and darted out of the poor excuse for a VIP room.

"You're really with him?" the bouncer asked Dana.

She nodded, slinking up to Jake. He slipped his arm around her, relishing the calm of having her next to him. For a moment knowing she was safe blotted out the darkness around him, but the bouncer's voice brought him back to reality. "You brought others?"

Jake nodded.

"Show me."

Dana followed Jake out to the main room, the bouncer on their heels. His mind raced through scenarios as he weighed his options. He could point Jo out. He wasn't blowing her cover. They'd walked in together. But still he didn't like it. If Dana had just landed them in the shit he suspected, Jake needed Jo to get out and get back up.

The lack of weight on his hip made him anxious. He hated being unarmed. Jo had her snub nose .38 in an ankle holster in her boot, but he and Dana were unarmed. She wasn't wearing enough to disguise a weapon, and he knew he'd be searched. That didn't leave Jake a lot of choices if the mouth-breather lumbering behind them pulled the Glock tucked into his waistband.

"Where are the others?" he demanded.

Out of time, Jake made his decision. "There." He pointed to Jo, who waved back with an easiness that couldn't have been better if they'd rehearsed this scenario.

"And?"

Jake held up his phone. "There are more. But they're not for your eyes."

"You got a name?" the bouncer asked.

"John," Jake said with a grin.

"Cute," he muttered. "Wait here."

Jake gave a salute which sent the bouncer lumbering away, muttering profanities under his breath. When he was out of earshot, Jake turned to Dana. "What the hell are you doing?"

"We're here to find Diablo, aren't we?"

Jo joined them. "What's going on?"

"We're either about to get what we came for or a whole lot worse."

32

IN THE FEW MINUTES BEFORE THE GIANT OF A MAN RETURNED, DANA, JAKE and Jo scrambled to cobble together a new plan, but the moment they were led out of the main room and up two flights of stairs it went out the window.

This was new territory. All the escape routes Jake had carefully mapped out in the event this was a trap—a view he adamantly expressed—no longer applied. His distrust was warranted, but Dana didn't let it deter her. She'd come here for answers, and it finally looked like they were about to get some.

The bouncer led the way up the dark stairwell. Jake and Jo followed with Dana trailing them. Another big man lumbered closely behind her. She could feel his breath on the bare skin of her back. It'd been hot in the club below. Here the air was chilled with emptiness.

It was clear that where they were going was starkly less inhabited than the bustling club. They climbed another flight, then another until the music below no longer reached her ears.

Not wanting to let Jake's paranoia take hold, Dana did her best to ignore the goose bumps racing up her arms. She took comfort in numbers and right now she had them. They outnumbered the two burly bouncers bookending them. Sure, they were huge, but brains beat brawn any day.

Finally, their ascent stopped. A door creaked open, and they were led into a dark room. It took a moment for her eyes to adjust. When they did, confusion rooted her to the spot. In the center of the dark space were several computer monitors, each one displaying video feeds. Fear hit her like a shockwave in the split second it took her to realize the feeds weren't live.

She watched the last few days play back before her eyes. Dana and Jake outside the J. Edgar Hoover Building. Dana, Jo and Claire leaving Jake's apartment. Dana, Jo and Claire at the landfill. Jake's SUV in the parking garage across the street. The three of them walking toward the front door of the Grave.

Jake was right. This was a trap. One that had been in the making for a while.

The room erupted into chaos as Jake and Jo came to the same conclusion. The bouncers anticipated as much, moving to block the door. Taking the two of them was feasible, but when three more men burst into the room from the opposite end, Dana let herself panic. Fleeing wasn't an option. Besides, hadn't she said she was done running? She'd come back to fight for what she wanted. It was time to prove herself.

She ran at the man closest to her, aiming to knock him off balance. It had the desired effect, but Dana went down with him. Luckily, she landed on top. Using her leverage, she tried to pin him onto his back, but he was too fast. His fist connected with her jaw, sending her sprawling. But she didn't stay down. She couldn't. They were outnumbered, and that was enough to make her ignore the pain searing through her jaw and keep fighting.

A quick glance past the man making another run at her showed Jake and Jo had their hands full. Getting out of here alive depended on each of them pulling their weight, and Dana refused to be the weak link. She wouldn't let Jake down. Not again.

This time she waited for her attacker to come to her. Striking at the last second, she heard the unmistakable crunch of bone as the heel of her hand drove upward into his nose. He lurched forward with an infuriated grunt, blood spattering the floor like a spilled drink.

The satisfaction of drawing first blood only lasted a moment. Fueled by rage, the giant lunged. He grabbed Dana by her hair before she could react and yanked her off her feet. Light burst like halos around the edges of her vision as her head struck the floor. She tried to catch her breath, but there was no time. The big man was atop her now, his weight pinning her arms to her sides, but she didn't let that stop her. Lashing out with her legs, she thrashed and kicked.

Laughing, her attacker grinned down at her. "I can see why he's going through all this trouble to get to you. You're a wild ride, sweetheart. I'm sure the boss won't mind if I take you for a spin first."

He shoved his hands under her shirt, tearing the lace of her bra.

Blind rage took over. The next thing Dana was aware of was blood raining down on her.

33

Jake's breath whistled through his nose. It was probably dislocated, but a small price to pay for still being on his feet, which was more than he could say for the other guys. He and Jo made short work of the two bouncers before taking on the remaining men who ambushed them. The one beneath Jake grunted as he slammed his fist into his windpipe one more time for good measure.

After tossing the guy through the bank of computer monitors, Jake used the power cord to incapacitate him. The guy groaning beneath him had gone three rounds with Jake's ribs. He was sure he'd pay for it tomorrow, but right now he had enough adrenaline flowing through his veins to lift a car. And that was before witnessing Dana yanked to the floor by her hair.

Jake saw red as he climbed to his feet. Halfway to Dana, Jo's voice rang out, calling his name. Jake looked back to see Jo struggling with another thug. She was still on her feet though, and he knew she had her snub nose in her boot. Dana was unarmed. The decision was made for him when his feet carried him swiftly toward Dana.

Grabbing a computer monitor from the wreckage, Jake raised it over his head, picking up speed. Baseball had been his favorite sport in high school. The idea of hitting a homer with this asshole's head would make his day, but Jake never got that far.

Three steps from Dana, the unthinkable happened. Jake watched her wriggle one arm free. It happened in slow motion. Dana inching her hand down to grab her shoe. Pulling it off with a steady hand. A second later her attacker screamed, pawing at the stiletto sunk deep in his eye socket. He spasmed, then slumped forward, his forehead slapping the floor above Dana's face, driving the heel even deeper into his skull.

Frozen, Jake could do nothing but watch the pool of blood ooze from beneath the man's massive frame. He looked back toward Jo, suddenly second-guessing his decision. She was doubled over on her knees, her attacker racing out the door. Jake had chosen wrong.

Dana was unarmed, and she never asked for help, even when she was in over her head. Jake was sure it was the right choice to help her over Jo. But now, as he stood in the silent aftermath, he saw things more clearly.

Climbing to her feet with a hiss, Jo limped toward Jake, her eyes wide as she focused on Dana's twitching limbs still pinned by the big man's dead weight. "Jesus! Jake, help her!"

Jake finally snapped out of it and moved to Dana's side, rolling the big man off her. She wheezed and coughed as Jake helped her sit up. Her top and bra were torn open, her chest slick with blood. Jake pulled off his jacket so she could cover herself. Dana took it gratefully, letting Jake guide her to her feet. His eyes met hers, not missing the sharpness of fear still present. "You good?"

She shook her head. "I killed him."

Jo stepped up, gripping Dana's shoulder firmly. "You did what you had to do. It was you or him. You made the right choice."

The bitterness in Jo's voice shook Jake, because he couldn't ignore the fact that she'd been looking at him when she said the last words. *He made the wrong choice.*

Jake pulled out his phone. There would be time for him and Jo to hash out rights and wrongs later. Right now, he was saving his arguments for Jenkins.

All business, Jake put his phone to his ear, preparing for the dressing down of a lifetime.

"It was an ambush," Jake explained, doing his best to keep his voice calm.

"And how was it you happened to stumble into an ambush?" Jenkins yelled.

"Right place, right time."

"Jacob Miller Shepard, do ya think I only got one leg in the water?" Jake braced himself when he heard the Louisiana twang slip into Jenkins' voice. Her southern roots emerged on rare occasions when she was too mad to hide them. "You're going to tell me exactly what happened here or it's your badge, and even then, I'm not making any guarantees. Keep in mind, I've already spoken to Claire. I know you didn't just happen upon this place by coincidence."

Claire had been Jake's second phone call. Whatever Dana's attacker said to her made her frantic to confirm the girl's safety. Claire promised that she was fine, but Dana had made Jake send another unit to her house just to be cautious. Jenkins had apparently taken it a step further and spoken with Claire herself. Not knowing what they talked about didn't bode well for Jake.

He glanced over Jenkins' head to where Dana sat in the back of an ambulance getting stitches. Both she and Jo were fine. He'd made sure their injuries weren't serious, but still, seeing that much blood coating Dana's skin ...

"Boy, do you have somewhere more important to be?"

"No ma'am."

"Then start from the beginning."

Sighing, Jake gave in, sharing everything from the tip Jo's CI gave them to how they ended up at the old laundromat and what they'd discovered inside. He shook his head in disgust. "I knew it was a trap."

"But you went in anyway? Without backup, I might add. You put your partners at risk and disobeyed orders."

"No one ordered me not to go in there!" he yelled, pointing at the building. "And you know what? I'd do it again. Did you see what was going on in there?"

"My vision's just fine, Shepard. The issue is your hearing. You were told to stand down. You're not even on this case anymore."

"So what? That means I'm just supposed to let this go unchecked?"

"You're supposed to do your job and call it in."

"I did my job, Jenks, and you know it. Eleven women got their freedom back tonight because I did my job."

"You're right. You helped eleven women. But you know who you ignored? The thousands of others you might've saved if you did this the right way. Everyone connected with this hell hole was gone by the time you called the cavalry. All you did was give me a dead body and a headache."

"Metro took more than twenty witnesses down to the station."

"Yes, junkies strung out on roofies! You know we're not going to be able to use anything they give us."

"What about the guy I tied up?"

"Who, the one calling for his attorney? You better pray he doesn't press charges or you're going to be facing more than a suspension."

"Suspension? Jenks, I can help."

"Trust me, Jake, you've done enough. The best thing you can do right now is go home."

He watched Jenkins walk away, disappearing into the flashing blue and red lights that had taken over two square blocks of the otherwise sleepy Shaw neighborhood.

A perimeter had been set up to search for the other creeps involved with the Grave. Jake, Jo and Dana had given descriptions of the doormen, bouncers and bartenders, but it'd been more than an hour since the police sirens drove everyone from the club. Whoever ran the place was long gone, slinking back into the shadows like the monsters they were.

"She's right, you know?" Jo commented, walking up behind him.

Jake's jaw muscles bunched. "I don't need another lecture right now. I fucked up. I get it."

"Do you?" Her keen eyes studied his. "I needed you in there and you left me hanging. I thought we were partners. More than partners."

"Jo, we are."

"It didn't feel like it." Her gaze drifted pointedly to Dana.

"I had a split second to make a decision. I made the logical choice. You had a weapon. Dana was unarmed."

"Jake, I need to know you have my back."

"I do." He tucked a strand of blonde hair behind her ear, cupping her cheek. "You know that, right?" She nodded, but her expression remained guarded as she took a step back, looking around to make sure no one had noticed the intimacy in his touch. "You were right about one thing."

"What's that?"

"This was a set up."

Jake nodded, his eyes seeking out the security cameras pointed at the scene. "Someone's been watching us for a while. They knew we were coming here tonight."

Jo's lips pressed into a thin line. "Needles."

"You think he sold you out?"

"I don't know, but I intend to find out."

34

Dana stared down at her plate of waffles. It worried her that even her favorite food couldn't provoke her appetite. The three of them sat in a diner, looking like extras from a zombie movie.

The bandage on her arm hid six stitches. She didn't even remember feeling the cut or how it happened. It must've been when she was getting tossed around like a ragdoll. It all happened so fast, but at the same time, certain images stood out like inkblots burned into her memory. The look on her attacker's face when the stiletto pierced his eye. The last sound he'd made before going still.

Jo slammed her phone down on the table. "The little shit's still not answering."

"What'd you expect?" Jake mumbled around a forkful of eggs. "He's a criminal."

"Yeah, well he's my criminal. We have a rapport."

"I think we should go down to the station. Talk to the witnesses."

"That's the opposite of what Jenkins told you to do."

"I know I can get the guy I tied up to talk. Don't you want to know who's been stalking us?"

Dana shoved her plate away, standing a little too quickly. Her hand caught the edge of the booth to steady herself. Jake was on his feet. "You okay?"

"Fine. Just need some air."

She didn't miss the look Jo and Jake exchanged on their side of the booth. Ignoring it, Dana grabbed her jacket and pushed her way through the diner's door, jumping at the cheerful sound the bell produced.

Closing her eyes, she leaned against the brick exterior, letting the cold air drive away her nausea. It was too warm inside the diner. Too casual. Her nerves were still on high alert, her muscles twitchy with excess adrenaline.

She didn't know how they did it. Jake and Jo sat inside, scheming up new plans over omelets like they hadn't just witnessed a murder. But Dana had done more than witness it. It was her hands that carried out the sentence.

She didn't even know his name, and she'd killed him. He wasn't the first person she'd watched die, and if things continued on this path, she had a feeling he wouldn't be the last.

This wasn't how it was supposed to be. Her deal with death was for access, knowledge. She'd never agreed to be the one holding the scythe. *You reap what you sow.* The old saying made Dana shiver as it settled into her bones.

She didn't want to be here, but she'd gone along with the plan to meet at the diner for a lack of a better one. What she really wanted was her bed. But she couldn't go home. Claire was there and seeing her like this wasn't an option.

Dana had caught her reflection in the rearview mirror on the drive over. The welt on her jaw was already starting to bruise, and the butterfly bandages above her eyebrow did little to distract from it. But the worst of it was the slice in her lip, where Dana had bit through her skin when her assailant had yanked her off her feet. Her whole body ached, and she wished she could sleep for a week, but keeping Claire safe was more important.

That's what I'm doing here, she reminded her scattered mind.

The last thing she wanted to do was revisit Needles. But if Jo's CI knew who set up the ambush at the Grave, they needed to find out. Jenkins and her team were analyzing the video footage Dana saw at the Grave. Despite Jake and Jo being in the films, Dana couldn't help feeling like she was the focus somehow. What her attacker said proved it. *No wonder he's going through all this trouble to get you.*

Dana hadn't repeated his words. She didn't know if it was fear or something more that made her want to keep them to herself. But she was certain that if she was the primary target, being around her could put the people she cared about at risk.

She looked down at the blue scrubs under her jacket. The clothes she'd worn to the Grave had been turned over as evidence. Not that she would've wanted to keep the blood-soaked outfit she'd bought specifically for the occasion. Except for the heels. Those had been hers. She'd never imagined how lethal the steel-pinned stilettos could be.

She shivered again, torn between going back inside where she'd have to pretend she wasn't shaken, or staying out here and freezing to death.

"Here."

Jake's voice startled her. He walked up to her; his jacket outstretched in his arms. She pulled hers tighter around herself. She'd been grateful when she found it waiting for her in Jake's SUV. "I'm fine."

"No, you're not."

She huffed a laugh, not fighting him when he draped his jacket over her shoulders. Arguing felt stupid, especially since Jake was right. And she knew he was talking about more than just her body temperature.

Their moment may have passed, but their connection survived. Their bond was undeniable. An altering of DNA at the molecular level. Or at least that's what it felt like when he looked at her like that; his eyebrows knitting tighter together, begging her to let him in.

Memories of everything she gave up when she ran away from him flooded back. But she'd made up her mind. Even if she wanted to change it, now wasn't the time. Madame Blanche told her a path must be chosen: *heartbreak or happiness.* But fate had chosen heartbreak long ago. The least she could do was leave Jake out of it.

She exhaled deeply, forcing a steadiness she didn't possess into her voice. "Jake, I'm fine. You can stop trying to save me."

"That's not what this is."

"It's not your fault. You're supposed to be the hero. I just don't need one." She handed his jacket back and shoved past him back into the diner.

35

Shadows from the streetlights fell through the large picture windows as they strode into the tattoo parlor. The sign on the door read closed, but it wasn't locked, and Jake had too much rage inside to wait for normal business hours before paying Needles a visit.

He didn't know if Jo's CI was the one who sold them out, but he was looking forward to shaking the piss out of him on the off chance that he was.

Being suspended had its advantages. He wasn't here in any official capacity, which meant technically he didn't have to adhere to the Bureau's rules. As far as Jake was concerned, Needles was the perfect punching bag for his bottled-up anger.

So far, the place appeared empty, but Jake hadn't expected anything else at this hour. The smell, however, surprised him. He'd assumed tattoo parlors needed to be moderately sterile. Needles' place smelled vaguely like a slaughterhouse. This wasn't exactly the best part of town, but still, health codes didn't discriminate.

Jo stopped shortly in front of him. "Something's wrong."

Jake had his gun drawn the moment the words left her lips. He didn't need a repeat of the Grave. One ambush was enough. Jo drew her weapon and moved into position, putting Dana behind them. For once the stubborn librarian cooperated, silently moving with them without objection. Jake moved systematically through the shop; knees bent, weapon ready.

After clearing the main salon, there was only one space left.

He headed toward the door to the backroom. He waited for Jo to cover him before kicking it open. He took one step into the room and fought to keep from gagging. In two more steps he found the source. "Clear," he announced, placing his arm over his face to muffle the scent of death.

Jo and Dana entered the room behind him. Both women gasped, an automatic response to seeing a corpse suspended in midair.

Needles hung from a vacuum cord by one ankle, his hands tied behind his back, his head removed. The severed skull sat a few feet below the body, mouth wrenched open unnaturally. Jake didn't have to get much closer to recognize the foreign object protruding where his tongue should be. A tarot card stuck partially out of his distorted maw. The illustration was the exact image Needles depicted. Jake read the card aloud. "The Hanged Man."

"Jesus!" Jo yelled, backing into Jake. "What is that?"

He turned around, staring at the gruesome pound of flesh on the workbench near Jo.

"It's a tongue," Dana answered. Her eyes moved to Needles, scrutinizing every detail. Watching her mind work was a beautiful thing. Even after all she'd been through at the Grave, she still couldn't turn it off: her quest for the truth.

Dana moved closer to the corpse, making a full circle around him before pausing directly in front. She spoke without turning around. "Jo, this tattoo ... he didn't have it when we last saw him."

Jo edged closer, looking at the deep blue art across Needles' throat. She read the words out loud, making Jake's blood run cold. "Loose lips sink ships."

Jo HUNG her head in her hands as they waited for the forensic team to finish up. For all her tough talk about Needles, it was obvious his death stung. He'd been her CI. Criminal or not, they'd built a relationship. Seeing it severed in such a brutal way wasn't easy.

"Well, we know he didn't tip off Diablo," Jake muttered. Forensics estimated time of death to be days ago, meaning the text Jo had received with the address to the Grave was from someone using Needles' phone.

"But he certainly pissed someone off," Jo answered. "Helping me."

"You don't know that."

"I do. You saw the tattoo. Someone knew he was a snitch. Whoever is watching us saw me come here. Needles risked his life to help me, and I was ready to give him up."

"Jo, we don't know what happened. This could have nothing to do with Diablo."

She glared at him. "You don't really believe that."

He didn't but rubbing salt in the wound wouldn't help. Sometimes these things happened. Working with criminal informants was a mutual risk. More often than not it wasn't the informant who got burned. When they did, Jake didn't lose any sleep over it.

He didn't know Needles, but he'd heard about the low-life cartel members he tagged. The guy had made a living taking dirty money from mob bosses and their minions. In Jake's eyes, he got what was coming to him. The only question he wanted answered was how it connected to their case.

The Card Killer, Diablo, the Grave, Ikemba, Santos ... there were so many players the game was starting to get out of hand. And the snitch who could've helped them make sense of it all had just been taken out.

"At least his death got me back on the investigation," Jake offered. Being first on scene would make it hard for Fuller to box him out of the investigation.

"Jenkins suspended you, Jake. Finding you here isn't going to make her reverse it."

"We'll see." If he could uncover something new that would give this case direction, he'd have a fighting chance.

The address to the Grave had been sent from Needles' phone. They'd been ambushed there, leading them to think Needles had sold them out. TOD eliminated that theory, putting Needles' death shortly after Jo and Dana first came to see him.

Was Needles just another pawn in a larger game?

An old scratch itched in the back of Jake's mind. This was starting to feel familiar and a little too personal. Catching Dana's eye, he led her away from the team processing the scene. "Does this feel familiar to you?"

"What do you mean?"

"I'm not sure yet, but the pattern ... it feels like we're being toyed with."

"You think it's someone you've dealt with before?"

"Could be."

She nodded slowly. "Based on the video footage, we have to assume someone is targeting one of us, but the clues don't make sense."

A gurney jostled past them, pushed into the back room by two guys in ME jumpsuits. It meant forensics had finally gotten everything they needed. It was time to cut Needles down. Even though they couldn't see beyond the closed door, Dana turned away. Jake could see the tattoo artist's death was a bitter pill for her to swallow. Especially so closely on the heels of what she'd been through in the Grave. "This isn't your fault."

"How? Our questions got him killed, Jake."

"I say good riddance," Jo said, walking up to them. "One less criminal in the world."

Jake appreciated her putting on a brave face. "I couldn't agree more."

Dana shook her head, the bewilderment in her gaze full of argument that never came. The sound of Jo's phone interrupted. "It's Jenkins." She answered. "Agent Walsh here."

Jake watched her eyes widen, followed by multiple head bobs. He tried not to take offense to the fact that Jenkins hadn't called him. He knew procedure and protocol were her bible. He'd been raised on the same. But it stung more than he'd expected being on the outside.

"Will do." Jo hung up, her expression blank for a moment.

"What's wrong?" Jake asked, prodding her back to life.

"It's Claire. She's in the hospital."

"Shit!" Jake's nagging feeling awoke. "This whole thing could've been a diversion to get to her."

Dana grabbed his arm. "You said there were police stationed at my house! They were supposed to keep her safe! How could they let someone get to her?"

Jo shook her head. "No one got to her."

"What do you mean?"

Jo's gaze hardened. "This was something she did to herself."

36

By the time they reached Claire's hospital room, Dana's fear had turned to anger. It was irrational, but she wanted someone to blame. The doctor who met them at Claire's bedside got the brunt of her wrath. When he was reluctant to share information, Dana had been ready to threaten the man with his own hospital stay. Thankfully, Jake's badge got the doctor talking before Dana made the situation worse.

"She's lucky to be alive," the doctor commented. "The amount of heroin in her system should've killed her. If the EMTs hadn't administered naloxone on scene we'd be having a very different conversation."

"But she's going to be okay?" Jake demanded.

"She's not out of the woods yet. We'll know more when she wakes up. But even then, someone with a history of this kind of drug use will have a long road of recovery ahead. You should be prepared to get her professional help."

After warning them that rest was the best thing for Claire's current state of recovery, the doctor excused himself, leaving Jake and Dana in shocked silence. "I want guards at her door," Jake muttered, striding from the room to make it happen.

Alone, Dana moved closer to the bed, still not quite believing this was real. She hadn't wanted to believe Claire would do something like this to herself. But the proof was hard for Dana to deny as she stared down at the pale girl in the hospital bed.

This might have been Claire's doing, but the blame didn't lie solely with her.

If Dana had been with her, this wouldn't have happened. Or maybe if she'd never left in the first place, Claire wouldn't have gone down this path. Either way, Dana was forced to face the truth. Claire's drug use was more than just recreational. She was using to mask something, something large according to the nearly lethal dose of heroin she'd taken.

If the police patrolling Dana's home hadn't checked on Claire when she didn't answer her phone, she might not have survived. As it was, she still might not pull through. Her body looked impossibly frail in the hospital bed. Dana sat down next to her, taking up one of her cold hands. Her fingernails were still tinged blue from loss of oxygen.

For a moment, Dana lost herself watching the IV pumping fluids into her veins. The EMTs and hospital staff had saved her life, but what if Claire didn't want to live?

If she'd wanted to give up before, Dana couldn't imagine things looking better from a hospital bed. Opioid withdrawal after prolonged addiction could have lasting effects on neuroreceptors in the brain. It's why the EEG glowed silently in the corner of the hospital room.

Claire had slipped into a coma after being revived at the scene. Her doctor assured Dana it was a normal side effect of overdose. *The body's way of giving itself a timeout to recover*, he'd said. But she knew what he really meant. There was no guarantee Claire would have the strength to fight her way back from this.

Dana gazed at her intern, her heart squeezing with sorrow as she realized if Claire woke up, she might not be the girl she remembered.

Guilt washed over her in waves as she sat in the silent room. She beat herself up for not pressing Claire harder about her drug use. And how had she missed her stash? She'd searched Claire's bag herself before leaving the house. She hadn't strip searched her, but Claire was a PhD candidate, not a junkie. Or maybe not. What other signs did Dana need before she stopped ignoring what was right in front of her?

Jake's arrival cut off her destructive thoughts. "Any change?"

"In the five minutes you've been gone?" Dana glared at him. Standing, she crossed the room to where he stood. "She took a lethal dose of heroin, Jake. She's lucky to be alive, though I'm not sure she'll see it that way if she wakes up." She'd added the last part under her breath, but Jake had caught it.

"You think she was trying to kill herself?"

"What else am I supposed to think?"

Jake shook his head. "She wouldn't do that."

"Like you'd know! You had no idea she was using or going to the Grave, or who knows what else!"

"Don't," he warned. "You weren't here. I did the best I could. You know what she's like. If you push too hard, she shuts you out."

"Clearly going easy on her isn't the answer!" Dana yelled, pointing to the hospital bed.

A nurse popped her head in, a look of disapproval on her face. "This is the ICU. You need to keep your voices down."

"You're right," Jake muttered. "Emotions are a little high right now."

"I understand, but perhaps the waiting room is a better place to sort them out. We don't allow visitors who aren't immediate family back here."

"I'm with the FBI," Jake argued.

"I've been told. That's your number on the board, correct?"

Dana gazed at white board on the wall. It wasn't Jake's phone number scribbled next to the notes about meds and vitals.

"It's my partner's number," Jake corrected.

"We'll call if there's any update," the nurse promised, herding them out the door.

37

Dana stormed past the guards stationed at the door, marching down the hall ahead of Jake, her phone in her hand.

"Who are you calling?" he yelled after her.

"Claire's parents. They should be here."

Jake's huff of laughter had her turning on her heels and stalking back to him. "Is this funny to you?"

"It must be nice to live up here," he said, tapping his temple. "Oblivious to everything going on in the real world."

His words hurt worse than if he'd slapped her. She was far from oblivious. If anything, she felt things too acutely. "You know that's not true."

"Really? Then I guess you know why Claire's parents aren't here, and why she wouldn't want them here." Jake took advantage of her baffled silence. "She hasn't spoken to them in over a year."

"What? Why?"

Jake sighed, his shoulders sagging. "They disowned her when she decided to continue interning for you. According to Claire, her parents told her it was time to give up dressing like a vampire and come home to help with the family business."

Dana blinked in utter shock. Claire's parents sold real estate in Seattle. Unless they dealt in haunted properties, she couldn't see Claire being an asset to their business. But that was beside the point. "Why didn't she tell me?"

"You're not exactly the easiest person to talk to, Dana. Plus, she knows how important family is to you. She was afraid you'd make her quit. Working with you means everything to her."

All at once, Dana's last remaining reserve of energy vanished. She sidestepped to a chair and sunk down into it. "And I fired her," she whispered.

Jake sat down next to her, the fight going out of him. "I'm not putting this on you, Dana."

"But you should. This is my fault. All of it. I left, not thinking about how it might affect her. I know how much her job means to her, but the first thing I did when I came back was fire her. If she was on the edge, I pushed her off."

Jake shook his head. "You're not responsible for her choices. She's an adult. Ultimately, what people do, good or bad, it's on them."

Dana pulled in a strangled breath, her chest tightening. "Then why does it hurt so bad?"

"Because you're a good person. And you want the best for the people you care about."

She nodded, feeling the burn of tears as she met Jake's gaze. "I do." She sniffled. "That goes for you, too."

He reached across the space between them and brushed her hair back. "I know."

His fingers lingered on her cheek, the warmth of his touch spreading through her like cracks in a dam; harmless at first but catastrophic if left unrepaired. Jake's touch was the only thing that could ever break through her defenses. Rather than risk the destruction of letting him in, she pulled away, wiping at her eyes. "Sorry."

"You don't have to be strong all the time."

Dana arched an eyebrow at him. "Says the man with the hero complex."

He huffed a laugh. "Okay, maybe we could both do better when it comes to that." Jake leaned his head back against the wall. "I've been an ass. The Grave ... this case ... it's getting to me. It's no excuse, but when I see women mistreated like that, it takes me back to my childhood."

Dana stilled, shocked Jake was voluntarily bringing up his past. She held her breath, afraid to disrupt his thoughts.

"The way my father treated my mother ... I could never understand why she put up with it. But when I saw those women at the Grave, beaten down and broken, I saw that same look in their eyes. The look my mother had." Leaning forward, he put his elbows on his knees and exhaled deeply. "I don't know how to stop it."

Dana reached over and took his hand. She wished she had an answer for him, some hope for him to hold on to. But she didn't. The harsh reality was the world was cruel and not everyone was granted access to the tools necessary to survive it. She thought of Claire, a bright young woman with her whole future ahead of her. If she could be swallowed by this kind of darkness, what hope was there?

Again, she wondered how Jake found the strength to do this job. They were up against insurmountable odds. Could anything they did really make a difference? "How do you keep going?" she whispered, unable to hold back her tears any longer.

His eyes burned with conviction. "I believe in someday."

He was being poetic, but she wanted facts, proof, something to give her the strength to get up out of this chair and keep fighting, because at the moment she only felt her losses, and they were weighing her down. Her parents, Dante, Meredith. Even Jake and Claire. They were still here, but she could feel them slipping away.

What good is someday when the people you want to share it with aren't around? Dana shook her head, driving away the depressing thought. "I don't think it's enough for me."

"What's the alternative? Giving up?" Jake sat tall. "I don't accept that. I know that if I keep doing my part, someday things will be better than they are."

She looked up at him, her throat aching with hope. "You really believe that?"

"I have to."

This time, when the tears fell, she didn't pull away. His arms wrapped around her, and she let the dam break, her sobs cradled in the safety of his shoulder.

38

Standing in the hallway, the three cups of coffee Jo balanced added to the rush of heat flooding her as she watched the intimate exchange between Jake and Dana. His arms encircled her, one hand rubbing soothing circles on her back while the other tenderly cradled the back of her head.

Jo wasn't the jealous type. Considering the situation, there were any number of reasons why Jake might be comforting his friend, but she couldn't deny the feeling of unease that twisted in her gut. Every instinct told her she was witnessing something more than a platonic embrace.

A lot of her job was trusting her gut. It's what made her a good agent. But she had to trust what instincts to follow and when. If what she was witnessing hadn't followed on the heels of what happened at the Grave, Jo might have thought nothing of it. But Jake had chosen Dana over her once already. That made her intuition harder to ignore.

But she had more pressing matters than her own mild insecurity to worry about at the moment. She was a professional and put the law first.

If there was something going on with her boyfriend and the FBI's infamous occult librarian, Jo would get to the bottom of it. But not here. Not now.

Straightening her spine, she resumed her confident stride, clearing her throat as she approached.

Dana stiffened, turning away to wipe her eyes when she saw Jo, but Jake's expression remained neutral. It quieted her nerves more than she expected when she didn't detect any shame. Shoving her personal feelings aside, she got back to business. "Do you want the good news or bad news first?"

"Bad," Jake answered.

"That guy you tied up at the Grave isn't pressing charges."

"I thought you said it was bad news?"

"I'm not finished. He's not pressing charges because he's MIA."

"What? How? I practically gift wrapped him!"

Jo shrugged. "Apparently the precinct was overrun with all the witnesses from the Grave. He slipped custody in all the chaos. Jenkins sent a team to follow up, but it turns out he gave a fake name and address."

"So we got nothing?"

Jo shook her head. "Jenkins is still going through the surveillance they recovered from the scene, but I'm pretty sure he's in the wind like everyone else from the Grave. Our only hope is tracking the IP address they were using to house the feeds. CS has it now."

Jo pushed past Jake's grumbling about the Bureau's cyber security department. She was ready to get to the good news. "However, I got a call from the team that processed the tattoo shop. Needles had a security camera."

"Please tell me we got an ID?" Jake asked, gratefully taking one of the coffees Jo offered.

She handed the other to Dana and pulled up the video on her phone. "No, but we got an eyewitness."

Jake and Dana huddled around the phone to watch the security video that had been forwarded to Jo. It was of the street view in front of Needles' tattoo shop. For ten seconds the video showed nothing out of the ordinary. Just sparse traffic, which was normal for that time of night. Then the front grill of a dark colored SUV came into frame. Then, nothing. The screen went blank, and the video ended.

"Okay, so we can probably get make and model from this, but I don't get it," Jake said. "Where's the eyewitness?"

Jo started the video again. Pressing pause and zooming in on the small park across the street. "See that house on the other side of the park?"

Jake squinted but nodded.

"Look at the front door," Jo instructed.

"I'll be damned." Jake straightened with the first grin on his face Jo had seen in days. "Sometimes, I love technology."

"What is it?" Dana asked, not catching what their trained eyes had.

"The neighbor has a doorbell camera," Jo explained. "It's aimed directly at Needles' tattoo shop. I'm sure it's just to monitor personal deliveries, but these cameras have been incredibly helpful at catching all kinds of criminal activity."

"Has anyone contacted the owners?" Jake asked.

Jo nodded. "They're expecting me."

"You mean us," he corrected.

"No, you're suspended."

"A technicality." Jake was already in motion.

Jo blocked his path. "Jake, you haven't been officially reinstated."

"I was first on scene with Needles. I'm a part of this."

Jo put her hands on her hips. "I'm not denying that. But if you keep cutting through all this red tape with a machete, you're going to do more harm than good. I know you don't want whatever we find thrown out of court on a technicality."

"Fine," he grumbled. "Then consider me your driver. Now let's go." Not waiting for an answer, he pushed past her, but Dana's voice called them back. "I'm going to stay here. If Claire wakes up, I don't want her to be alone."

Jake walked back, pulling Dana into a quick embrace. He said something in her ear that Jo didn't hear. Dana nodded, then sat back down, wrapping her fingers around her paper coffee cup.

39

JAKE'S EYES WERE ON THE TAILLIGHTS IN FRONT OF HIM. HE GRIPPED THE wheel, reminding himself to slow down. Jo made contact with the owners. The recording would be there waiting for them. No reason to drive like a madman.

"Were you and Dana ever more than partners?"

Jo's unexpected question nearly made him swerve into the other lane. Keeping his eyes on the road, he shook his head.

"Then I guess I don't have to ask if you're more than that now."

This time Jake glanced at her. "Why would you think that?"

She shrugged. "I saw you two at the hospital. You looked … close, that's all."

"We *are* close. You know better than anyone how this line of work bonds people."

"Dana's not in our line of work."

"I know. That makes this harder for her."

"How do you mean?"

"She didn't choose this life, it chose her, and no one prepared her for what it's like … hunting monsters, pulling a trigger. She took someone's life today and almost lost a friend. Guilt is weighing on her. Finding a way to live with that isn't going to be easy for her."

"I'd be worried if it was."

Jake exhaled and grabbed a piece of gum from the center console, popping it in his mouth. "All I'm trying to say is, today was hard on her. I was just trying to be a good friend."

Jo reached over and squeezed his hand. "You *are* a good friend, Shepard. She's lucky to have you. Maybe we can have her out once we get settled in Denver."

Tugging at his seatbelt, Jake fought the claustrophobia settling over him. "Yeah. Maybe."

"Getting out of the city always does me some good," Jo quipped, gazing out the window. "Ah, here we are," she said as he pulled up to the address she'd given him.

"I'm coming in with you." It wasn't a question.

Jo heard the conviction in his voice and was smart enough not to waste time arguing. "Fine, but let me do the talking."

"No problem."

She inhaled, and he knew she was letting the adrenaline of the unknown fuel her. He did the same. Jo gave him a wink as they walked toward the house. "Let's make these next forty-eight hours count."

He didn't need to be reminded that with each passing hour the trail was getting colder. It's why he was out here running on empty. He spit out his gum and finished the rest of his coffee, which was now cold. What he really needed was sleep, but even as tired as he was, he knew when he closed his eyes, sleep wouldn't come. It never did when he had a case like this.

He'd spent the last few nights staring at his ceiling, his mind juggling the few pieces of the puzzle he had. His head felt like a snow globe, shaking up clues and letting them land over and over to see if he could make something fit. Rival mobs, drugs, prostitutes, playing cards, tarot cards, headless thugs, body dumps, kink clubs, and now a dead tattoo artist.

Jake shoved his jumbled thoughts aside and knocked on the door, hoping to find a few more pieces inside.

40

"I'm sorry, I wish I could be more helpful, but I wasn't home. That's why we got the cameras. My husband and I work at Sibley Memorial. We rotate who's on nights so someone's always home with Matthew, but our sleep schedules overlap a bit." She quickly added, "It doesn't happen often and never for more than an hour."

"Matthew?" Jo asked.

"My son. He's upstairs, asleep."

"How old is Matthew?"

"Ten."

"Do you mind if we ask him some questions?"

The woman's brow creased with worry. "Can't it wait? He's sleeping."

Jake spoke this time. "Mrs. Royston, if your son saw something it could help us apprehend a very dangerous criminal who's been terrorizing the city."

Her hand flew to her chest. "Oh my god! You mean the Card Killer. You think that's who you'll find on my camera footage?"

Jake slipped his notebook back into his pocket. "We're not making any assumptions, ma'am. But we would appreciate your cooperation in this matter."

She frowned, obviously struggling with exposing her child to a line of questioning that might connect him to the Card Killer. As usual, the media wasn't doing Jake any favors. He hadn't turned the news on since the disaster of a press conference Fuller called, but he knew the press was still churning out unreliable propaganda to support their personal and political agendas.

"I don't know," the young mother started. "If Matthew saw anything, he would've mentioned it."

The sound of the stairs creaking had Jake on his feet, hand already at his hip. A little boy with messy black hair stared at him through wide eyes. "I'm sorry, Mom. I wanted to tell you, but ..." Jake relaxed his posture, taking a step back to encourage the boy to come down the stairs.

He hovered in the middle of the staircase, apprehension in his big brown eyes as he looked from Jake to Jo to his mother. Jo spoke first. "Hello, Matthew. I'm Agent Walsh, and this is my partner, Agent Shepard. Your mom was just helping us answer some questions."

"Is she in trouble?" he asked.

Jo shook her head. "No one's in trouble. Actually, we're very grateful for all the help your mom has given us."

Mrs. Royston opened her arms, and Matthew ran to her.

"Would it be all right to ask you some questions, Matthew?" Jo pressed.

Mrs. Royston nodded, and Jake sat back down, pulling out his notebook again. He let Jo run the questioning. She was better with children than he was, less intimidating. He didn't like working with kids. Their minds were too impressionable. Questions had to be asked just so or they could unwittingly alter a child's fragile memories.

Jake let his gaze wander the Royston home as Jo went through the questions meant to gain the little boy's trust. Birthday, favorite color, superhero he liked, etc. She was good at it, and it made him wonder if she wanted kids. It wasn't a subject they'd broached. But if he was considering moving across the country for her, shouldn't he know the answer?

"What about last night?" Jo asked, snapping Jake's attention back to the present. "Did you get to watch any of your favorite TV shows?"

Matthew looked down at the floor.

Jo spoke gently. "What happened last night, Matthew?"

"I was supposed to be asleep. My dad was sleeping, and my mom was at work, but I wasn't tired, so I came downstairs to watch TV."

"And did you?"

"No."

"Why not?"

"I heard a noise."

"What kind of noise?"

"Like when we make microwave popcorn," Matthew said. "Pop! Pop!"

"Just two pops?" Jo asked.

He nodded.

"Then what happened?"

"I stopped and listened. When I didn't hear anything else, I went to the door."

His mother sucked in a breath, but Jo silenced her with a stern look. They needed Matthew to keep going. "Did you open the door?"

The little boy shook his head vehemently. "I'm not allowed to open the door without Mom or Dad."

"That's smart," Jo encouraged, earning an appreciative nod from the boy's mother. "So what did you do?"

"I peeked out the curtain." He pointed to the heavy window covering on the door's sidelight.

"And what did you see?"

"A big black truck. It was parked in the street, and I thought that was weird."

"That is weird," Jo agreed. "Then what happened?"

He shrugged, like the story was getting boring. "A bunch of guys got into it and drove away."

"How many guys?"

"I don't know. Three?"

"Where did they come from?"

Matthew's face scrunched up as he tried to remember. "That place with the neon sign, I think."

"Can you point to it?" Jake asked.

Matthew looked at him, hesitant for a moment before finally nodding. The three adults rose and followed the little boy to the front door. Jake crouched down to his height and pulled the curtain back. Matthew pointed, his little finger leaving smudge marks on the glass. "That one."

"The tattoo shop?" Jake asked.

Matthew nodded. "Yep. Oh, hey! That's the truck!"

Jake followed Matthew's gaze to where his SUV was parked in the driveway. "You're sure?"

"Yep," he said again, nodding emphatically.

Jake stood, his eyes meeting Jo's. Her gaze held the same trepidation. So they were looking for a black SUV in D.C. Talk about a needle in a haystack. They had the video footage from the Royston's front door, but it was doubtful the angle would give them a clear view of the license plate on the vehicle Matthew saw parked outside Needles'. Without it, the vehicle list would be a mile long. Even with make and model, black SUVs made up the majority of the vehicles on the streets of D.C. They needed something more to go on.

"What about their clothes?" Jake asked. "What were they wearing?"

"They were dressed like bad guys," Matthew answered.

Jake frowned. "Bad guys?"

"Yeah. All black," the little boy said.

Jake slipped his notebook back into his pocket, his lips still pulled down.

"Thank you," Jo said. "You've been very helpful, Matthew."

"I hope you catch the bad guys."

Jo smiled, handing his mother her card. "Me too."

41

The *tick, tick, tick* of the wall clock made Dana wonder why hospital time defied the laws of nature. There was no other place where minutes could move so slowly, yet too fast.

She'd managed to talk her way back into Claire's room. It helped that her name was listed as Claire's emergency contact. A notion that brought an unexpected surge of emotion, which was currently lodged in Dana's throat.

It'd been over an hour without any change. It gave her too much time to mull over the words Jake whispered before he left with Jo. *Don't give up.*

Those three little words felt deadly as Dana sat in the hospital room, watching Claire's chest keep a steady rhythm, rising and falling in tune to the steady beeps of the monitors. No nurses barged in to administer drugs. No doctors stopped by for updates. Not a word from the guards outside the door.

Dana took it as a good sign. It meant Claire was stable. She wasn't getting worse. But she wasn't getting better.

Another glance at the clock made Dana's stomach tighten. She counted the minutes as they dragged by, realizing they'd never be enough. Not when each one could be Claire's last.

There was so much more Dana wanted to tell the girl she'd called her intern for the past three years. Claire was so much more than someone she worked with. She was her protégé, her confidant, and most importantly, her friend. She'd been there for Dana even when she hadn't asked her to be. She cared for her in all the little ways that were often missed but counted more than she ever knew.

Claire was there by Dana's side throughout her recovery after Cramer. She was there last year, when Dana grappled with Meredith's disappearance and the aftermath that followed. If it hadn't been for Claire's intuition at the catacombs, Dana might not have survived that nightmare.

Years of memories together flooded Dana, and a singular theme emerged. Claire just wanted to be part of something; a notion Dana knew well. Yet she recognized now how she'd pushed her away. She'd done it out of love, thinking Claire would be safer if she was on the outside.

The past had proven that the people Dana was closest to usually paid the heaviest price. That was something she'd never wanted for Claire. Yet here they were. Dana, sitting by her hospital bed, praying she would open her eyes.

She squeezed Claire's hand, knowing how cliché bedside bargaining was, but unable to stop it all the same. "I'm so sorry, Claire. I promise, if you come back to us, we'll do better."

Sorrow crowded Dana's chest as the reality of her lie settled in the silent room. Whatever happened with Claire it would only be Dana left to see her through. Jake would be in Denver.

"*I'll* do better," she amended. "I won't let you down."

42

Jake paused at the door, not wanting to wake Dana. Her head rested on Claire's hospital bed. The image made his mind flash back to the last time he was in a hospital with them. That time, it had been Dana in the bed.

He hated thinking about how close he'd come to losing her that day. His only solace was knowing the people who'd hurt her got what they deserved. The Priory of Bones wouldn't be able to torment anyone else thanks to Dana.

Jake continued to watch her steady breathing, wondering if the price she'd paid to silence them had been worth it.

After their first case, Dana had been haunted by nightmares. Everything she witnessed in their next case only made things worse. Or at least he assumed it did. Dana hadn't opened up to him about it. She'd been too busy rushing out of town, which he could admit now was partially his fault. It was too much too soon, and he should've known better.

Hell, he'd wanted to disappear too when he found out Vega had once again slipped free of the trap they'd set for him.

The bastard is going to haunt me forever.

Jake pushed thoughts of Terrance Vega from his mind. He'd wasted enough time chasing ghosts. He needed to stop being paranoid. He'd already exhausted that angle as soon as Claire's friend Sadie turned up dead.

Anytime a prostitute went missing or was killed, Jake picked up Vega's file again. But nothing had changed. He was still in the wind. Which was fine with Jake. One less monster lurking in his city. For now, Jake was focused on the case before him.

He stepped further into the hospital room, keeping his footsteps quiet so he wouldn't wake Dana. He'd come to fill her in on what they'd found at the Royston place, which as of now wasn't much. Since there wasn't anything she could do to aid the investigation at the moment, he wanted to let her sleep. He knew she needed it. He sure as hell did.

Yawning, he paused in front of the whiteboard, reading through the notes scribbled there by the hospital staff; not that he understood any of it. The extent of his medical training in the Army boiled down to dressing field wounds. Slow the bleeding and keep moving, was their motto. Thinking back, it was a miracle any of them made it back home. A festering flesh wound could kill a man as fast as a bullet. But Jake knew better than to let his mind dwell too long in the darkness of those memories. He had enough trouble to deal with in the present without dredging up the past.

Deciding his time might be better spent assisting Jo at the lab, Jake turned to leave, almost plowing into the nurse who walked into the room. It was the same one from earlier, and her stern expression was anything but welcoming. "I thought I told you family only?"

Jake held up his hands. "I was just leaving."

"Jake?" The sound of Dana's drowsy voice stopped him. "Did something happen?"

The nurse crossed her arms, her scowl deepening. Jake smiled at her, appreciative of her diligence. It was good to know Claire had someone so dedicated looking after her. "No. Just came by to check on you two. Let's go get a coffee," he suggested when the nurse cleared her throat.

Dana followed him out of the room and down the hall toward the bank of vending machines. Jake fed a ten into the one marked Gourmet To-Go. He knew the coffee gurgling out of the nozzle would be anything but gourmet, but as long as it was hot and highly caffeinated, he wouldn't complain. "Any changes with Claire?"

Dana shook her head and Jake caught a glimpse of the angry purple bruise on her jaw.

"Well, no news, is good news, I guess."

"I've never understood that saying," she mused, accepting the piping hot cup of coffee Jake offered. "No news is just no news."

He retrieved his cup from behind the acrylic door and walked the short distance to the empty waiting room area. "Yeah, but no news means everything gets to stay as is."

"And that's a good thing?" Dana took a seat next to him in a row of worn blue vinyl chairs.

"It can be when you're in a hospital."

"Or things can easily take a turn for the worst."

Jake exhaled, setting his cup on his knee so he could give Dana's his full attention. "She's going to wake up. Claire's a fighter."

Though she didn't look convinced, Dana nodded and took a sip of her coffee. "What happened at the Roystons'? Did you catch anything on the footage?"

"Jo took it to the lab. They're analyzing it now. She'll call if there's anything worth hearing."

"What about eyewitnesses? Did anyone see anything?"

"Jenkins has a team going door-to-door, but the Roystons didn't see anything. They both work nights at the hospital. Wife was on, husband was home, asleep. Only one who was awake was their ten-year-old son. According to him, a black SUV pulled up in front of the tattoo shop. He heard two pops, then three guys dressed in black ran out."

"Pops? Gun fire?"

Jake shrugged, sipping the bitter coffee. "We'll see if the video from their doorbell confirms his story."

"You don't believe him?"

"I didn't say that. But he's a kid. Not exactly an expert witness."

"Actually, children that age have remarkable memories. His cognitive recollection is fully matured, but not yet altered by external cues like the complex society pressures of adolescence and adulthood."

Jake held back a smirk. "I didn't know you were an expert in child psychology."

"Hardly, but a general knowledge is relevant to certain areas of my studies."

Jake wanted to tell her they had different interpretations of "general knowledge," but a different question came to mind. "Do you want kids?"

Dana paused, her coffee halfway to her split lip. "Where'd that come from?"

He rubbed his face. "I don't know. This case … it just has me thinking. Like today, we went to this shit house, in a shit neighborhood, where a kid probably witnessed a murder and he's as happy as can be, talking about superheroes and catching bad guys."

"What's wrong with that?"

"Nothing. It's good, but ironic when you think about it. Claire grew up somewhere safe, nice, with money, and look where she ends up. So depressed she tried to kill herself." He shook his head. "It feels wrong to bring kids into this world, but then I meet someone like Matthew Royston and I think, maybe some kids turn out alright."

"Claire's not a kid, Jake."

"I know. But sometimes it feels that way. I try to look out for her, protect her. But how do you protect someone from themselves?"

"I don't know." Dana wrapped her long fingers around her paper coffee cup, her thumbnail scratching at her cuticles. "But if being a parent means feeling this terrified all the time, it's not for me."

"Nah." Jake bumped his shoulder into hers. "You'd do all right. You have that tough love thing down."

She rolled her eyes, a smile almost peeking through. "What about Jo?"

"What about her?"

"Does she want kids?"

He should know that answer. Or at least want to know. The warmth Jake had regained sitting next to Dana drained away as the harsh truth settled over him. He needed to face it, but now wasn't the time. He was running on caffeine and adrenaline. Skirting the truth, he shrugged. "It hasn't come up."

43

Jake's coffee had long since gone cold, but their conversation continued. He was grateful Dana kept the focus on their case. Easing back into the comfort zone of partnership, he reiterated the details of the Royston visit at Dana's request. "I looked at the video footage before we left. The tattoo shop is so far away, I'm not sure it'll be much use." Dana's puzzled expression stopped him. "What's wrong?"

"Needles wasn't shot. He was hung."

"So?"

"You said the Royston boy heard pops."

"Yeah. Doesn't mean Needles didn't get off a couple of shots before someone beheaded him, hacked out his tongue and strung him up."

Dana cringed and Jake regretted his callous tone. He'd been desensitized a long time ago. Death might be her profession but studying it and witnessing it were two very different things.

"We should go back to the crime scene and look for the bullets."

"Already have a team on that," he answered. "If shots were fired, the gunman knew enough to collect the brass, but we're checking into any GSWs reported at area hospitals and clinics in case Needles got a piece of his attackers."

"Does this mean you're officially back on the case?"

He smirked. "For now."

"Officially or is this your own brand of Shepard justice?"

"Officially, but I like the sound of Shepard justice."

Dana rolled her eyes again.

"Jenkins called me on the way here and lifted my suspension. But I'm on thin ice according to her."

"So now what?"

"Now we wait."

Dana sighed. "It feels like we're getting nowhere."

"Hey, no news is good news, remember?"

But Dana didn't smile this time. She stared into her coffee; her deep brown eyes lost somewhere far off. Finally, she looked up at him, the sorrow in her gaze making him ache. "Why did you never call?" she asked. "About Claire, I mean."

There was no accusation in her voice this time and Jake's defenses slipped, letting the truth out. "I picked up the phone a dozen times." He scrubbed a hand across his tired features. "I guess I let my stubborn pride keep me from making the call."

"Why?"

"You didn't need us." He tried to shrug off the sting those words still evoked. "I guess I wanted to prove that we didn't need you. Stupid, I know."

Dana was looking at him now. "Jake, that's not why I left. If anything, I think I needed you too much and that scared me."

Jake remained silent, anticipating the truth he'd waited six months for. After all they'd been through, he deserved honesty, and she finally seemed ready to offer it.

Setting her coffee down, Dana took a deep breath and faced him. "I've been on my own for a long time. Letting people in, depending on them ... it's not easy for me." Her eyes filled with emotion, and she looked down. "Especially when someone you thought you could trust turns out to be someone else entirely."

Jake knew she was referring to Meredith's betrayal. He remained silent letting Dana gather her thoughts.

"What happened with Mere ... it really messed me up. I couldn't face what she'd done, what I'd almost done. I just wanted to outrun it for a little while. When the book tour came up, it seemed like the perfect excuse to get the space I needed to sort my head out."

Again, Jake regretted not waiting to confess his feelings. Dana had been on the edge and instead of offering her a parachute, he'd told her to jump. The timing hadn't been right, but for them, between their jobs and their scars, it might never be right.

He'd already lost too much to poor timing. He'd taken a risk, and he'd failed. Those were the chances. He had to figure out how to live with them. But it seemed Dana was still struggling to find her footing. Her brown eyes darkened with emotion. "I'm sorry, Jake. My intention was never to hurt you or Claire. I just wanted to find a way back to myself. I can see now how selfish it was."

"Don't apologize for taking care of yourself." He would never fault her for that. Self-preservation was a rule the Army instilled in him. *You can't help anyone if you can't help yourself.*

Sentiment tightened his throat and he wished he had the words to tell her he understood. He'd been in her shoes. He hadn't taken the time to heal. It's why he was constantly at war with himself and would be until he dealt with the part of him that hadn't come back from his last tour. The part of him that still lay on that blood-soaked spit of sand in Ghazni holding what was left of his best friend.

Ramirez's eyes sparkled with laughter in Jake' memory. *It's your funeral.* It was one of the last things Jake's best friend said to him. It shouldn't have been a big deal. It was something they said all the time: a joke, a dare, a battle cry. But it was never supposed to be a goodbye.

Jake caught Dana's hand, threading his fingers through hers. He didn't have the words to convey everything she meant to him. Instead he said, "Place the mask over your own mouth and nose before assisting others."

She forced a smile and squeezed his hand, repeating the phrase his Special Ops team uttered before each mission. He'd never shared it with anyone but her. It felt right hearing her say it. The same way his next question felt right.

"When this is over, do you think you could do something for me? Do you think you could come with me to see Ramirez?"

Dana's hand remained in his, her eyes searching. "It would be my honor."

He squeezed her hand, his chest feeling lighter. However, the levity didn't last.

"I hope you find everything you want in Denver, Jake. You deserve to be happy."

"Dana, Denver's not—" The buzzing of his phone cut him off. Seeing Jo's name on his screen brought reality screeching back. He took the call. "Shepard."

"Jake, you need to get down here. We found something."

44

DANA STARED AT THE VIDEO SCREEN. IT WAS PAUSED ON A STILL THAT showed a black SUV parked in front of the tattoo shop. Jo had just finished explaining how the lab techs were able to enhance the video footage from the Roystons' enough to get the license plate from the vehicle.

"And get this," Jo continued. "It's registered to Lieutenant Allen."

Jake stiffened. "That can't be right."

"I checked it twice," Jo insisted. "And that's not all. His wife reported him missing."

Jake muttered a swear. "Then we have a problem."

Dana didn't follow. "Who's Lieutenant Allen?"

"Arthur Allen works homicide. He assisted me on my first case with the Bureau."

A chill slid down Dana's back as she connected the dots. "Your first case? That was Jenni James."

Jake nodded, his gaze heavy with implications. "And Vega."

Unprepared for the shockwave that name sent through her, Dana reminded herself to breathe. Six months ago, Terrance 'Ivy League' Vega had turned her life upside down. The notorious sex trafficker was the only one who'd slipped through the net she and Jake used to ensnare one of the world's most dangerous secret societies. If he was back in D.C. ... "Jake, if this is Vega, he's come back to finish what he started."

"My thoughts exactly."

"Somebody needs to fill me in," Jo demanded.

Dana was grateful Jake stepped up. Her mind was too busy swimming with the horrors she'd witnessed the last time she'd crossed paths with Vega.

"Terrance Vega was involved with the secret society we took down six months ago. He ghosted when we got too close. It saved his hide, but with him on the run we were able to shut down the drug and sex trade empire he'd built in Deanwood."

Jo caught on quickly. "The territory Ikemba and Santos have been fighting over?"

Jake nodded.

"And what, you think he's come back for revenge?"

"That's what he does, Jo."

"You really think he'd risk being caught just because of some vendetta?"

"I do. This war started a long time ago. My first case with the Bureau was a prostitute Vega killed. We brought him in but couldn't make the conviction stick. Letting him walk still haunts me."

"Jake, I'm not saying this scumbag doesn't have a dartboard with your face on it, but I've got a dead CI and a missing cop. You said Vega was sex crimes. What makes you think this is him?"

"Because, that missing cop was the one who arrested him all those years back."

Dana's heart dropped to her stomach. Jake's revelation made it impossible to deny the evidence before her. "Arthur Allen arrested Vega?"

Jake ran a hand through his hair making it stand on end. "Allen was just a beat cop back then. He'd seen the warrant on Vega and brought him in on a parking violation of all things. He was in the room when I interrogated Vega."

"Okay," Jo said, pacing as she spoke. "I can see the connection, but Jake, it's loose. Are you sure about this?"

"I wish I were wrong, but it's him. I know it. He's been planning this all along. The cartel war between Ikemba and Santos was the perfect ruse. Not only did he throw us off his scent, but he set two of his rivals up to take each other out so he could get his territory back and make a grab for theirs as well. He's smart and patient, he only strikes when he knows he can inflict the most pain."

Jake's words made Dana inhale abruptly. She grabbed his arm. "Claire! He's going to come after Claire!"

In the next breath Jake was on the phone barking orders to the guards at her room. After being reassured her condition hadn't changed, he was on the move. Dana followed on his heels even though she didn't know where they were headed.

Jo chased them into the hall, asking the question for her. "Jake! Where are you going?"

He turned back. "To warn Jenkins. She worked that first case with me. If Vega's cleaning house, she's on his list."

"Okay. You get to Jenkins. I'm going to help the team searching for Allen."

Jake held up his phone. "Stay in touch."

Jo nodded, heading off in the opposite direction, her footsteps matching the rapid beat of Dana's heart.

45

"I don't know." Jenkins tapped her manicured red fingernail to her chin.

She sat behind her desk in the pristine interior of her office in the J. Edgar Hoover Building, listening patiently while Jake relayed his theory. Not being able to read her neutral expression grated on Jake's fraying nerves.

"Jenks," he pressed. "It's him. Vega is behind this. You know I'm right."

Even now while he compelled her, it was hard to know where her head was. Finally, she pushed back from her chair and stood, her eyes moving to Dana before settling on Jake. "I'll admit, it fits," she concluded, but she was quick to cut off Jake's triumphant grin. "You may be right, but Jake, you know I can't issue a manhunt on a hunch."

"It's more than a hunch and you know it," he shot back.

Jenkins straightened a stack of papers on her desk. "I've got the surveillance report right here."

Jake crossed his arms. "Let me guess, another dead end."

Her silence told him he was right. He swore, standing so abruptly his chair tumbled backward.

"Sit down," Jenkins ordered.

"I'd rather stand."

"Tracing the surveillance footage was a bust, but the ME's report has shed some light."

She had his attention.

"First, there were traces of GSR on Needles."

Jake blinked. So the kid had been right, the poor bastard had tried to fight back. "And what else?"

"No casings. No weapon."

"Great. So no chance to run ballistics."

"There's more," Jenkins added. "They've identified fourteen different remains from the landfill. One of them is Rafael Santos."

Jake was stunned silent. He righted his chair and sat down. "Jenks, we have no weapons, no witnesses, no leads. Tell me this doesn't have Vega written all over it?"

"You can keep saying it, Shepard, but until you get me proof, my hands are tied."

"Come on!" he implored. "We're wasting time. Work with me here."

"Trust me, Jake, I am working with you. And after that stunt you pulled at the Grave, I might be the only one willing to. If you do this any other way than by the book, it'll be your job. And this time, not even I can save you."

"I never asked you to stick your neck out for me," he clipped, his voice low with anger.

Jenkins shot him a look that simmered with disappointment. "You didn't have to. We're family. That's just what we do."

The words pierced Jake, each of them a knife to his heart. Remi Jenkins was as close to family as it got. And she'd always treated him as such. She didn't deserve his wrath. Not when it was Vega who incited it. "You're right," he muttered. "But this is Vega. I know it, and I can't stand the idea of letting him slip away again."

"All the more reason to do this the right way," she argued, walking around her desk toward the door.

"Where are you going?"

Pausing, Jenkins turned to face him, wearing a look of annoyance. "You're aware I'm the assistant director of this department, correct?"

The question had been rhetorical, but Jake nodded anyway.

"Then you understand that this case isn't the only iron I have in the fire."

Jenkins headed toward the door, but Jake charged after her, catching the sleeve of her expensive blazer. Her eyes met the fire in his, but he kept his voice even. "Jenks, didn't you hear what I said? If this is Vega, you're a target?"

"I'm aware. And you should damn well know by now that I can take care of myself."

With that, she walked out of her office, the door shutting in Jake's face. He wanted to chase her down and drag her back to her desk. He'd tie her to it if he could. There was a monster loose in D.C. painting a target on the backs of everyone Jake cared about.

It was killing Jake that he couldn't have eyes on each of them. He heard Wade's voice in his head. *Putting all your eggs in one basket only gives the wolf a bigger meal.*

Jake knew it made more sense to spread out the targets. Years of military combat engrained that in him. Logistically, a spread formation was most successful. But logic didn't factor into his mind at the moment. His heart pounded beneath his ribs, rattling against the cage that kept it from leaping out to defend those he loved.

Jake wanted Jo, Dana, Jenkins and Claire where he could see them, where he'd have a fighting chance at protecting them if need be. Currently Dana was the only one willing to accommodate.

Turning his attention to her, he was suddenly aware of her unusual silence. Even more baffling was her cooperation. At the moment, it felt like she was the only one who believed him. But her reserved attitude was worrisome. In the past she'd been his mental sparring partner. Was this what it felt like to be on the same page as the brilliant librarian?

It was unnerving, but he decided not to pull at that thread. He had enough to worry about. Grabbing their coats, he opened the door and held it for Dana. "Come on."

"Where are we going?"

"To find Vega. He's out there, Dana. Whether I can prove it or not, I know this is him. I can feel it in my bones."

"Jake, I believe you, but Jenkins is right, we have to find proof and go about this carefully. Otherwise we're playing right into his hands."

The irony wasn't lost on him. Jake was usually the one reminding Dana of the repercussions of straying outside the rigid lines of the law. But desperate times called for desperate measures.

Jake flexed his jaw, cracking his neck from side to side as he marched down the hall. He paused in front of the elevator and jabbed the button. "I don't know about you but I'm tired of playing games."

Dana gazed up at him, her eyes full of determination. "So am I."

Jake grinned. "Then let's go get this bastard."

46

"Jake, I know you do your best thinking when you're driving, but we've been at it for an hour."

"Rome wasn't built in a day."

Dana resisted rolling her eyes. "I'd feel better if we could swing by the hospital and check on Claire."

"I thought we agreed. She's safer if we keep our distance."

Dana sighed. Jake had explained his *eggs in a basket* theory already. It's not that she disagreed with him. Based on her starring role in the surveillance footage and what her attacker at the Grave whispered, she knew she had a target on her back. But she couldn't shake the nagging feeling of dread that filled her each time she thought of Claire. She was alone and defenseless in a hospital bed. There were guards at the door, but that did little to ease her mind.

Driving around aimlessly only exacerbated Dana's desperation. *Not aimlessly,* she reminded herself. Jake was diligently canvassing Vega's old stomping grounds, though Dana didn't hold much hope of uncovering anything.

She tried to keep her skepticism from her scowl, but Jake knew her too well. "Dana, I know that look. If you have something to say, just say it."

"Vega's not going to be at his old hideouts. It's too predictable."

He glared at her, frustration rolling off him in waves. "If you've got a better idea let's hear it."

"I don't know if it's better but I've been thinking about the tarot cards."

"What about them?"

"I don't know. That's the problem. They're the only thing that doesn't make sense."

Jake's dark brows furrowed. "The only thing?"

"Well no, but it doesn't seem like Vega."

"I thought we established this already. He used tarot to make sure you'd be part of this case."

"I get that, but he could've picked any occult icon to draw me in. Why tarot cards?"

"I sense you have a theory?"

"I'm working on one."

"Let's hear it."

"Well, tarot cards tell stories. They show us our destiny, paths our future might take."

"And what, you think Vega's taken up divination?"

"No, but it's like you said. He's smart, patient. Someone that meticulous wouldn't just leave tarot cards at his crime scenes for no reason. I think he's trying to tell us something."

"Yeah, that he wants us dead," Jake grumbled.

Dana shook her head. "It's more than that. I think he could be giving us clues that we're not seeing."

"Clues to what?"

"I don't know yet but think about it. When he was working with the Priory of Bones, Vega spelled out their entire master plan. He was taunting us, letting us know we had the answers if we could decipher the code. I think he's doing the same thing here."

Jake was silent, his jaw muscles bunching while he mulled over Dana's words. "He does seem to get off on being one step ahead of us."

"It's a common trait in narcissistic personality disorders. Showing that he's superior to law enforcement inflates his sense of self-importance."

Jake cut his eyes at her. "If you're suggesting this asshole can get off by pleading insanity, I don't want to hear it. He's brutally murdered people. There's no excuse for that."

"I'm not excusing him, just trying to understand him. A personality disorder is just one possible explanation for his actions. It's common among cult leaders. And it could explain why his plans are escalating. If we can find his motivation, we might be able to predict his next move."

"Okay, so what does a narcissistic psychopath who traffics drugs and women do next?"

"It's not what he'll do, it's what he wants."

"That's easy," Jake answered. "Power, notoriety, fame. It's what all these scumbags want."

"How would someone like Vega get that?"

"Beheading cartel members in D.C. seems to be working for him."

Dana shook her head. "If he just wanted our attention, he would've made sure we knew he was behind the murders. He's gone through excessive lengths to hide his identity."

"So what then?"

"He wants power and notoriety, but he still wants to get away with it. I think he wants to rub our noses in his genius one last time before he takes us out. He has an exit plan."

Jake snorted. "It's not going to work. You don't go after cops if you plan on getting away with murder. No one's letting a cop killer walk in this city."

The sharp ringing of Jake's phone sounded through the stereo. He hit the speakerphone and answered. "Shepard."

"Jake." Jo's voice echoed through the SUV. "We found Allen."

"And?"

Her pause gave Dana the answer before Jo confirmed it. "We were too late."

Jake punched the steering wheel, his knuckles turning white as he gripped it tighter.

"I'll text you the address."
"On our way."

47

THE KILL WAS SLOPPY, THAT MUCH WAS EVIDENT FROM THE MOMENT JAKE walked onto the scene. Blood spattered the walls; arterial spray from the looks of it. Drag marks and indentation on the carpet showed the furniture had been rearranged.

Did Allen fight back or is Vega just getting theatrical?

It sickened Jake to see the officer slumped over in his chair. He looked like a broken mannequin, propped there under the soft yellow glow of lamp light. It almost looked like he was waiting for the show to begin. Actually, much of the scene looked staged. But for whose benefit?

"Walk me through," Jake ordered, wanting to get Jo's take on the scene before he gave his own assessment.

"Two glasses of whiskey, two cigars, playing cards." She pointed to the items on the coffee table between the chairs. "Insinuating the victim knew his attacker. Good news is we might be able to lift prints or DNA."

Jake shook his head. "Look again. No smudge marks on the glasses and I don't smell cigar smoke. You're not gonna find any DNA. These are props."

Jo frowned. "How do you know?"

"Do we have TOD?"

"ME estimated ten to twelve hours ago."

Jake pointed a gloved hand at the cold cigars. "If someone was smoking that ten to twelve hours ago, we'd smell it. And there's no ash. This was staged to look like another mob hit."

"It looks like it could be right out of *Goodfellas*, for fuck's sake." Jake turned to see Officer Hartwell behind him, face pinched in anger. He shook his head. "Allen was one of the good ones."

"You knew him?" Jake asked.

Hartwell nodded, tapping his badge. "Same precinct till he made LT."

"My condolences," Jake said, meaning it. "Who was first on scene?"

"Hernandez." Hartwell waved a young, round-faced officer over. On a good day, his honeyed skin tone probably held a healthy glow. Today, he looked as green as his age.

Jake introduced himself. "Agent Shepard, FBI. I understand you found Lieutenant Allen?"

Hernandez nodded. "Yes, Sir."

"Did you disturb anything?"

He shook his head. "I checked for a pulse, that's all."

Jake looked down at the officer's uniform. Sure enough, his pants were dark around the knees. He'd knelt in Allen's blood when feeling for a pulse. "Make sure you turn over your uni as evidence. It'll need to be processed. We're looking for any DNA that doesn't match Allen's."

"We've got zilch in the way of DNA at the other scenes. You really think the Card Killer got sloppy all of a sudden?" Hartwell asked.

"We don't even know this is the Card Killer," Jo interjected.

"Yes, we do." Dana spoke for the first time since they'd entered the condemned row home. She pointed to the cards fanned out on the glass coffee table. "There's an extra card at the bottom of the deck."

Jake looked closer, not seeing it at first. But then ... He swore as he saw the detail Dana caught. A chill swept over him as he moved closer. "The first card in the deck. Representing the first time Vega got arrested?"

Dana nodded. The card was face down, with the same white border around the edge as the rest of the deck, but it was larger. Something Jake hadn't noticed at first thanks to the way the cards were arranged; fanned out, one edge overlapping the next.

"Has this been photographed?" An evidence marker sat on the table next to the cards, but Jake wasn't taking any chances.

His anger threatened to bubble over when he didn't get an answer. If he had to ask again, he was going to start busting heads, and he really didn't want to sucker punch Hartwell again. Dana came up with a solution before it got that far.

Pulling a compact from her small crossbody purse, she crouched near the coffee table and slipped the mirror beneath the glass. Jake joined her. Anger rippled through him when he deciphered the illustration. A lone man sat on a throne, a sword in one hand, the scales of justice in the other. The word beneath the figure was reversed in the mirror, but it only took Jake a moment to untangle it.

"Justice," Dana murmured, her eyes meeting Jake's.

He shook his head. "Not yet. But it's coming."

Standing, Jake stalked out of the room, phone already to his ear.

"JAKE! STOP!"

Jo chased after him, but he ignored her. He was too angry to stop moving.

"Jake! You heard, Jenkins. This doesn't prove it's Vega!"

Running out of real estate, Jake jerked the door of his SUV open. "It's him, Jo! And I'm not gonna sit on my ass and do nothing while we wait for him to kill someone else."

"We're not doing nothing," she argued. "The team is processing the scene. It takes time. You know that."

"Yeah and I also know a cop is dead. What I don't understand is why I'm the only one motivated to do something about it?"

Jo dipped her head, her gaze sympathetic. "That's not fair, Jake. We all want justice for Allen."

"Justice." Jake hated the bitter taste the word left in his mouth now.

The moment he'd seen that image on the tarot card any shadow of a doubt that Vega was behind this vanished.

The illustration on the card was the same one carved into the courthouse where Jake had stood side by side with Allen and watched Vega walk free.

In his memory, he could still see that cocky smile on Vega's face. It made Jake want to punch something. His phone call to Jenkins hadn't helped. He'd called her immediately after making the connection to the image on the tarot card. She'd been at the courthouse that day, too. She should be as pissed as he was. But Jake heard nothing but disappointment in her voice when he described Allen's scene. Despite the undeniable connection, she still refused to order a manhunt for Vega.

Jake didn't know what he'd been expecting. Jenkins was doing things the way she was supposed to, the way he used to, by the book. His gut told him this was Vega, but he didn't have proof. Not anything solid, anyway. But he'd find something, even if it killed him.

He climbed behind the wheel, but Jo followed so he couldn't shut her out. Her hand caught his before he could get to the ignition. "Jake, stop. Come back and comb the scene with me."

"I can't. This is personal. You don't understand."

"The hell I don't! I'm in this with you. We're a team, remember? You're not the only one who feels responsible for this shit show! It's my CI in the morgue. And I understand what it means when we lose one of our brothers in blue. No one is taking this lightly. We're all out here doing our jobs, the best we can. The only person I don't see pulling his weight is you."

Heat crept up Jake's neck until his ears burned. He didn't enjoy the tongue lashing, but he could appreciate being called out when he needed it. Rubbing his face, he muttered into his hands. "You're right. It's just ..." His rage bubbled over, and he punched his horn. The blare echoed down the desolate street. "It's him, Jo. It's fucking Vega, I know it. Not being able to prove it is killing me."

"Then come back inside and help me find some proof." Her bright green eyes were pleading. "Just give me one more hour at the scene. After that we can leave and go wherever you're rushing off to."

Considering he had no clue where he'd been planning to go, Jake gave in. Exhaling heavily, he got out of his SUV, savoring the brief feeling of Jo's hand in his. "I'm on your team, Shepard."

"I know." He gave her hand a quick squeeze dropping it before someone noticed. It was rare that he regretted having to keep their relationship hidden, but right now, he craved contact, warmth, anything to remind him what he was fighting for.

He leaned against the cool metal of his vehicle, letting it soothe the anger still simmering beneath his skin. "Thanks for talking me down. I couldn't do this without you."

She grinned. "Yes, you could. You'd probably be more than suspended by now, but you don't need me. That's what I love about you. You're a loner, like me."

That got a smirk out of him. "Come on. Let's go take a stab at that teamwork thing I'm always hearing about."

48

Dana blinked, her eyes adjusting to the glare of the diner's fluorescent bulbs. It was a harsh contrast to the dismal crime scene. Her empty stomach growled, but there was no way she could eat after what she'd just witnessed.

Jake and Jo didn't have that problem. The two of them washed down their plates of fried food with coffee, causing her to wonder if their stomachs were lined with lead. Sipping at her coffee, she pulled tiny pieces off her chocolate croissant, letting the dusting of powdered sugar melt on her tongue. The nutritional value was non-existent, but at least the calories would breathe some life back into her; something she desperately needed after being surrounded by so much death.

It often snuck up on her how different death was in the real world. The deaths she studied in her library were neat and orderly. They told her stories, linking history to culture; things she could make sense of. But here it leapt off the pages.

There was nothing orderly about the senseless ways people killed each other. That notion surrounded her with a deafening stillness that felt like it could suck the light out of the world.

Having wielded death by her own hands, Dana was starting to wonder if she'd become a magnet for it. Perhaps losing her parents at such a young age marked her in some way that attracted death. It was a relatively common occurrence that upon witnessing death, one saw it more readily; a loss of innocence never to be regained.

There was no denying she'd seen more than her fair share of death lately. It seemed drawn to her like a moth to a flame. Or was it the other way around? Was she the flame or the moth?

Realizing she wouldn't find the answers inside the brightly lit diner, Dana closed the door on her morbid musings, forcing herself to tune back into the conversation at the table.

"Okay," Jo hedged. "If it's really Vega and he wants notoriety, why's he still trying to throw us off by setting up such an elaborate crime scene?"

Jake dredged a french fry through gravy and popped it in his mouth. "I don't know. Maybe he's still angling to get the cartels to take each other out so he can scoop up the spoils when he's ready to step back in and claim his throne?"

Jo snorted. "You realize how insane that sounds, right? *If* Vega is the Card Killer, he's killed six people, including a cop. He's not stepping into anything, unless it's a jail cell."

"It's not insane," Dana offered, causing them to pause, both with food hovering before their mouths. She felt suddenly self-conscious. She must've been lost in thought for longer than she'd expected to elicit such a reaction. She rushed to fill the awkward silence. "The definition of insanity is doing the same thing repeatedly while expecting different results. Vega hasn't repeated his MO once."

Jo shook her head. "Decapitations. First three vics and Needles all had the same mutilations."

"Yes, but only the first two were mailed to you. They may have been from the same Nigerian cartel, but they each were sent with different playing cards in their mouths. I believe each one represents a message. And since the murder scenes on the first two haven't been discovered we can't make an accurate assumption of how the victims were killed."

"Okay, but—"

Dana held up her hand to silence Jo. She was just getting started. "Victim number three was found in an alley, not mailed. Another deviation from modus operandi. Then, we have the fourth victim, Sadie Azeez. She was stabbed in public, a severe deviation from the first three killings. Based on the message on the tarot card found at Jake's, I believe Claire was intended to be the fifth casualty. But it was a threat, not a murder. Then he jumps to Needles, the sixth victim. He was decapitated but left with his body which was in full inverted display, emulating the tarot card found with him. Plus additional mutilations with the removal of the tongue and tattooed message. That's another escalation of MO."

"What about Allen?" Jake asked, his interest piqued.

"Allen was also arranged in the manner of the tarot card found with him, but he wasn't decapitated and no written message was found at the scene. That's a total of seven unique victims."

"So what's your point?" Jo asked.

Dana wrapped her fingers around the mug of coffee, soaking up the remaining warmth. "My point is, insanity is the last term I'd apply to this killer. If anything, I'd suggest we're dealing with a highly intelligent individual who's acting out a revenge fantasy that he's been planning for quite some time."

Jo's pale eyebrows reached skyward. She looked from Dana to Jake. "She's scary."

"Scary good," Jake added with a wink, popping another fry in his mouth. "The only thing you missed is the fact that we know who the killer is."

"I agree," Dana added. "This feels personal, and a little too close to the last case that led us to Vega."

Jo shook her head. "Look, I'm all for gut intuition, but until I see concrete proof, I'm keeping an open mind and you should, too. Letting your emotions lead can make you blind to the truth."

"Emotions often help the blind see," Dana offered in defense.

Jake grinned, gesturing to her as though there was nothing more to discuss. Jo had other ideas. "I'm not saying it can't be Vega. I just want proof."

"I get it," Dana offered. "But this is how Vega operates. He stays in the shadows, pitting people against one another, getting others to do his dirty work. He's like a conductor, orchestrating a masterpiece of sadistic mind games. Ensnaring people is his specialty, and he always makes it personal." Her throat tightened. "He lured me in with a case he knew I couldn't pass up, then made me choose between saving my partner or my best friend." Storm clouds invaded Jake's piercing gaze, and Dana swallowed thickly. "And now …"

Jake reached across the table, his warm hand closing over hers. "I'm not going to let him do it again."

For a moment, Dana savored the warmth of his touch before she pulled away. Settling her hands in her lap, she nodded.

Concern creased Jake's brow. "Dana, I won't let him get to you."

She lifted her gaze to meet his, conviction burning in her eyes. "He's not going to get to any of us."

•

49

Jake slapped cash onto the chipped red tabletop. Standing, he pushed his chair back. His appetite left the moment he heard the pain in Dana's voice. Guilt filled his stomach, bathing his greasy meal in a pool of regret as he thought about what he was putting her through—again.

Whatever she'd come back to D.C. for, it wasn't this.

He and Jo chose this career, but Dana hadn't. She'd merely been trying to shed light on the darkness death had colored her life with. Getting wrapped up with the FBI and the kinds of monsters they hunted was never her plan. He'd been the one to drag her down this twisted road.

If he took his ego out of it, he could understand why she'd left after their last case. Hell, some days he could see the appeal of packing a bag and driving south until the ocean stopped him.

"I'll meet you at the car," Jo said, flipping her long blonde ponytail over her shoulder as she headed to the ladies' room.

"Me too," Dana added, moving to follow her, but Jake reached out, catching her elbow.

"Dana, I don't want to make you relive this."

"Reliving it implies I've finished living it once already." The warmth drained out of her eyes. "I live it every single day, Jake. For everyone who didn't survive the Priory of Bones. And for the few who did."

She was referring to Meredith, and that only deepened his remorse. What happened to Dana's best friend wasn't his fault, but sometimes blame didn't matter. Memories of Ramirez crowded his mind, sharpening the sting of guilt. Jake had buried his best friend. Dana hadn't gotten the chance. Meredith Kincaid might still be alive, but the woman Dana knew her to be was long gone. Jake had witnessed it that day on the hill. He'd seen the wild fury that controlled her. If Dana hadn't taken that shot, Jake would be in the same cemetery as Ramirez.

He owed Dana more respect than he'd shown her. It was time to channel his anger in the right direction. "This time we finish it. For Meredith. For Jenni James. For all the others who deserved better."

The gold flecks in Dana's eye blazed to life. "What makes you believe we'll get Vega this time?"

"Because it's about damn time we got some redemption."

A hint of a smile tugged at her lips. "Careful, Jake, you're starting to sound like someone who believes in second chances."

"I never said I didn't believe in second chances." It's why he'd joined the FBI.

"Right, just not promises or apologies."

"Dana ..."

She held up her hands. "Don't worry. I'm not asking for any. The only thing I want is proof this is Vega so we can end it for good."

"Then we're on the same page."

She nodded. "It's hard to ignore the similarities between the Card Killer and our last case."

Jake agreed but convincing anyone who hadn't lived it wouldn't be so easy. "Human trafficking and secret societies, to drug cartels and mob hits ... it's a leap and one that won't be easy to sell if we don't find something incriminating."

"We both know Vega's too smart to leave something behind."

"Then how do you suppose we prove he's behind this?"

"We go back to the beginning."

"You want to reopen the Kincaid case?"

"I think it's worth comparing what we've got on the Card Killer with the evidence from our last case. We might've been looking at it all wrong. With a suspect in mind, the pieces might fall into place."

And lead right to Vega!

"You're right!" That familiar rush of blood that always followed chasing down a lead pumped through Jake's veins. "Plus, it beats sitting on our thumbs while the task force circle jerks the evidence."

Jake expected it would take twice as long as it should for the evidence they'd collected at Allen's place to be combed through. With a cop dead, each agency would want to put their stamp on it, which meant multiple examinations.

He didn't mind being thorough, it was wasting time he had a problem with. Every second could mean Vega was getting closer to his next kill or further from Jake's reach. He wasn't sure which he hated more. "Let's go back to my office. We can request the Kincaid files and compare them to our on-going investigation."

"Or we could go to my library," Dana suggested.

Jake raised his brows. "You have a copy of the files?"

Dana didn't even bother to look embarrassed when she nodded. "For research."

Sure, more like obsession. Jake held back his sarcastic comment. "Less questions from Jenkins always sounds good to me."

He doubted she'd sign off on his request to pull the Kincaid files anyway. Their family had been through enough. Pulling the file would reopen old wounds and raise alarm in the political world—not something Jake was eager to do. He needed to keep the few friends he still had on the Hill.

He helped Dana into her jacket and led the way toward the exit. "To the bat cave." Grinning, he added, "Is it weird that I was kinda starting to miss your creepy library?"

Dana rolled her eyes, but he didn't miss her ghost of a smile.

Jo was already outside when Jake followed Dana through the door to the parking lot. She crossed her arms tightly over her chest against the cold, a blast of arctic air making the fine blonde hair around her face dance. Noting the excitement in Jake's gaze, she frowned. "Oh no. I know that look. What's going on?"

"Road trip."

50

"Spooky," Jo mused, peering out of the lab to Dana's beloved collection of rare occult books and artifacts housed beneath the Smithsonian.

Dana did her best to block out Jo's enthusiasm as she set up their workspace. From the moment the petite agent stepped off the elevator and into Dana's world, her chatter had been endless, which wasn't something Dana was used to here.

One of the things she loved most about her underground library was the peace and solitude it offered. Both were a requirement in order for Dana to do her best work.

"I can't believe you actually work here every day," Jo continued. "There's no sunlight. Don't you ever get creeped out being underground?"

Dana shrugged. "Jake doesn't like it either."

"It grows on ya," he replied, his tone almost defensive.

Jo laughed. "Yeah right! All those tunnel missions you ran? I don't know how you set foot down here, Shepard. You're more claustrophobic than I am."

"This is a resort compared to Tora Bora," he answered.

Curiosity lifted Dana's gaze from the files she was sorting on her gleaming white lab tables. Jake rarely spoke about his time in Afghanistan and from the pain filling his faraway look, she knew better than to pry. But that didn't stop her from wanting to steal glimpses when he revealed slivers of the life he'd once lived.

"Tell me about it. Those caves became tombs." Jo gave a slight shiver and walked over to Jake. Placing a hand on his cheek she leaned in and whispered something in his ear.

He nodded, closing his eyes as he pressed his lips briefly to her forehead. It was a reminder of the bond they shared. What Jake experienced in the Army was something Dana would never understand. And as much as it pained her to admit it, she was envious Jo was privy to those secrets.

Thankfully, Dana had more pressing issues to distract her. She preferred to focus on facts over feelings anyway. She'd intended to compare her copy of the Kincaid files with what they currently had on the Card Killer, but already she found something that needed her attention. "This doesn't fit."

Jake broke away from Jo, their brief moment forgotten as they walked over to the images Dana had pulled up on her smart board. She'd arranged each Card Killer victim in the order they were attacked. Next to each photo was the card that had been found with them.

Keller Kent - Ace of Spades.

Azi Udo - Joker.

Marcus Silva - Tower.

Sadie Azeez - Wheel.

Claire Townsend - Death: *You're next.*

Vincent 'Needles' Dega Pinkerton - Hanged Man: *Loose lips sink ships.*

Arthur Allen - Justice.

Seeing Claire's face next to six other victims who were no longer breathing forced Dana's mind into a frenzy of analytical thinking and she didn't like where it was leading.

"What doesn't fit?" Jake asked.

"The first two cards. The killer used playing cards rather than oracle cards for a reason."

"They'd be easier to come by," Jake suggested.

Dana shook her head. "It means something. Cartomancy has been around since 1360. It was a favorite pastime of European royals. It uses the classic 52-card deck to discern destiny the same way tarot is used. Suits set the themes, while the face or numerical cards direct the story. Each card is assigned a meaning, but unlike tarot, there are no major arcana cards, making the readings much more black and white."

Jake crossed his arms. "Okay so Vega wanted to be clear about his message."

"Yes, but I still can't figure out what it is and how the two different decks come into play."

"I know you don't want to hear this," Jo started, "but the simplest explanation is usually the right one."

"Meaning?"

"This is two different killers."

She shook her head. "The point of this exercise is to operate under the assumption we have one killer, Vega. And he doesn't do anything without reason. This is all a game to him. We just need to figure it out before he makes his next move." Dana's gaze traveled to the board, snagging on Claire again. At the very least they needed to figure it out before he went back to clean up a failed move. "When was the last time you heard from the hospital?"

Jake answered. "Claire's security detail checked in on the hour."

His assurance brought only a modicum of relief, but it was all Dana would get until she could lay eyes on Claire herself. Knowing she was of more use here, she turned back to the board, uncapping the dry-erase marker with her teeth. She ticked numbers down the board next to each name.

"Number one, we have the Ace of Spades, sent to Agent Joanna Walsh's office inside the mouth of Keller Kent, known enforcer for Nigerian cartel leader, Obasi Ikemba. Next, we have the Joker, sent to Agent Jake Shepard's office inside the mouth of Azi Udo, same associates."

"No," Jo interrupted. "The second head was sent to me as well, it just got forwarded to Jake's office with the rest of my department mail."

Dana froze. She turned to Jake. "Is that true?"

He nodded, rifling through the evidence spread out on the lab tables until he found what he was looking for. He held up the photograph displaying a cardboard box, the shipping label visible. Ice formed in Dana's veins stealing her breath. "He was already watching us."

Jake set the photo down. "What?"

"It explains everything. He knows you and Jo are dating. It's why he sent her the first head. He knew targeting her would ensure you got pulled into this case."

"Then why send the second head to me if he knew I was already at Jake's?" Jo challenged.

"That was a bonus he wasn't counting on. But when he figured out you were sharing Jake's office, it meant Vega could wait to show his hand. He wanted everyone to take the bait that this was just a drug feud between rival cartels." Dana shook her head, turning back to the board. Her hand shook as she gripped the marker. "He set a trap, and I walked right into it."

"What do you mean?" Jake asked, but Dana was too busy scribbling names next to the list of victims and cards.

1. Keller Kent - Ace of Spades - Joanna Walsh
2. Azi Udo - Joker - Jake Shepard
3. Marcus Silva - Tower - Dana Gray

"Dana, where are you going with this?"

She whirled to face him. "The third body is where Vega switched to tarot cards. It's how he planned to pull me onto the case."

Jake scratched his head studying the board, but Jo spoke up. "You'd just gotten back into town the day forensics kicked back the results on the tarot card."

"Exactly. It proves he was watching us all along."

51

Light sparked behind Jake's eyes as Dana's theory began clicking into place. The video footage at the Grave was just the tip of the iceberg. If she was right, he'd probably been keeping tabs on them since the Priory of Bones. Jake was a fool for not seeing it. "All Vega had to do was track your credit card activity to know when you bought your airline ticket."

Dana pulled her phone from her pocket, bringing up a travel app. "I bought it a week before I came home."

Jake took one look at the date and his pulse began to race. He rifled through the papers on the lab tables again, pulling Keller Kent's file. He flipped open the first page and jabbed his finger at the date. "Christ! Kent was killed the same day Dana bought her ticket."

"Just playing devil's advocate here," Jo said, "But that could easily be a coincidence."

"There are no coincidences in science," Dana whispered. It was an old mantra Jake had heard her use before. This case was no doubt dredging up ghosts she preferred to keep buried. It's why they needed to find something concrete to stop Vega before the body count grew.

"I was right," Jake muttered.

Jo cocked her head. "About what?"

"When you brought me this case, I said someone's trying to get your attention."

"Not Jo's attention," Dana corrected. "Yours, Jake. Look at the cards. He sent the Joker to you with the second victim."

"So Vega's calling me a fool?"

"No, you're taking it too literally." Dana was back at the board, scribbling notes alongside the cards. "Just like the Fool in a tarot deck, the Joker in cartomancy symbolizes the seeker, or the person the reading is about. The card represents the main character beginning a quest. One Vega set up specifically for you."

Jake leaned his palms on the table, his knuckles tightened around the edge. "He's making it personal."

"If you're the Joker, I'm the Tower," Dana explained, pointing to where she'd written her name after Silva's and the tarot card they'd found with his severed head. "Vega knew the upheaval my return would cause. He's trying to orchestrate chaos. Plus, look at the card." She pointed to the plummeting figures. "Two people are falling from the tower. His plans involve us both."

Jake nodded, pacing as he studied the board. "He clearly wants payback for what we took from him when we shut down the Priory of Bones. But," he paused, pointing to the Ace of Spades. "What's Jo's role in this?"

"To ensure you got involved in the Card Killer case," Dana replied.

Jake shook his head. "Then why not come after me directly?"

"We know Vega likes to hit where it hurts. He's not above coming after those we care about."

"Yeah, but why the Ace of Spades?" Jake asked.

"I'm not entirely sure. Spades represent challenging tasks to come, the Ace determines those events will bring misfortune or endings," Dana explained. "He could've been setting the narrative."

Jake looked contemplative. "I guess that fits if Vega was trying to foreshadow six murders."

"It's more than that." Dana and Jake both turned at the chilled tone of Jo's voice. "Ace ... it's my nickname."

"What?" Jake stalked around the table to her. "Since when?"

"Always. It's what my dad calls me." Jo swallowed thickly, looking suddenly shaken. "If this is Vega, and he's been watching us like you say, then he'd know that. And ... shit, my dad! He could be in trouble!"

Jake swiveled back to Dana, but she was already turning to write the rest of the names next to the cards on the board.

1. Sadie Azeez - Wheel - Claire Townsend
2. Claire Townsend - Death
3. Needles - Hanged man.
4. Arthur Allen - Justice.

She turned back to explain, but Jo's attention was lost to a phone call. "No, I won't hold," she hissed into the phone. "Tell him it's his daughter."

"Explain," Jake demanded, pulling Dana's attention back to the board.

"The fourth victim was found with the Wheel card. It represents the many life cycles we can experience. I think Vega meant this card for Claire. He was showing us how easily Claire could end up like Sadie."

"Then why leave the Death card at my apartment and threaten her?" Jake argued.

"If the pattern fits, it was to draw another person into the case."

"Who?"

"Jenkins? She was part of both the Jenni James and Priory of Bones cases."

"Jenkins was on the case from day one."

Dana capped her marker and stared at the board, fear hardening her expression. "Jake, I think Vega failed with Claire."

"What do you mean?"

"What if she was supposed to OD?"

"What would that prove?"

"I don't know yet, but she's the only name on the board twice." Dana circled both places where she'd written Claire's name, then drew lines connecting the cards between them.

The Wheel and Death.

Jake didn't like the unsettling picture taking shape in his mind. If Vega was masterminding a death wheel, Jake wanted no part of that ride. Not when each spoke carried the names of people he cared about.

Dana's brown eyes searched his. She looked as lost as he felt. They were trying to force a square peg in a round hole; anything to grasp a shred of proof that would stick to the slippery bastard Jake had been hunting since he started his career with the Bureau.

As much as he hated to admit it, everything they had was still circumstantial.

Dana chewed her nails as she stared at the board. "I can't shake the feeling that Vega's not done with her, but it doesn't make sense. Why Claire?"

"Because Vega's a psychopath. Who knows why he does anything?"

"He has a reason," she replied. "We just haven't figured it out yet. Another thing that's been bothering me are the drugs. I searched Claire and her things. If she had heroin on her I would've found it."

Jake shook his head. "You'd be surprised where a junkie can manage to hide their stash."

"But Claire's not a junkie. You know her. We both do."

"So why make it look like she is?"

"I don't know. To hurt us?"

Jake swore. "Jesus. We can't rule it out. If he staged an OD, it would've sent me off the deep end."

"You would've done anything to make sure Vega paid, and he knows that." Dana uncapped her marker again as she walked to the board and added Jenkins' name to the list. "Which meant Jenkins would've had to intervene. Each murder is meant to bring one more person he has a vendetta against into the case, closer to the kill zone. And I don't think he's done."

Jake pinched the bridge of his nose. "If that's the case we're talking about dozens of people. Vega's had a long career in D.C."

"But he has one more kill in mind."

"Only one?" He stared at the board. "What am I not seeing?"

Dana wrote the number eight with a question mark next to it. "There are eight arcana in tarot."

Jake swore. "That's why he used them. He's given us a timeline. He has one more kill planned, but he means to wound three more people with it."

1. Keller Kent - Ace of Spades - Joanna Walsh
2. Azi Udo - Joker - Jake Shepard
3. Marcus Silva - Tower - Dana Gray
4. Sadie Azeez - Wheel - Claire Townsend
5. Claire Townsend (failed) - Death – Remi Jenkins
6. Needles - Hanged man - ?
7. Arthur Allen – Justice - ?
8. ?

Jake vaguely heard Jo's hushed phone conversation behind him as he mind churned with a million scenarios Vega might have up his sleeves. He hated this part of the job. It required he let his own inner demons out to play. It was effective, but the danger was reeling himself back in. It was easier said than done.

Staring at Dana's morbid list, he saw victims, people he loved and the cards that connected them. There was a pattern forming. But it wasn't complete.

He focused on the empty spaces after the sixth and seventh victims. "If this spiderweb you've concocted is correct, then Vega's not done. Who else is he planning to bring into his game?"

Dana's gaze shifted to Jo. "Could her father be one of them?"

"He's the DA. It's possible Vega crossed his desk."

"One way or another all the names on the board can be linked to Vega."

Jake agreed. "Jenkins, Allen and I worked the Jenni James case. You and Claire were dragged into the crosshairs with the Priory of Bones. Jo, Needles, her dad? It's a reach."

"Unless we're just missing the connection." Dana was back at her board drawing lines between the three names Jake just listed. "Needles was Jo's informant. He did tattoos. Didn't Vega tattoo the women who worked for him?"

A bitter laugh forced its way past Jake's lips. "*Worked* isn't really a term that applies to sex slaves, but yeah. He branded his women with an ivy leaf."

"If Needles did the ink that connects him. With Jo linked to him and dating you, it's enough reason to put a target on their backs."

"So, you think Vega is just tying up loose ends?"

"What other reason would he have for coming back?"

Jake scowled. "We need to talk to the DA."

52

"Those cases are confidential, Agent Shepard."

"I understand, Sir, but you were lead prosecutor on the case. We need it unsealed so we can establish Vega's intent. It's the proof we need to move forward with this investigation."

"I'm sorry, son, but I need a little more than intent if you want me to open sealed records."

Jake looked like he wanted to punch something as he stared at the unassuming cellphone in Jo's hand. District Attorney Stone Walsh was a formidable man. Dana had easily determined that from the tone of his voice and the length of the conversation. They'd only been on the phone with him for a few minutes before he shut them down. Even his daughter seemed unable to penetrate the public prosecutor's rigid detachment.

It'd been easy to research Stone Walsh's meteoric rise through the ranks of D.C.'s legal offices. His popularity and the sheer longevity of his career made it difficult to weed through his case load, but eventually they'd found the right keywords that led them to a case involving a sixteen-year-old boy charged with a death of a prostitute.

Terrance Vega's first kill?

Right now, it was purely conjecture, but Dana couldn't shake the feeling that they were close to unlocking another clue in Vega's sadistic game. Unfortunately, him being a minor at the time the crime was committed meant the records were sealed. And it seemed no amount of pleading was going to get DA Walsh to circumvent the system. "The best I can offer is a review, but only if you get a judge to grant you access after you've submitted a formal request."

"Fine," Jake muttered. "I'll start the paperwork right now. In the meantime I need to arrange protective custody for you."

Walsh laughed. "I'm the DA. I'm not going into hiding."

"Dad." Jo's voice was pleading. "This is serious. We already have six homicides, and we have reason to believe you're on Vega's list."

"If I went into hiding every time I pissed off someone I brought charges against I'd never get anything done. I've been doing this a long time, Ace. I can take care of myself."

Dana watched Jo flinch at the use of the once beloved nickname. Now it would forever been tainted. She knew the feeling. Remembering her parents without seeing Cramer's face was nearly impossible. *Even after the monsters are gone, they continue to devour the good pieces they left behind.*

"You're not listening to me, Dad. He has surveillance on us. And probably on you, too."

"I told you, send a subpoena to Judge Bryson. He's fast, and he owes me a favor."

"If we find evidence your home surveillance has been tapped, will you accept protective custody?" Jo asked.

The DA's laugh was sympathetic this time. "Let me put it to you this way. I'll go into hiding when you do."

"Dad, it's my job to chase down the bad guys so you can put them away."

"Don't give me that you bag 'em, I tag 'em, line, Joanna. This is your last case in D.C. You've worked too hard to get to HRT. I'd love it if I could send you to Denver in one piece."

Denver. The word stung, bringing back to light the reality Dana had managed to bury beneath the chaos of the Card Killer. But this wasn't some unknown suspect. It was Vega and he was hunting her and the people she cared about.

Even if they somehow managed to stop him, when this was over, she couldn't go back to the life she'd come back for. Jake would go to Denver with Jo, taking any hope of righting the wrongs she'd set in motion the first time Vega pulled Dana into his dark world.

It was his fault she fled the first place she'd considered her home since losing her parents. She refused to let Vega take anything else from her.

When Jo finally hung up the phone, her face was ashen. She spoke only to Jake, but her words carried through the silent lab. "I need to go see him."

"I don't think you'll be able to talk sense into him. He's even more stubborn than you are." Jake squeezed Jo's shoulder, but she pulled away.

"Still, I have to try. He's my dad."

"I get it."

"I'll put in the subpoena on the way."

"Good. Let me know when we get approval. I want to go to Jenkins with this."

Jo headed toward the door, holding her phone in the air. "Stay in touch."

"Roger that." Jake turned back to Dana. "Feel like popcorn?"

"What?"

"Once the surveillance subpoena comes through, we have a lot of grainy security footage in our future."

His words hit her like a bolt of lightning. "Jake! I know where we should start!"

53

"So, if he's been watching us this whole time," Jake mused, his fingers drumming the steering wheel impatiently at the traffic light, "it's feasible to assume he's watching us now and knows we're going back to this voodoo shop."

"It's a mystic shop."

"Same difference. My point is, he could be waiting there to take us out."

"No. He's planning something bigger. Like you said, he likes to hit where it hurts. He got Jo with her CI, and now he's targeting her father. He tried to get us through Claire."

Jake cut her off. "I have no doubt he wants to drag her down with us, but her drug use could have nothing to do with this."

Dana shook her head. "I don't know what to believe anymore."

"That's what he wants. You said it yourself. The Tower card was meant for you. It represents chaos, upheaval."

"So?"

"So, he's trying to shake you. Don't let him."

Jake's assessment only fueled Dana's fears. No matter how many times he assured her they would get Vega this time, she had a hard time believing it. Mostly because her worry for Claire was clouding her ability to think.

There was a team of trained agents standing guard at her door, but still, Dana ached to be back at the hospital with Claire. It was irrational. What would she do other than hover and chew her nails? But what could she do here?

Dana hated feeling useless. She wished they'd found solid answers at the library, but this case was out of her depths. The tarot cards had seemed relevant at first, but they might be nothing more than a distraction, most likely meant to draw Dana into the case where Vega wanted her.

He was obviously orchestrating his own narrative. Whether Dana interpreted it or not wouldn't change anything. Six lives had been taken. Her mind flashed back to the landfill. More than six. The truth was, she was scared. This time, it was more than her life on the line. This time it was personal.

She had been just as instrumental as Jake and Jenkins in dismantling the empire Vega was trying to build with the support of the Priory of Bones. Now that they weren't around, Vega was aiming to take out the last remaining obstacles that could stop him from rebuilding what he'd lost. She could almost understand the strategy. It was something conquerors had done for centuries. The thing that bothered her was Claire.

Dana couldn't stop seeing her intern's name on her smart board. It was the only one on there twice. What did that mean?

"You're sure you saw cameras at the voodoo shop?" Jake asked, dragging Dana from her spiraling thoughts.

"Mystic shop." She remembered the white signs with bright red letters. They weren't subtle. *All readings are recorded for authenticity and legal reasons.* "Yes, there were definitely cameras."

"Did you actually see the cameras, or just signs? A lot of places use signs and fake cameras as theft prevention, but they aren't actually recording anything."

"There's a tv behind the counter. I saw the footage."

"Then we better hope the shop owner hasn't deleted it."

"Do you have a current photo of Vega so we can ask the owner to identify him?"

"I don't want to go that route unless we have to."

"Why not?"

"You never know who he's got on his payroll. I don't want to risk tipping him off."

Dana bit her lip, mulling over Jake's logic.

"What were you doing at a mystic shop anyway?" he asked, his curious gaze meeting hers momentarily.

"It was after Jo took me to meet with Needles. I saw the shop across the street and wanted to get a tarot deck to see if it would help me make sense of the clues."

A blue minivan swerved in front of them, and Jake slammed on the horn as hard as the brakes. Dana grabbed the dash, grateful the distraction got her out of answering more questions about her visit. Vega's game may have brought her back here, but she had no intention of telling Jake about her reading.

54

The star-shaped bells hanging from the windchimes inside the shop jingled a celestial tune when Jake and Dana walked in. The place was exactly as he expected—cramped and creepy.

Tiny, mismatched tables were crowded with teetering towers of candles, tea, stones, orbs, crystals and jewelry. Bookshelves spilled over with art, statues, books, cards, Ouija boards and other witchy items. Masks and wings hung from the ceiling like they were suspended in time, waiting for Halloween or perhaps some more sinister occasion.

The whole place was overwhelmingly weird. It felt like intruding on a voodoo yard sale. Of course, Dana would only correct him if he said so. There probably wasn't an ounce of voodoo in the place, not that he could tell the difference. Which was why he'd come with the expert.

Attention on Dana, Jake nodded to the black and white video feed showing on an ancient twelve-inch tv screen mounted above the cash register. "Guess you were right about the surveillance."

Seeing the split-screen footage streaming on full display behind the counter made the visible cameras and shoplifting signs seem like overkill. But everything about the place was overdone, including the cloying scent of incense filling Jake's lungs. He just knew it would linger, clinging to the fibers of his suit long after they left. His skin crawled as he wondered what else would follow him from this shop.

The patchwork curtains behind the counter rustled and a woman wearing a colorful headscarf came out. Jake had to stifle a laugh at the carefully curated image she was trying to exude. She reminded him of the genie in the coin operated fortune teller game at the boardwalk.

In his experience, anyone who put that much effort into trying to convince others of their identity was a fraud. But if she knew how to work the surveillance system Jake didn't care if she thought she was Cleopatra.

The woman's dark eyes lit from within when they landed on Dana. She stepped around the counter and reached out, catching Dana's extended hand with both of hers.

"Madame Blanche, I'm Dr. Dana Gray."

"Yes, I remember, Cher. I'm glad you came back. Did you choose a path, or have you come for more clarity on your crossroad?"

Jake shot Dana a perplexed look, but she ignored it, making introductions instead. "Madame Blanche, this is Special Agent Jake Shepard with the FBI. We're here hoping you might be able to assist us with an investigation."

Madame Blanche stepped forward, extending her hand to Jake. When he took it, the old woman's eye sparkled with delight, her gaze returning to Dana. "Ah, this is him, isn't it, Cher?"

Jake pulled his hand back, shooting Dana another look of confusion. "Uh, what's she talking about?"

Again, Dana ignored him. "We're not here for a reading, Madame Blanche. We need access to your video surveillance."

"I'm sorry, Cher. Those are confidential."

Jake held up his badge. "Not today."

Madame Blanche pressed her lips into a tight line as she scrutinized his FBI shield. "Do you have a warrant?"

"Don't need one." Jake pulled up the subpoena Jo had emailed him on the drive over. She must've used her pull as the DA's daughter to get it so quickly, but if they found what they were looking for, it would be worth it.

Madame Blanche's exasperated sigh was the last of her resistance. She led Jake and Dana behind the counter and gestured to the dusty VCR unit beneath the cash register. "Help yourselves."

"Actually, we're looking for the surveillance from a specific date. How much does each tape record?"

"I use a new tape every day. I store a year's worth in the back. Anything older than that will be in my storage unit."

Jake scratched his head, his mind boggled by the antiquated system. The woman was paying for storage units full of video tapes when she could essentially boil all her surveillance data down to a few backup drives the size of his wallet. For someone all-knowing, she was certainly in the dark when it came to technology.

"What date do you have in mind?" Madame Blanche inquired.

Dana spoke up. "Let's start with the day I was here."

"Of course, Cher."

"Why not earlier?" Jake questioned once Madame Blanche pushed her way back through the patchwork curtains.

Dana shrugged. "If Vega's been watching us like I think, he would've been waiting for me to come here."

"Then or now?"

"Both," Dana replied. "Look at the name of the shop. I should've seen it right away."

Jake read the gold letter stenciled on the mirror behind the counter. *Mystic Tower.* That old feeling in his gut twitched awake, the one that had saved his ass more than a time or two. His instincts told him Dana was right. But rubbing salt in the wound never helped. "We're here now."

"Yeah, but if I'd realized it sooner—"

"Dana, we don't even know what we'll find on the tapes."

"We'll find him. I know it. The same way I know he sent me the Tower," she protested. "He meant for me to figure it out."

"He meant to taunt us. Don't let him get to you. If we're gonna figure out his next move I need you here with me, not caught up in his mind games."

Madame Blanche returned with a tape. Thanking her, Dana took it, reaching for the eject button on the VCR. "Hold up." Jake turned to the dark-eyed woman. "Do you have anywhere we could view this where there aren't surveillance cameras?"

Looking put out, Madame Blanche crossed her arms. "There's the break room."

"I don't expect you have a VCR in there, do you?"

"Of course. How else can I watch my telenovelas?"

Jake grinned, gesturing for her to lead the way.

"What was that about?" Dana asked, following him and the waddling fortune teller into the bowels of her witchy lair.

"If Vega's watching us, he either found a way to hack into surveillance systems or he's got eyes somewhere else."

He watched Dana's throat roll as she nodded. "Good point."

He couldn't blame her for being on edge. Knowing the private moments of their lives had been invaded by someone was unnerving. Knowing it was Vega was what nightmares were made of.

55

Her dry eyes burned. It felt like she hadn't blinked in hours. Dana wanted to take her glasses off and rub them, but she was too afraid she'd miss something.

Watching the video footage from Madame Blanche's security system was like watching paint dry. To make matters worse, it was split into four sections. Each showed a different area of the shop. Two cameras filmed the main shop. One the register. One the fitting room she used to do her readings.

Jake was concentrating on the top half of the screen, while Dana trained her eyes on the bottom, which showed the reading room and the register. There wasn't a lot of action.

At first, they'd tried to fast forward, but it went so fast they were missing things. And when Jake tried to rewind the tape, it made a high-pitched squealing sound that ended their plans to speed through the footage.

They couldn't risk ruining the tapes. Not when they might finally be able to pin something incriminating on Vega.

Jake yawned as he leaned back in his chair. He threaded his fingers behind his head, making his back pop loudly. She glanced at him, noticing the bags under his eyes. She knew she didn't look much better.

The lack of sleep made it feel like she'd been back in D.C. for months, not days.

She should offer to go on a coffee and donut run. Food was the last thing on her mind, but Jake's appetite seemed to know no bounds. His stomach started growling an hour ago. She briefly wondered if that was an Army thing; learning to eat when the opportunity arose. It was a survival technique she'd never had to master.

"You hungry?" she asked.

He raised an incredulous eyebrow. "Always."

She forced a smile. "It looks like we'll be at this for a while. Why don't I go pick up some coffee?"

"I can go."

"Let me get this one." Dana knew what was happening wasn't her fault, but she couldn't help feeling slightly responsible. If Vega had been lying in wait, it was her return that prompted him to put his plan in motion.

She stood, but Jake caught her hand. "Wait! It's you."

Turning back, she watched herself walk into the shop. Dana sank back down into her chair, her eyes trained on the black and white image of herself. She didn't waste time, immediately locating the tarot cards, then making her purchase. But that's where her curiosity got the best of her. She watched the silent conversation exchanged between her and Madame Blanche and then she watched herself follow the woman into the reading room.

Jake leaned closer to the screen. "You didn't tell me you got a reading."

"It's not important." She pressed the fast forward button, not wanting to relive the painfully accurate fortune Madame Blanche was about to spell out with her cards. Fortunately, there was no sound on the recordings, but that didn't stop the words from replaying in Dana's mind.

Two roads converge, a path to be chosen.
Heartbreak or happiness.
You must look inward for the answers you seek.

Jake was about to argue when Dana sucked in a breath. She hit play, pointing at the screen. "Jake! Look!"

A grainy black and white figure sat down in the same seat Dana had been occupying in the reading room moments before. The man wore a baseball cap pulled low, the collar of his trench coat popped to help obscure his features, but Dana would know that face anywhere. It was one of the many who starred in her nightmares.

Jake's eyes widened. "Christ. Is that who I think it is?"

"Fuller." Dana's voice was breathy with disbelief, but there was no denying what she was seeing.

"What the hell is Mike Fuller doing here?"

Her gut told her she already knew the answer, but her mind made her follow a path of logic. "Maybe he was checking to see if any of Needles' neighbors saw something that night."

Jake shook his head. "Look at the date stamp. It's before we found Needles. And I read his reports. No one mentioned this shop by name."

"Jake ..." Dana couldn't even get the words out as tension built in her stomach. She didn't know how to express what she was feeling, only that somehow, finding Fuller here felt worse than if they'd walked in on Vega himself.

"Come on," Jake ordered, snatching the tape from the VCR. "I've got some questions for Madame Blanche."

"Oh yes, he's one of my best customers. Comes here every week. Sometimes more."

"Why?"

"Sometimes for readings. Sometimes he just visits the prayer wall."

Jake met Dana's gaze. "Prayer wall?"

"Yes, it's where customers can make a donation and light candles for loved ones or leave offerings."

"It's not on the surveillance tapes."

Madame Blanche looked appalled. "It's a sacred space. That would be an invasion of sanctity."

"Show us," he ordered.

A moment later they were standing in the back of the store. An old wooden upright piano had been fashioned into a makeshift altar, housing rows of colorful glass votives. Some lit, some not. Above the piano altar was a large, framed board where photos, prayers, wishes, and money were pinned, along with a rabbit's foot keychain, rosary beads and all sorts of other occult accoutrement. But the offerings that stood out to Dana were the cards. Each one familiar to her.

The Ace of Spades.

The Joker.

The Tower.

The Wheel.

Death.

The Hanged Man.

Justice.

And one new card.

The Eight of Swords.

"Jake, this is how they've been communicating," she whispered. "Vega could easily send someone in here to leave these messages for Fuller."

"They're not messages. They're kill cards."

"What?"

"I did some digging into Fuller when you told me about your history with him. Most of his files have been redacted, but he was a Marine before he joined the Bureau, then the CIA."

"Why is that relevant?"

"Marines leaving kill cards on victims to claim their kill."

"Morbid."

"That's not what they were originally meant for. Soldiers carry them because they contain vital information like blood type, name and unit number. They're meant to save lives, but somewhere along the way it became a twisted way to claim enemy kills. Kind of like a bragging right."

"And you think Fuller took part in this?"

Jake shrugged. "In the late eighties to early nineties, US intelligence agencies recruited heavily from the military. That's when kill cards started popping up stateside. Fuller fits the timeline."

Dana's eyes drew back to the Eight of Swords. "If you're right, a new card means a new kill."

"Or the order for one." Jake was already in motion, phone in hand as he snapped a few photographs, then started to make a call.

"Who are you calling?"

"Jenkins."

"Wait. If Fuller's working with Vega we need to be careful."

"Dana, they've been watching us this whole time. They more than likely know we're here putting two and two together. The time to be careful is over. These bastards have been orchestrating this whole thing right under our noses, and now we have proof. I'm not gonna be careful with it if it means saving another innocent life."

Unable to argue, she followed him back into the night.

56

Taillights blurred by like red comets as Jake accelerated up the onramp. The dark streets of D.C. only added to his desperation. 11th was the most direct route to HQ from Shaw, but the openness of the interstate called to him. Besides, breaking the sound barrier was more acceptable on 395. And right now, the speed limit wasn't even on Jake's radar.

He needed to get to Jenkins and relay the information they'd found. It wasn't the most solid case he'd ever built, but with a new kill card on the table, he couldn't wait. Not when the next target could be someone he knew.

Again, he hit the speed dial for Jenkins. Again, it went to voicemail.

"Where the hell is she?" he yelled, punching the wheel.

It wasn't like Jenkins to go off the grid in the middle of an investigation. Jake didn't like the notions rattling around his head. Her phone could be going to voicemail for a million different reasons, but he couldn't ignore that one of them could be because Vega or Fuller had already gotten to her. "No theories on who the eighth card is for?"

Dana shook her head. "The victims are all over the map. Some were decoys, some were loose ends, some were revenge."

He knew she was referring to Lieutenant Allen. Jake could still picture the tarot card they'd found at his scene. *Justice! What a crock!*

Someone was toying with him and everything he stood for. His finger itched to call in an APB to apprehend Fuller and Vega. A cop had been killed. Issuing a city-wide manhunt would be easy. Making charges stick to the two slippery scumbags, not so much.

Jake was tired of catch and release justice. He wanted the real deal.

"Have you heard from Jo?" Dana asked.

"Not since she sent the subpoena."

Dana shook her head. "Maybe her father is right. She should cut her losses and go to Denver while she still can." She paused. "Maybe you both should."

Jake could feel her staring at him, but he didn't dare take his eyes off the road. Instead he asked, "Why did you ask Madame Blanche for a reading?"

"It's not important."

Somehow, he doubted that. Dana was frugal with her time. She did things with purpose, and if she stopped to ask about her future in the middle of a murder investigation it meant something. "She said something about crossroads and choosing a different path. That feels kind of important."

"It doesn't pertain to our case."

"That's not what I asked."

"Jake."

"Dana." He kept after her, trying to hide his stubbornness with humor. "Doth the lady protest too much."

She laughed, her voice full of disbelief. "Did you just quote Shakespeare?"

"What? I'm not a jarhead."

There was just enough light in the car for him to make out her rolling eyes. It was strange to realize he missed the rare tick of annoyance she let slip. It made him want answers more than ever. A nagging thought told him this might be his only chance. If they survived this case, and that was a big if, he was headed to Denver. A lightbulb instantly lit in his mind. *Different paths.*

"Why won't you tell me about your reading?"

"Because it's personal."

"Since when is personal off limits with us?"

"Jake, just let it go, okay? It's not important."

"I know you pretty well, Dana. You took time out of a murder investigation to sit down with a fortune teller. That makes me think whatever you asked her was pretty important. And despite my behavior lately, if something's important to you, it's important to me."

He could feel Dana staring at him. A glance in her direction caught the slow roll of her throat as tension stiffened her posture. She exhaled. "You're relentless, you know that?"

"I'm told it's a loveable quality."

"In dogs maybe."

He laughed and the pressure between them thawed. Jake reached for Dana's hand and squeezed. "What's going on, Doc?"

The old nickname slipped out, melting the last of the tension between them.

"Denver." Dana whispered the word with caution.

"What about it?"

"It's where you see yourself?"

Jake felt the angel on his shoulder, but it was his devil that did the talking. "Dana, I don't even have a job offer yet. There's a lot still up in the air. Honestly, I have too much going on right here at home to think that far ahead."

"Does Jo know that?"

His chest tightened at the accusation in her voice. It wasn't misguided.

The truth was, he hadn't made up his mind. But that was mostly due to the fact that Dana still refused to tell him why she'd come back. There was an answer he was waiting for. One that would change everything if he could just make her say it.

"Dana ..." Jake's phone rang through the SUV, breaking the inch of progress he'd made. Seeing Jenkins' name on the caller ID made up for it. Jake hit the speaker phone. "Where the hell have you been?"

"Jake. I'm at the hospital."
His focus boiled to a knife's point. "Why?"
"It's Claire."

57

She's awake. She's awake. She's awake.

Dana held on to Jenkins' words as they rode the elevator to Claire's floor, trying not to think about the other friend she'd once visited here. Meredith's fate would not be Claire's. If Dana had to will it into existence she would.

The brief information Jenkins offered over the phone wasn't enough, but they'd been unable to convince her to say more. Jake's disregard for the speed limit had gotten them to the hospital in record time. And now that the elevator doors slid open, only a short distance of polished white vinyl kept Dana from the truth.

Jenkins met them outside Claire's room. Her hand collided with Dana's chest, keeping her from rushing inside. Two FBI agents flanked Jenkins, looking like they'd be happy to restrain Dana further if given the command. But Jenkins had other ideas. "Why don't you boys take five. And bring me back a coffee while you're at it."

Jenkins waited until the agents were out of earshot before she spoke again. "When Claire woke up, she was hysterical, spouting all kinds of nonsense. The agents on duty had the good sense to call me. By the time I got here her doctor had given her a sedative to calm her down.

But all I could ascertain from her babbling was she has a statement to give, one she'll only give to you, Jake."

"She has good reason not to trust just anyone," Dana muttered.

Jenkins crossed her arms. "Meaning?"

"We'll fill you in after we talk to Claire," Jake insisted, pushing past his boss into Claire's room.

Dana was on his heels. Her breath whooshed from her lungs when she saw Claire's pale blue eyes open upon their arrival. The adrenaline that had been keeping Dana's body upright guttered out like a flame. She clutched the hospital bed rail for support as Claire began to sob.

The girl opened her boney arms for Jake, and for an instant his large frame engulfed her. Dana watched his hug blot her out like a lunar eclipse. She ached to join them, but her defenses were up. Discovering Fuller's involvement, almost telling Jake why she'd returned to D.C., and now this. If Dana let her emotions surface, she might fall apart, and that wouldn't do them any good.

Pulling in a calming breath she compartmentalized yet another situation and waited for her emotions to numb.

Jake sat back, and Claire looked up at him through large, watery eyes. "You came."

"Of course."

"Claire," Dana started. "Jenkins said you wanted to talk to us?"

Jake shot her a look of warning. She knew he wanted to tread lightly, give Claire time to collect herself before they grilled her, but Dana had a feeling they didn't have that kind of time. Not with another card out there, a kill order sent by Fuller or Vega or both.

Claire startled when her gaze settled on Dana. "What happened to your lip?"

Dana had done what she could to disguise her other injuries, but there wasn't much she could do about her lip. "I bit it," she answered, skipping over the details so they could stay on task. "What did you want to tell us, Claire?"

"I-I didn't do it," she stammered.

"Do what?" Dana pushed.

"Try to kill myself. I didn't put that needle in my arm."

"Then who did?" Jake asked.

Claire's eyes fell, and she picked at the threads of her blue hospital blanket. "I know no one's going to believe me, but I swear I'm not making this up."

Jake reached out, closing his hands over hers. "Claire, you can trust us."

"It was Fuller."

Dana felt the air pressure in the room drop as Claire's words settled over her.

"What was Fuller?" Jake was shaking his head, his confusion clear, but Dana understood.

It made perfect sense. It's why Vega had chosen to work with him. He could get him access to anyone or anything. Including Claire.

Dana's voice was quiet, but steady. "Fuller came into my house?"

Claire's eyes met hers, and Dana saw the truth written in her fearful expression. The girl gave a single nod and pulled up the sleeve of her oversized hospital gown, exposing the bright purple track mark on her arm. "I never shot up," Claire explained. "Sadie and I, we just smoked H. It was just for a thrill. I'm not a junkie. If I was, I'd have more track marks. But I'd be smart enough to hide them. I'd never put a needle here." She gestured to the angry vein radiating from the crook of her elbow to the middle of her gaunt forearm. "Only someone with nothing to lose would be this careless."

In that moment, Dana knew Claire was telling the truth. After their heart to heart there was no doubt in Dana's mind that Claire would intentionally try to overdose. Not when she'd just gotten clean and had her job back. Plus, she wanted to see Sadie's killer brought to justice. None of that sounded like someone who wanted to give up.

Dana turned to Jake. "Who was patrolling my house when Claire was found?"

"Carter and Molina."

"Aren't they on the task force?"

"Yeah."

"Then they wouldn't question Fuller if he said he needed to go check on a witness."

"Shit." Jake stood, roughly dragging his hand through his hair. After a moment of pacing he headed toward the door.

"Where are you going?" Dana called after him.

"Jenkins needs to hear this."

58

JENKINS ROSE FROM THE CHAIR NEXT TO CLAIRE'S HOSPITAL BED; THE scowl she wore fit the situation. Jake could hardly believe it himself. He knew Fuller was a first-rate asshole, but he'd never expected this. Not only was he ex-military, but he'd been a Fed and now a Spook. All institutions built on trust and made up of individuals who followed the code to protect and serve. But after Claire reiterated her story, and Jake and Dana added what they'd found at the Mystic Tower, there was no way to overlook his true colors.

Agent Mike Fuller was a traitor and a murderer. Or at least attempted murderer.

Jake squeezed Claire's hand, grateful that a scrappy fighter lived inside her small frame. There was no doubt in his mind that Claire wasn't meant to survive the dose of heroin Fuller had given her.

Cracking his knuckles, Jake let himself imagine how good it would feel to punch Fuller's teeth down his throat. If he was foolish enough to show his face, Jake might not have to imagine it.

Joining Jenkins at the window, he spoke in hushed tones. "I want someone from our team on Claire's door from now on."

"We already have guards out there."

"No, I mean Feds. Our guys. No one from the task force. There's no telling how far Fuller's corruption reaches. And I want back on this case, no restrictions. I'm the one who's gonna bring that asshole in."

"Look, Jake, if you're right, no one wants Fuller's head on a platter more than me."

"*If* I'm right?" Anger flashed in his veins. "Jenks, we have him dead to rights."

"No, Shepard. What you have is video footage of a CIA agent visiting a tourist shop. For all we know he was there following up a lead."

Jake shook his head. "That's bullshit, and you know it. The shop owner said he's a frequent customer."

"Fine, so he believes in astrology or some shit, that's not a crime. And it's certainly not enough to bring him in."

Jake looked back toward the hospital bed, where Dana sat with Claire. "What about what Claire said?"

Jenkins gave him a tired look. "You know as well as I do what'll happen if we put a junkie's word against a CIA agent's."

Jake swore, knowing that's what Fuller was banking on. "She's not a junkie. Fuller and Vega are using her as a pawn in all of this."

"You might be right, but I told you, we can't afford anything but concrete proof if you're gonna go after these kinds of heavy hitters."

"So, what do you suggest?"

"For now, I suggest you stand down."

He laughed. "That's not gonna happen."

Jenkins moved closer, her voice a deadly whisper. "I'm not saying you're wrong, but I need you to trust me and not poke this bear."

"Care to share with the group?"

"I've already said too much. Stay out of this, Jake. Stay here and look out for Claire. That's an order." She turned toward the door then paused, looking back. "Now if you'll excuse me, I need to go see about arranging protective custody for the DA."

"He agreed to it?"

Jenkins put her hands on her hips. "Let me guess, I have you to thank for this frivolous favor?"

"It's not frivolous. Vega's targeting people close to me who worked his cases. DA Walsh ticks both those boxes."

"Doesn't hurt that he's your girlfriend's father either."

Jake flinched then quickly followed Jenkins to the door. "How'd you know?"

"It's my job to know," she hissed, mercifully keeping her voice to a whisper. "The only reason I haven't pulled both your badges is because it'd derail her HRT transfer, and I owe your uncle some pretty big favors, but you're burning through them like daylight, boy. You need to back off this case and let me handle it."

"I can't. Not when Vega's got Fuller going after the people I care about. That includes you."

Jake expected his words to soften Jenkins' demeanor, but her jawline only hardened. "Did you ever stop to think that it's not Vega at all?"

"What are you talking about? It all lines up."

"Because you want it to. Jake, if you're desperate to see something, chances are you will. But that doesn't make it true. It just means you're crazy enough to create your own self-fulfilling prophecy."

He heard her but was unwilling to let her words penetrate. "It's him, Jenks. I'd stake my career on it."

"Yeah, well you might have to."

"Come on, work with me. All I'm asking is you put a tail on Fuller. If I'm right and he's working with Vega, he might lead us right to him."

"You need to stand down, Shepard. There are things at play here you don't know about. Leave it be. That's an order."

Jake watched her walk out of the room, baffled. He looked back at Dana and Claire. Apprehension shone on both women's faces. Jake didn't have the heart to say he'd failed them. Not while there was still breath in his body.

"I'm gonna go back to headquarters with Jenkins," he lied. "We've got our guys right outside the room. Stay here. You'll be safe."

He could see the questions forming in Dana's eyes. It was why he turned his back on her and headed out the door, determined to return with answers.

59

Dana's gaze stayed fixed on the door long after Jake disappeared through it. She knew he'd heard her call after him, but he'd chosen to ignore her, which meant he was about to do something stupid.

Truthfully, she itched to be by his side. Chasing down the next lead, doing whatever it would take to end this, but she'd made a promise to herself when she came back to D.C. She wasn't the girl who ran headlong into danger anymore. She wanted a different life, something sustainable and stable.

She'd lived too long in a darkness of her own making. All the death she'd witnessed had taught her many things, but most importantly, that one day it would come for her, too. Before that happened, she wanted to be sure she found a way to live.

At best, she'd been living a half-life. But if she wanted something more, the change would have to start with her.

Reminding herself of her resolutions, she turned her attention to what was important. The girl sitting right in front of her. *Another life she'd almost lost.*

Dana had no plans of wasting this second chance.

Turning to Claire, she brushed a strand of dark hair from her face.

It was something her mother used to do. Dana had always loved her mother's touch. It was something that had been burned into her memory, and she was grateful it remained. "Can I get you anything, sweetheart?"

Claire shook her head, her eyes still fixed on the door. "When is Jake coming back?"

Dana wished she knew the answer. She hadn't heard the conversation between Jake and Jenkins, but their body language had spoken volumes. Even with Claire's statement about Fuller, the proof Dana and Jake uncovered wasn't enough. But that was the last thing the girl needed to hear. "I'm sure he's gone to make sure your statement gets into the right hands. He'll be back once everything is in order."

Claire dragged her gaze from the door to look up at Dana. "So you believe me? About Fuller."

"Yes." She'd known for a long time what kind of man Mike Fuller was. It was unfortunate that now Claire did, too. "I'm sorry if I made you doubt my trust, Claire."

"You didn't. It's just … after everything, I wouldn't believe me either."

"From the moment we got the call about your OD it felt off."

"What do you mean?" Claire asked

"I don't know. I kept thinking about where you'd hidden the drugs or when you'd had time to get more. After everything we talked about, it felt like things were back on track again. I just couldn't make it fit." She gave a tight-lipped smile. "But I guess that's because it didn't."

"I don't get it. Why would Fuller do something like that to me?"

He wanted you dead. Dana didn't want to lie to Claire, but she also didn't want to cause her more stress. She settled for a half-truth. "You heard our theory about Terrance Vega?"

She nodded. "The drug trafficker from your last case."

"I think this started then and now Vega's come back for revenge. He's using Fuller to help him take out the people who got in his way. Me, Jake, Jenkins …"

"And me?"

Dana paused, uncertain whether to go on, but Claire's eyes were clear and full of yearning to understand. That look was why Dana hired her over the dozens of other applicants. Claire had a thirst for knowledge and never shied away from the truth. "I don't think I was meant to survive the catacombs, but thanks to you, I did."

"That's what put me on Vega's list?"

"I believe so."

Claire was silent for only a moment, before her eyes met Dana's, blazing with conviction. "I don't regret saving you. I'd do it all over again in a minute."

A wave of emotion crashed over Dana, and she pulled Claire into her arms. For a moment, the two women clung to each other, reassured by the solid form of the other. It struck Dana how easily she could've been denied this moment if Fuller had been successful, or if Vega had been all those months before.

It was yet another reminder of how precious moments like these were. Her moment with Jake may have passed, but Claire was right here, offering her another chance to carve out the kind of bond that made life worth living.

Overwhelmed with gratitude, Dana released Claire and sat up so she could brush her hair back from her forehead and place a kiss there. "We're going to end this for good this time. I promise. And then things can go back to normal."

Claire exhaled, her exhaustion evident. "Normal never sounded so good."

"Why don't you get some rest?"

"You look like you need it more than I do." Claire shifted in the bed, making room for Dana. She patted the empty space beside her, and Dana's heart squeezed. Claire, the girl who hated human contact, was inviting her in. It was an honor Dana couldn't refuse.

She climbed into the creaking hospital bed and let Claire curl into her. Closing her eyes, Dana shut out the images of Meredith, the only other friend she'd ever truly let in.

Forcing the memories away, Dana opened her eyes and focused on the vase of lilies she'd just noticed. They sat on the rolling table, beneath the television that silently displayed the news. The cheerfulness the bouquet added to the sterile room was undeniable. But who sent them?

She asked Claire as much, but the girl was already drifting off to sleep, and Dana wasn't far behind.

60

Jake stalked down the halls of the J. Edgar Hoover Building, mildly surprised his key card still worked. He wouldn't put it past Jenkins to deactivate it to keep him in the dark. She was hiding something; he was sure of it.

The woman wasn't the type to back down from anything, not even going toe-to-toe with another agency. Being promoted to administration made lesser agents wary of ruffling feathers, but not Remi Jenkins. Her loyalty belonged to her country and that meant upholding justice, no matter what.

The war vet always had his back, he knew that, so why was she keeping him out of whatever angle she was working? His success with the Priory of Bones case was largely due to the fact that he pulled Jenkins in on it. It was a courtesy he expected her to return when necessary. And if Vega was involved, it was necessary.

He'd helped Jenkins chase that lowlife all over D.C. It was the first case they'd worked together. Years later he still hadn't shaken the bitter taste of that loss. He'd had Vega, but the prick walked because of lack of evidence.

Jake knew it was why Jenkins was being such a hardass now, and he didn't blame her. He wanted something concrete to nail the bastard too, but he knew they'd have better odds of finding it together. And that's what he planned to tell her—after he put together his official report, including Claire's statement.

Jake rounded the corridor to his office about to greet Margot, but the television in the small reception area caught his attention. "Turn that up."

Margot startled. "The news?"

"Yes. Now."

Hearing the shortness in his voice, she did as directed.

Authorities now believe Terrance Vega is connected to the famed Card Killer deaths that have claimed six lives so far, including D.C.'s own, Lieutenant Arthur Allen.

Rage sang through Jake's veins as a photograph of Vega filled the screen next to the reporter's head. "How the hell did the press get a hold of this?"

The question was rhetorical, but Margot stuttered a response. "A-are they right?" Her hand moved protectively to her pregnant belly. "Is Vega the Card Killer?"

"Thanks to the ill-timed media coverage we might never find out." Leaking this kind of information would spook Vega. The last thing Jake wanted was for him to disappear again. Which was why law enforcement knew better than to share this kind of information.

A thought bubbled up like air racing to the surface, blocking out Margot's chatter. *Fuller!* He could've orchestrated the leak to the press to get a message to Vega that Jake was closing in. It fit with the surveillance theories. If Fuller was the one watching the surveillance, he'd have seen Dana and Jake at the Mystic Tower, and known they were putting it together.

But then another idea dawned on Jake, this one even more disturbing. Why would Fuller turn the heat up on Vega if they were working together? Jake had been operating under the assumption that Fuller was Vega's lapdog, helping him return and rebuild what he lost. But what if it was the other way around? Could Fuller have something on Vega? Or did he just decide to turn on him?

Jake walked into his office, his mind spinning with questions.

Sinking down into his chair he had to consider Jenkins' accusations. Maybe Vega wasn't involved at all. Maybe Jake just wanted him to be the mastermind behind the disaster he found himself in; professionally and personally.

Picking up his phone he dialed Jo's number. It was too late to ask her father to issue a gag order on the press, but if he could get him to grant them access to that sealed case of Vega's it might give him something else to go on. Without something to connect Fuller and Vega, he was grasping at straws.

TWENTY MINUTES of groveling paid off. It was most likely Jo who'd persuaded her father to unseal the court records, but Jake had been the one to sweet talk the judge into rushing the review.

He jogged down the steps outside the district court office, determination returning to his stride with the promise of finding something of use in the records being sent over to him at this very moment. For the first time since this case started, Jake felt like he wasn't chasing his tail and he was going to hold on to that feeling. At least that was his plan until Mike Fuller's ugly mug got in his way.

The arrogant CIA agent was leaning against Jake's SUV, looking like he didn't have a care in the world—something Jake's fists ached to change. "What are you doing here, Fuller?"

"Just enjoying some fresh air. It's a free country, isn't it?"

"For now."

Fuller grinned. "I heard you've been asking about me."

Jake threw his words back at him. "It's a free country."

"Whatever you think you know, you don't."

"I know about the Mystic Tower. And I know why you left it out of your reports."

Fuller's grin turned into a sneer. "I don't report to you."

"Funny you bring that up, 'cause I've got a few questions about who you report to."

Anger turned his ruddy complexion molten. Jake savored the tiny victory. He was getting under Fuller's skin. Which meant he was on the right track.

Jake smirked. "Don't want to tell me? It's okay, I'm pretty good at figuring things out on my own. You'll see."

"If you know what's good for you, you'll listen to your boss and keep your head down before you find yourself without one."

"Is that a threat?" Jake cracked his knuckles praying for an excuse to pound Fuller's face in.

"I don't make threats," he growled.

"Well I do. And if you come near Claire again, you'll be the one in the hospital."

Fuller was a lot of things, but stupid wasn't one of them. He wisely backed down from a fight he knew he wouldn't win. Jake only had so much restraint. If the Spook kept pushing him, he'd be glad to remind him who the superior agent was.

A mist of icy rain began to fall as Jake stood there watching Fuller skulk away. Letting him go wasn't easy, but he had faith in due time, he'd get his chance. But first he needed to see what was in Vega's sealed records.

With any luck, it would lead him back to Fuller so he could serve vengeance in the form of a life sentence. That would be the only thing more satisfying than bashing his face in.

61

DANA WOKE, THE WARMTH AND COMFORT OF HER SURROUNDINGS FOREIGN. It took her a moment to place the white walls and whir of machinery. The nurse by the white board startled her, but her presence helped Dana place the setting. She was in the hospital, and the warm body next to hers was Claire.

"You're really not supposed to be in her bed," the nurse said, her tone laced with contempt.

"Sorry," Dana whispered, untangling herself from Claire's grasp, but her carefulness was unnecessary, as the nurse roused the girl a moment later to take some blood. It was one of the many things Dana hated about hospitals. They preached rest as the best medicine, but it was impossible to get any due to their ceaseless poking and prodding.

"Can I get you anything?" Dana asked Claire, when the nurse finally flipped off the light and left them in peace once more.

"Do you think Thaiphoon delivers to the hospital?"

Dana grinned. "I don't know, but I'll find out."

She picked up her phone to dial when she saw she had three missed calls from Jake. *Shit.* Her phone was on vibrate. She must've slept through his calls. She was just dialing him when the door to Claire's room burst open.

"Jake!" Claire's voice was full of joy, but Dana's cheeks warmed with guilt the instant she saw relief douse the fear in his gaze.

His eyes were trained on Dana. "You didn't answer your phone."

"I'm sorry. I fell asleep."

His expression softened, which only made her feel more guilt-ridden. He'd been run as ragged as she was. If anyone deserved a rest, it was him. Getting to her feet she offered him her chair. "I was just going to see if I could get us something to eat. Why don't you stay and keep Claire company?"

"Can't. I'm waiting on a file from the clerk of courts."

Her eyebrows rose. "You got it unsealed?"

He nodded.

"How'd you get Walsh to change his mind?"

"I can be charming."

She huffed a laugh to mask the flush of heat that filled her veins. "Glad to hear you're using your powers for good. Give me a minute to run out to the front desk and find out about deliveries."

Jake nodded and Dana pushed past him toward the door. When she returned, he was seated next to Claire's bed, the two of them grinning like thieves. It melted her heart and filled her with envy all at once.

She wished she could have such an easy way with either of them. Maybe someday she would. *Not with him,* her subconscious reminded her.

Stuffing down her selfish desires, she rejoined them. "So good news and bad news. Thaiphoon doesn't deliver here, but Wiseguys does. I ordered two pies. A Margarita and a Nashville hot chicken, in case you're hungry, Jake."

He brought his hand to his heart, feigning discomfort. "You know I can't resist Nashville hot chicken." He stood up and ruffled Claire's hair. "I wish I could stay but I've gotta meet Jo to access a file. Save me some pizza, okay?"

She nodded and Dana did her best to ignore her disappointment. Jake walked toward her, and she moved aside to let him pass, but he paused, his hand wrapping around her arm. Warm breath tickled her ear as he spoke, his voice low and stern. "Keep your phone on."

"Jake, I'm sorry. I didn't mean to ignore your calls."

"I know." For the briefest moment, he let his head rest against hers. "I thought …"

"The worst," she finished.

He straightened, his blue eyes burning with words unsaid. "I'll call you after I access the files."

"Okay."

Jake didn't say goodbye, but Dana preferred it that way. Goodbyes were final. And things between them … well, they were anything but.

She watched him walk through the door, nodding to the agents standing guard outside. For a moment she was lost in her thoughts, only to have them shattered by Claire's scream.

Dana whirled around and Jake raced back to the room, getting to Claire's side at the same time Dana did. She grabbed the girl's trembling hand. "What's wrong?"

Claire's gaze was fixed on the television, a shaking finger pointing at the screen. "That's him. He was here."

Dana and Jake exchanged an uncertain glance before returning their attention to the news report. Terrance Vega's mugshot stared back at them, the crooked grin on his face taunting.

"Vega was here?" Jake demanded. "In your room?"

"Not in my room, but he delivered my flowers. I saw his face in the doorway, but the guards wouldn't let him in."

"You're sure it was him?" Dana asked.

"Yes!"

"Claire!" Jake snapped. "Why are you just telling us this now?"

"I'm sorry. I didn't know it was him. He looked familiar, but I couldn't place him until just now." Her gaze was back on the news report. "It's him. I'm sure of it."

In an instant Jake was moving. Slipping into agent mode he barked orders to his men. "Nelson. Vassar. Get in here." He pointed to the television. "Is this the guy who delivered flowers here earlier?"

"I don't know," the shorter agent replied. "We just started our shift."

"It was him!" Claire insisted, her voice taking on a frantic quality. "I'm not lying!"

Jake turned back to face her. "I don't doubt it, but I need to establish a timeline. When did the flowers get delivered?"

Claire glanced at the clock on the wall. "About six hours ago."

"Nelson, get access to the hospital's CCTV. You're looking for visual confirmation of Terrance Vega. Roll the footage back. When you find him, I want screen grabs with timestamps. Vassar, call in backup. I want teams stationed at all the hospital entrances and exits."

"Jake," Dana interrupted. "We're not leaving Claire here."

"She'll be safe here."

"Are you crazy? Vega knows where she is. He almost got into her room!"

"He's just trying to make us think he can get to us."

"Well it's working!" Dana yelled, unable to fight her panic. "I'm checking her out as soon as her doctor okays it."

"And take her where? Fuller's already shown he can access our homes."

"It's the best option we have."

"I disagree."

Dana was about to launch into an argument when a thought occurred to her. Her mouth fell open as her eyes locked on the flowers. There, nestled among the lilies, was a card. Dana rushed toward it. She was about to grab it when Jake stopped her. "Wait. Gloves."

She grabbed a pair from one of the boxes in the convenient wall dispenser. Donning the blue latex, Dana faced the bouquet with shaking hands. Pulling the white envelope from the plastic pick she carefully slid a finger beneath the tab.

Was it too much to hope Vega had been foolish enough to lick it, leaving DNA behind?

The tab pulled free and Dana reached inside, already knowing what she would find. She pulled out the tarot card. It was identical to the one they'd seen pinned to the board at the Mystic Tower. The Eight of Swords: a symbol of being trapped as a result of one's own failures.

Slowly, she turned the card over. A gasp escaped her as she read the words written there.

One, or many? You decide.

A date, time and address were scribbled beneath the riddle, roughly giving them 72 hours to decipher it. But Dana didn't need that much time. She knew what Vega wanted. She'd guessed at it earlier when she'd circled the only name she'd written on her board twice.

Vega wanted Claire. And he wasn't going to stop until he got her.

62

"We got him," Jake announced, walking triumphantly back into Claire's hospital room. "We're gonna nail the bastard."

He held up his phone to show Dana the screen shots of Vega they'd captured from the hospital security footage.

Vega, entering the hospital.

Vega on the elevator.

Vega in the hallway on Claire's floor.

Vega exiting.

They hadn't gotten lucky enough to capture footage of his vehicle, but this was enough. Jake had already sent the images to Jenkins, and this time she was satisfied.

The hospital surveillance footage was the smoking gun he'd been looking for, and Jenkins issued an interagency APB for the capture of Terrance 'Ivy League' Vega.

Vindication was sweet. Now all he had to do was keep the status quo until Vega was apprehended. Jake wanted to be on the street, hunting down the monster who'd been terrorizing D.C. for more than a decade, but he was needed elsewhere.

Claire's doctor had been quick to sign off on her discharge. It was obvious the hospital didn't want to be dragged into the media shit storm Vega's manhunt would spawn. Jake couldn't blame them.

For now, Dana was getting her way. Jake and two teams of hand-picked agents would be accompanying him back to his place, where Jo, her father and Jenkins planned to reconvene to review their options. Jake put in a request for a safe house, but Jenkins had other ideas. Ones she apparently couldn't discuss over the phone.

"You ready?" Jake asked, slinging an arm around Claire. The girl gazed up at him looking surprisingly calm despite everything she'd been through. He'd picked up a t-shirt and sweats for her at the hospital gift shop, and Dana had lent Claire her coat. It only added to her overall appearance of a child playing dress-up.

Jake planned to pack her full of calories once he got her somewhere safe. She was much too pale and thin for his liking. Her stint in the hospital hadn't helped. Maybe Dana was right about wanting to take her away from the fluorescent lights and white walls. It only exacerbated Claire's frailness.

"Come on. Let's go home."

TRAFFIC HAD BEEN MERCIFULLY LIGHT. An hour later Jake was back in his skyrise apartment, surrounded by the comforts of home, a dozen containers of Thai food and the people he loved ... and DA Walsh.

Meeting a girlfriend's father for the first time was unpleasant enough. Meeting him under these circumstances took awkwardness to a whole new level. Jake had stared down terrorists who'd looked at him with less hostility.

Man up, Shepard. He's just looking out for his daughter.

Thankfully, Jake had more pressing matters to distract him, like Dana's attempt to undermine his good mood. They'd had video footage of Vega delivering a threat and thanks to the unsealed court records a way to connect him to Fuller. Albeit a loose connection, but still she was unsatisfied.

"The documents don't list Fuller by name, and the only witness is dead," Dana argued.

Jo looked to her father. "Do you remember anything else about the accomplice in that case?"

The DA laughed. "You don't honestly expect me to remember the details of a thirty-year-old case."

"It's Fuller," Jake argued. "Right here." He pointed to the passage he'd underlined in the copy of the court document he printed. "Mikey, aka Mikey D, Mikey the Devil, was seen exiting the premise where Kaitlynn Ward's body was discovered with Terrance Vega. The witness placed both Mikey and Terrance Vega as frequent visitors of 214c."

"A known bordello in those days," Walsh added.

Jake glared at him. "You knew why this file was sealed. Not because Vega was a minor, but because Fuller was a Marine, turned Fed, turned CIA. He's Diablo and he's been cleaning up after Vega since they were teens."

"I'm not sure I like your tone," Walsh answered.

"I'm not sure I like your assistance in this cover up."

"Jake!" Jo scolded. "My dad would never do something like that."

Walsh stood up. "I don't need to defend myself to you, but she's right. Besides, if you knew anything about the judiciary system, you'd know I'm not the one who gets to decide what cases are sealed."

"Let's stay on topic," Jenkins ordered. "We're all on the same team, so let's keep our allegations on the criminals."

Jake knew he was pushing his luck, but he didn't care. Not when he was this close to the truth. "Someone sealed those records so we wouldn't connect Fuller and Vega."

"I don't know," Jo started. "I guess it's possible."

"Sounds too easy," Walsh answered.

"Face it, Vega's only human. We knew sooner or later he'd slip up, even with an inside man helping him," Jake rebutted. "We got lucky Claire recognized him at the hospital. And she can even pin Fuller with the drugging charges."

"Jake," Jenkins cut in. "Let's leave Fuller out of this for now and focus on the hard evidence. We have Vega on tape, attempting to commit a crime."

"That's just it," Dana argued. "It's almost like he wanted us to catch him. He didn't even try to avoid the cameras."

Jake couldn't deny that. At one point, Vega had stared directly at the camera in the elevator. "What do you want me to say? The man has a god complex. He thinks he's invincible. Waltzing into a hospital is just another example of his arrogance."

"Or it's part of his plan."

Jenkins crossed her arms. "What are you getting at, Gray?"

"I think Vega is targeting Claire."

"Why? She has the least to do with him. Jake and I are the ones who've been hunting him all these years."

"I don't know why she's caught his attention. It could be that she helped me escape the catacombs, or because of her involvement in our research into the Priory of Bones. And we can't forget she's the reason we knew about the Grave and were able to dismantle another of Vega's human trafficking rings."

"And let's not ignore that Vega likes to hit where it hurts most," Jenkins added. Her gaze landed on Jake. "He knows Claire's someone important to you. And with your history of protecting helpless women—"

"I'm not helpless," Claire interjected.

"I don't mean to imply you are, darlin', but in Vega's eyes you're someone under Jake's protection, and that makes you a target." She shot a glance at Jo and Dana. "All of you are."

DA Walsh harrumphed, muttering under his breath. "You always know how to pick 'em, Ace."

"Dad!" Jo hissed.

Jake ignored the rude remark. "It doesn't matter why Vega's after Claire. He's not going to get her."

"You can't just will that into existence," Dana argued. "He's given us an ultimatum. We need a plan."

Claire spoke up. "I think we should give Vega what he wants"

Shock colored Dana's voice. "Excuse me?"

"Oh, come on, his message was clear. One or many." Claire crossed her arms. "If we don't give him what he wants, he's going to keep killing and I don't know about you, but I don't want that on my conscience."

Dana put down her takeout container. "Claire, you can't be serious. We're not going to let you sacrifice yourself."

"Well, I expect you all to swoop in and save me before it comes to that, but yeah, I'll gladly be the bait if that's what it takes to catch this monster."

"She has a point," Jo added.

Jenkins looked thoughtfully at Claire. "It could work."

"Oh my god!" Dana yelled. "I'm not hearing this."

"Neither am I," Walsh muttered. "I'm the District Attorney for heaven's sake. I can't be a part of discussions like this."

Jo scurried to her feet, following him toward the door. "Dad, where are you going?"

"Home, where I strongly suggest you head as well."

"I'm in the middle of a case."

"A case that will be turned over to another division now that you have a suspect connected to six serial murders. Go home, Joanna. Pack your bags and step into your future, while you still can." Walsh's glare landed on Jake for an uncomfortable moment before he stepped out of the apartment with his daughter on his heels.

63

"Absolutely not!" Dana shouted, but Jake and Jenkins continued to ignore her.

They were sitting in Jake's living room running through FBI sanctioned sting scenarios, but they were wasting their time. There was no way Dana was going to sign off on using Claire as bait. The fact that Jake was even entertaining the thought was appalling.

It wasn't just his poor judgement that was bothering her. This farce was nothing but a waste of time. Almost twenty-four hours had gone by since they'd found the tarot card clue in Claire's hospital room. Vega's deadline was drawing near.

The full force of the FBI should be concentrating on finding Vega, not putting together an operation that would endanger someone else that Dana loved. "This is too risky!"

"I know it's not without risk," Claire replied. "But I don't see what choice we have."

"We can put you in a safe house and let the FBI do their jobs."

"Vega's shown he can get to me if he really wants to. Isn't it better to play his game, so we can beat him at it before more people pay the price?"

"At least this way, we'll see him coming," Jenkins added.

Jake nodded. "They're right, Dana."

"No!" She stood. "Nothing about this is right! I'm not going to stand by and let you do this."

She stomped to the bathroom and slammed the door, hating that it was the only room left with a modicum of privacy.

Jake's home had been turned into a command center with FBI agents milling about, going over strategies with Claire despite Dana's valid arguments.

Leaning over the sink, she turned on the faucet and splashed cool water over her face. She refused to back down. Not when Claire's life was at stake. A knock at the door had her grumbling. "Just a minute."

She dried her face and looked at her tired reflection. She'd looked better, but she'd also looked worse. Exhaling, she pulled her shoulders back, regaining her poise. Fear had chased her from D.C. Painful soul-searching had brought her back. Progress required evolution, and Dana had evolved into someone who would no longer accept losing those she cared about.

Opening the door, she was surprised it was Claire's face that greeted her. Instead of letting Dana out of the bathroom, the girl pushed her back inside and shut the door. "Claire! What's wrong?"

"You!" she whisper-hissed. "Why won't you just let me do this?"

"Play sacrificial lamb to a sex trafficker?" She laughed. "If you have to ask, you're even less suited for this than they think. This isn't a game, Claire. It could cost you your life."

"That's why I have to do it. Don't you see? It's my fault we're in this situation."

"How do you figure?"

"I befriended Sadie. I brought Diablo or Vega or whoever he is into our lives."

"Yeah and that's because I left you to fend for yourself. If we're playing the blame game you can lump me in. Jake and Jenkins, too. We've all played starring roles in Vega's twisted game. Which is why it makes no sense to put this kind of pressure solely on you."

"No one's pressuring me into this. I want to help. It's the only way I can redeem myself and prove that I'm trust-worthy again."

"Claire, you don't have to prove anything."

"Yes, I do. I have to prove it to myself. I need to do this. And I need you on my team. If even one more person dies, when I could've stopped it ..." A sob cut off Claire's words before she could stifle it. "I can't live with that kind of guilt."

Dana pulled Claire into her arms, holding her thin frame as the girl sobbed. "I'm on your side, Claire. Always."

She looked up at Dana through watery eyes. "Then you'll stop fighting me on this?"

"I'll never stop fighting for you, but if you're determined to do this, I'm going to make them exhaust every option until it's foolproof."

"Thank you." Claire grinned. "I'm not gonna lie. I'm over sitting in that room full of meatheads."

Dana sighed, knowing exactly what she meant. Jake's apartment looked like a casting call for the next All-American hero blockbuster. The sheer amount of muscles and testosterone would intimidate anyone. Especially someone like Claire, who mainly interacted with books, academics—*and the occasional cult clubbers.*

Still, Alpha Male was not in Claire's wheelhouse. It wasn't in Dana's either, but for Claire, she'd do her best to make sure every one of the intimidating agents was using the muscle that counted most when it came to putting together a plan to bait Vega.

She hadn't resigned to going along with Claire's well-intended notion just yet. If there was a way around it, she'd find it. But not while hiding in the bathroom.

"Come on," she said, opening the door. "Let's go back out there and show those meatheads how to work smarter, not harder."

64

Jo's presence in the living room made Dana pause when she and Claire rejoined the agents assembled in Jake's apartment. She hadn't returned after her abrupt departure with her father last night. If she'd called to say anything to Jake afterward, he hadn't shared it with them.

Dana was curious where the female agent would stand on all of this. Like Jake, she was a by the book, rule follower, who liked procedure and protocol as much as he did. Yet, Jake had thrown his normally cautious demeanor out the window when it came to Vega. Would Jo do the same?

Jake was about to conduct a logistics meeting. If Jo had objections, Dana could measure them here. With any luck, she'd be one more ally in Dana's corner to come up with a plan that didn't involve using Claire as bait.

Tapping the white board, Jake called everyone to attention. "Listen up, we have less than 48 hours to pull this off. That means I expect your full focus. Now is the time for questions. When you get onsite, you need to have this plan locked and loaded. Understood?"

The enthusiastic reply from the assembled agents was as frightening as it was encouraging. Dana's stomach knotted as Jake continued addressing the team he was entrusting with Claire's life.

"Alpha team, you'll take the high ground here. Beta and Gamma teams, you'll be here and here. Delta team, you'll be holding the perimeter. Teams are to remain out of view at all times. We have no idea how many decoys our Tango is employing so know your friendlies. And keep the package in sight at all times."

Jo spoke up. "What about civilians? The Metro runs right through there. It'll be swamped at that time of day."

"We have the transit authority's full cooperation."

"They're shutting down the Green Line?"

"They're delaying that section of the line during our sting."

"Won't that alert Vega that we're on to him?" Dana asked.

Jake shook his head. "No. Transit authority will announce that they're servicing the lines but continue sending dummy cars so as not to alert Vega of any change in schedule."

Dana pulled up the Metro app on her phone, studying the timetable for that section of the Green Line. She knew exactly where it was. A desolate stretch of rail between the Navy Yard and Anacostia Park.

She could picture the dilapidated pedestrian bridge that led over the Anacostia River. She'd gone up there once in grad school with a lab partner who swore the view was worth the risk of tetanus the rusty structure promised. It wasn't.

That section of the mud-brown water was littered with trash and the foul smell left behind by the people who partied there. It was the perfect place for a crime.

Jake's voice drew Dana's attention back to the board as he fielded questions. Despite Jo's earlier reservation, she didn't raise any more red flags, though Dana wished someone would. There were too many variables.

Vega could easily be hidden somewhere waiting to pick them off one by one until no one was left to guard Claire. Or if killing her was truly his end game he'd only need one bullet and good aim.

Then there were the unknowns, like what if he showed up with a hostage? Or what if this whole thing was a ruse meant to keep their attention in one place while he struck in another?

But she'd already voiced her concerns, each of which were shot down with acute experience.

It wasn't that Dana didn't trust Jake or his team. She'd witnessed them in action before. Their tactical precision at Candlestick Lake was the only reason not one of the hostages had been harmed. But this was different. This was Claire.

She looked over to where the girl stood a few feet away. Her clear blue eyes were trained on Jake and even though a mess of black hair obscured most of her features, it was easy to read her determination.

Dana pulled up the Metro map again, sharpening her own determination as an idea formed.

65

Jake caught Jo's eye, giving her a nod to take her time as he walked to the opposite side of his crowded apartment. He didn't want to interrupt the conversation she was having with Harris. The Alpha team leader had served with Jo, and he knew better than to get between Rangers and their war stories.

Walking over to his floor-to-ceiling window, he gazed out at the National Mall as dusk settled across the capital. Muscle memory had him itching to walk to his wet bar and pour himself two fingers of Blanton's.

This was the calm before the storm. He wouldn't get another chance. Having a drink to quiet his mind was his pre-mission routine, but that was something he preferred to do in private, when his weaknesses were less on display.

Besides, tomorrow was too important. He needed his focus laser sharp.

You'll be sharper if you sleep. Jake ignored his inner demon's whispers. There was no doubt a stiff drink would take the edge off and help him get some shut-eye, but it would have to wait.

He'd operated on little to no sleep before. He could hold out a while longer. His indulgences could wait. They'd taste sweeter when this was over anyway.

Finished catching up, Jo ambled over, her hand touching the small of Jake's back only for an instant. Still, it made him flinch. Jenkins might know about them, but the rest of his unit didn't, and he preferred to keep it that way—less complicated was always better.

For a while she stood next to him, shoulder to shoulder staring out at the fading light as the agents thinned out. When they were relatively alone, she finally spoke. "Jake, I can see you've put a lot of thought into this, but I think you're being hasty."

It was a blow he hadn't been expecting. "Vega's the one who set the timeline."

"Yeah, but you're playing right into his hands."

"If you have a better idea, you're a little late to the table. We hashed out the specifics yesterday. *After* you left."

He hadn't meant for his words to have so much bite, but it was no use trying to backpedal when he stood by his statement.

"I had my own matters to attend to yesterday."

He could see it in her eyes. She was starting to check out. "I'm sure you did."

"What's that supposed to mean?"

He shook his head, a bitter laugh escaping. "You've already got one foot in Denver, Jo. I don't need that kinda half-assed energy on my team. You're either all in or you're not."

"I'm *not* in, Jake. That's what I've been trying to tell you. This mission has Charlie Foxtrot written all over it. You're just too close to see it."

"Christ, Jo, way to shit in my cereal on parade day."

"You're not gonna make it to parade day if you keep up this cowboy BS."

"I suppose you've got a better idea?"

"Yeah. Turn this over to BAU and let them do what they do. It might take longer, but you won't be forcing a friend to risk her life."

"I'm not forcing Claire to do this. She volunteered."

Jo took Jake by the hand and dragged him out of his living room, down the hall to his bedroom like a child in need of scolding. It was humiliating, despite the fact that only Dana, Jenkins and Claire remained to witness it.

Once inside his room, Jo closed the door. Jake opened his mouth to voice his displeasure, but Jo held up a hand. "No! You listen to me. Claire is a civilian, Jake. She has no idea what could go wrong. She's who you swore an oath to protect and serve, and now you're throwing her to the wolves so you can get yours?"

Pinching the bridge of his nose, Jake exhaled, reconsidering his choice to forgo a drink.

"I'm right, and you know it," Jo pushed. "BAU is going to take over now that Vega is the prime suspect in the Card Killer case. They found his DNA on the vase in Claire's hospital room. My guess is they'll find it on the tarot cards at the Mystic Tower, too. If that happens this case is as good as over for us."

"What about Fuller? He's involved in this, but we haven't made a concrete connection. I can't just let it go. Not until I know it's over."

"Why do you have to be the one to end it?"

"Jo, I can't walk away from something unfinished when people I care about are in the line of fire."

"I didn't say that."

"That's exactly what you're saying."

Her nostrils flared. "I'm such an idiot." She paced away from him, turning back before he could ask what she meant. "Did you ever plan on coming to Denver?"

"Jo, I can't. Not right now. I'm needed here."

"Yeah. And I'm needed there. So where does that leave us?"

Jake looked at the ceiling, wanting to scream. He settled for grabbing his hair. "I don't know. Maybe when this is over, I can come out there and—"

"Don't bother. It's already over."

"Jo—"

She held up her hand again. "Just tell me one thing. Was any of this real to you?"

"What? Of course it's real, Jo. I care about you."

The anger drained out of her. "Just not enough."

"What's that supposed to mean?"

Her green eyes drifted past him to the door, as if she could see through it. "I've seen the way you look at her. You might care about me, but you care about her more. I'm not a consolation prize, Jake. I deserve better." She grabbed her jacket from his bed. "Don't bother looking me up again unless you get your priorities straight."

"Jo! Where are you going?"

"To convince my father to take a vacation day and help me pack."

"Don't leave. Not like this."

She rested a hand on his chest. When she caught her breath she leaned in, pressing a kiss to his cheek. "No hard feelings, soldier. The timing just wasn't right." Forcing a smile, her bright green eyes glimmered with unshed emotion. "Who knows, maybe someday it will be."

Someday. He hated that word and all the false hope it promised. He didn't do promises or apologies, but he felt he owed Jo his best effort. "I never meant to hurt you."

"I know, but it didn't stop it from happening." She squeezed his hand. "Figure out what you want, Shepard. Before it's too late."

Then she was gone, walking out of his life as easily as she'd walked into it.

66

Inky black darkness engulfed Dana the moment she flipped the lights off. She'd wanted to leave the nightlight on, but Claire insisted she liked the dark. The girl drifted to sleep almost immediately, leaving Dana alone with her thoughts.

It wasn't her favorite place to be these days. Echoes of her fortune floated back to her, driving her from the dark room. Closing Jake's bedroom door silently behind her, Dana made her way down the hallway to the kitchen. Jake stood there, facing his whiskey collection, his internal struggle evident from the set of his jaw.

"Jenkins left?" she asked.

Jake nodded. "A few minutes ago." Abandoning the bar, he walked to his kitchen and flicked on the coffee pot. "Want some?"

Dana closed the distance between them and flipped the switch off. "Do you plan on getting any sleep tonight?"

He shrugged. "It'd be nice, but I've got a lot on my mind."

"I know what you mean." She reached for the kettle on the stove, filled it and returned it to the burner, turning it on high. "I've been thinking about Claire's role in all of this ..."

Jake's groan cut her off. "Dana, she's made up her mind. The mission's been finalized. We're running sims tomorrow. We can't keep changing things at the eleventh hour."

"I know. Just hear me out."

His muscles bulged as he crossed his arms, but she held her obstinate look. Sighing, Jake took up one of the barstools at his kitchen island. "Let's hear it."

Dana stalled long enough to locate a pair of clean ceramic mugs and scrounge up some tea bags from his sparse pantry. "What if I told you that you could keep the same plan for your mission to take out Vega without Claire being in any danger?"

His brow furrowed. "I'm listening."

The kettle boiled giving Dana time to reconsider if she really wanted to cut Jake in on her plan. The old Dana wouldn't have, but she'd come too far to go back to the scared woman who never let anyone in. At some point, she'd have to trust someone. It was the only way to keep evolving. And if anyone was worthy of her trust, it was Jake Shepard.

Pouring the scalding water into the mugs, she set the tea to steeping and turned to face him. With a hopeful exhalation, Dana laid out her plan in detail.

It'd come to her while listening to him brief his team, and if she could get him on board, she knew it would work. When she was done, she clasped her fingers together to keep from fidgeting.

She wished she knew what way he was leaning. The entire time she'd been talking he'd remained quiet, his eyebrows knitting closer and closer together. Now the crease between them was so deep she felt she could disappear into it.

Finally he spoke. "You think Vega will buy it?"

"Long enough for you to take him out."

He began nodding. "I think it could work, but there's one problem."

"What's that?"

"Claire will never go along with it."

"That's why we're not going to tell her."

"Dana ... She'll never trust us again."

"Better to lose her trust than her life."

Jake glared at her. Dana knew it was a low blow, but at this point she'd use any means necessary to keep Claire out of harm's way. "She's not just going to stay here and go along with this."

"I know."

"So what's the plan?"

Dana looked down at the two mugs of tea in front of her. They were done steeping. She spooned out the used tea bags and passed a mug to Jake, letting the warmth of her own mug soothe the chill that ran through her. "Remember the tea I used to help her sleep through her detox?"

Jake's eyes bulged. "Christ. You're scary, you know that?" He shoved his tea away.

"I didn't drug yours. You watched me make it."

He shook his head. "I think you missed your calling. The CIA could use someone like you on their team."

"Very funny." She took a sip of her tea. The hot beverage burned a path down her throat to her stomach. "Speaking of spooks. Are you sure Fuller won't catch wind of this?"

"This mission isn't exactly black ops, but we've kept it tight for obvious reasons. Besides, Jenkins let me know she'd been doing her own digging into Fuller. Apparently, he's been under IA's microscope for a while now. Jenkins is helping with the investigation. Our theory tying him to Vega through the Mystic Tower was enough to bounce him off the task force. He won't be a problem come mission day."

"And you think Jenkins will go along with our new plan?"

"She'll be on board." Jake shook his head. "I'm actually surprised she didn't suggest it herself. It's scary how similar you two are."

Dana took another sip of tea to disguise her grin as she let the compliment fill her with warmth. Relief spread through her now that she and Jake were in agreement. If they could pull this off, Claire would be safe. But one thing still nagged at her. "Fuller's a bigger part of this than we can prove."

Jake shook his head again. "Don't worry. He'll get his once we bring

Vega in. The guy has no loyalties. He'll flip on anyone he can to plea bargain his way out of a life sentence."

"Can that happen?"

"Not on my watch. And especially not with DA Walsh as prosecutor."

Dana winced at the mention of Jo's father. It'd been too easy to slip into that comfortable space with Jake again. Spending time at his house, learning her way around his kitchen. It wasn't smart. "What does Jo think about all of this?"

Jake stared at his untouched tea, silent for a beat too long. His broad shoulders rose and fell on a heavy exhale. "Not much considering she'll be in Denver when everything goes down."

"What?"

Jake stood, abandoning his tea for a glass at his wet bar. He poured himself a drink with a heavy hand and downed half of it in one gulp before turning back to face her. "HRT needed her."

Dana wanted to turn away from the pain flickering in his eyes, but she couldn't. She had too many questions. "Oh. When are you joining her?"

"I'm not."

She blinked. "What do you mean? I thought you were moving to Denver together."

"So did I." He gave a shrug and took another drink. "Plans change. People leave." He shrugged again and finished his drink, placing it back on the counter with force. "I guess the timing wasn't right."

Dana was left speechless as Jake stalked to his gigantic windows to stare out at the glowing lights of the capital. She was still processing what he said when he abruptly turned to face her, his eyes bright with anger. "Are you ever going to tell me why you came back to D.C.?"

"I told you, it's not important."

"Maybe it is, Dana. Maybe it's the most fucking important thing in the world. If I had anything to do with it, shouldn't I get to decide?"

Dana's chest was in her throat as Jake stalked toward her, his heart beating for her to see. She wasn't ready for this. And neither was he. Things had just ended with Jo. He wasn't in his right mind.

Even with the island between them, Dana backed up until the kitchen counter prevented her from putting any more space between them. She forced steadiness into her voice when she spoke. "Jake, now's not the time to get into it."

His laugh was dry. "Well, when's a good time for you? Because apparently I suck at timing."

"Jake ..."

"No!" He stalked around the island, not stopping until he was right in front of her. She could taste the warmth of the whiskey on his breath. "You owe me the truth, Dana."

"I know," she whispered. "And someday, you'll have it. Just not today."

Anger crackled in his eyes like lightning over a storming ocean. He turned away from her, gripping the side of his sink so hard she expected it to crack. Dana held her breath as his head sank between his heaving shoulders.

For a moment everything was quiet; her holding her breath, him sucking all the oxygen from the room. Then the combustion she expected culminated as Jake smashed his whiskey glass into the sink and stormed down the hall.

She stayed put until she heard the bathroom door slam shut and the shower turn on. Heart pounding, Dana walked to the sink and began cleaning up the pieces of shattered glass. Once the remnants of Jake's temper were gone, she turned on the faucet to wash her hands. Her eyes snagged on the jagged scar across her left palm and a tidal wave of memory pulled her under.

She and Jake in this same kitchen.

A broken glass.

A forged bond.

She'd been the one doing the breaking that day, leaving Jake to pick up the pieces.

It was her turn to return the favor.

Turning off the water, Dana dried her hands and shut off the lights before taking up her spot on the couch. She pulled a blanket over her and stared out at the lights of the city below as her finger absently rubbed the scar on her palm. It was a reminder that trust and terror could be woven together.

Jake was never the thing she feared. Her heart was. There was nothing more terrifying than trusting it.

67

A SLIVER OF BLUE SKY SPLIT THE CURVED CHAIN LINK CAGE. RUST AND graffiti stretched out as far as the eye could see above the rippling brown water of the Anacostia. The pedestrian bridge looked worse than Dana remembered. But then again, she'd never viewed it this way.

She stood by silently while Jake addressed the two dozen or so agents and technicians in the FBI's simulation hangar. He explained the footage recently obtained via drones provided a 360-degree view of the mission site.

Apparently, this was common practice, but Dana felt like she'd slipped into an alternate dimension as the simulated landscape spun around her like a bad theme park ride. The motion of the virtual scenery made her nauseous, but Claire seemed to be enjoying it.

A Metro train blurred by in the reflection of Claire's glasses, her eyes wide with intrigue. "This is incredible," she whispered.

Jake's voice rang through the hangar, putting an end to their conversation. "The footage you're watching was collected yesterday," he explained. "It was too risky to do in-person recon at the site, but we managed to send undercovers on the Green Line, and they can confirm the intel we have is accurate."

Dana caught the subtle nods of three agents who stood near Jake, hands clasped behind their backs. She didn't know them. Besides Jenkins, Jake and Claire, there were few familiar faces in the room.

She barely recognized the four groups of teams from Jake's apartment. Today they'd traded their suits for tactical gear. The sight was jarring against the metropolitan landscape. Dana didn't like thinking of D.C. as a war zone, but today, for all intents and purposes, it was exactly that.

"The point of these simulations is to flush out any possible obstacles. We'll rehearse multiple scenarios to ensure we're prepared for anything. Success is the only acceptable outcome, people, am I understood?"

"Yes, Sir!"

Jake nodded to Jenkins, and she gave the signal to the technicians. Sim day was underway. Dana helped slip a jacket identical to hers over Claire's slender shoulders. Convincing her to wear it was the first part of her plan. She was grateful Jake made it sound like a seamless part of his tactical strategy. "It makes sense from multiple angles. The jacket is easy for the team to track and assuming Vega has eyes on us, he's already seen you wear it home from the hospital."

Claire bought it hook, line and sinker.

The jacket she wore today was a duplicate. Half a dozen of them hung on the wall near the technicians. Dana didn't like thinking why more than one might be necessary. Pushing her morbid thoughts away she smoothed the jacket's collar and gave Claire's shoulders a squeeze. "You ready?"

"Yes." The waver in her voice said otherwise.

Dana stared into her clear blue eyes. "Claire, you don't have to do this."

"Yes, I do." Dana tried to object, but Claire cut her off. "I'm doing this for myself as much as anyone. I'll be fine. It's just a simulation. I can do this."

Nervous energy tightened Dana's stomach as she watched Claire walk to her spot on the scaffolding that was meant to represent the pedestrian bridge. Today might be a simulation, but tomorrow would be real. The guns would hold live rounds, not paintballs.

Once everyone was in their places, Jenkins announced, "Live drill!" and the simulation came to life. The roar of the trains and the river filled the hangar. One of the technicians hit a button that activated an industrial fan strong enough to lift Dana's hair.

Chills rippled up her spine as she stood on the safety of the sidelines watching the mission unfold. The agent impersonating Vega climbed the scaffolding and approached Claire. The sight was enough to stop Dana from drawing breath. Her only comfort was knowing that tomorrow, it wouldn't be Claire up on that bridge.

Claire might end up hating her for what she planned to do, but in Dana's mind, the ends justified the means.

One or many? Vega hadn't specified who had to be the one. The moment she figured out he wanted Claire, Dana had made her choice. Having Jake back her up on it only solidified that she was doing the right thing.

Chewing her nails, Dana counted the seconds that ticked by much too slowly. Without an earpiece she couldn't hear what was being said over the team coms, but she watched Claire hold her hands up; the signal that she'd identified the approaching target.

A moment later two shots rang out and an explosion of red erupted on the target. One on his right shoulder, the other on his left knee. He dropped his weapon and fell to his knees. A siren buzzed and the hangar lights flooded the space, washing out the simulated scenery.

"Good work, everyone!" Jake hollered, walking back to the center of the room. "Reset. Sim two stations." Before he disappeared into the shadows with the rest of his team, he caught Dana's eye. His gaze was full of questions, and she knew what he was asking.

She swallowed her fear, doing her best to exude confidence as she nodded. They'd set a course, and she meant to see it through.

"Reset. Sim eleven."

Dana's confidence grew with each successful mission she watched.

Jake threw every situation she could imagine at his team, and each time they adapted, giving him the successful outcome he demanded.

"He's good at this," she said quietly to Jenkins.

The seasoned agent stood next to Dana, arms crossed, jaw hard, legs wide. She oozed authority as her keen eyes surveyed the scene. "He is," she admitted. "But let's see how he does with something out of my playbook." She pressed the com button on her earpiece and issued a command Dana couldn't decipher.

A few seconds later the simulation went live. Right away, Dana saw what Jenkins had up her sleeve, but no one else did. Before Dana had the chance to object, gunfire echoed through the hangar, followed by the sound of Claire's scream.

Dana was in motion before the siren buzzed to signal the end of the drill. She rushed onto the scaffolding and pulled Claire's crumpled form into her arms. The girl squeaked and hissed as she sucked in shallow breaths. "Claire! It's okay. You just got the wind knocked out of you. Take deep breaths through your mouth."

But Claire was too hysterical to listen. She raised her shaking hands, her eyes bulging at the red liquid covering them. It was just paint, but Dana understood the fear the image evoked. To Claire, it was a very realistic glimpse into her future if things went wrong tomorrow.

Having experienced the searing pain of the real thing, Dana knew the sting of paintballs was nothing compared to a bullet tearing through flesh. But she didn't need to terrify the girl more than she already was. "Come on," Dana said, trying to help Claire to her feet. "We're done here. Let's go home."

Claire looked at her through wide, watery eyes shaking her head frantically. "I can't," she whispered, her voice cracking. "I think ... I ..."

Dana followed Claire's line of sight to the stain darkening the inseam of her pants. The poor girl had wet herself!

Heart twisting with guilt, Dana almost let the truth slip. She would've blurted out her plans to keep Claire safe tomorrow if Jake's angry voice hadn't drowned out her words. He was charging toward Jenkins. "What the hell was that?"

"Kayaker," Jenkins replied, nodding to the agent in an orange life vest who'd taken the shots.

"That wasn't part of the drill," Jake seethed.

"Prepare for every outcome," she replied calmly.

"Christ, Jenkins! She's a civilian!"

Jenkins moved her gaze to the scaffold where Dana and Claire were perched. "She should know what she's getting into."

"She does."

"Doesn't look like it."

Jake turned, his eyes locking with Dana. Jenkins knew Claire wouldn't be on the bridge tomorrow. So what was she playing at? Was she truly trying to exhaust every scenario they might face, or was it something more?

Dana squared her shoulders. It didn't matter what message Jenkins was trying to send. She wasn't changing her mind.

She helped Claire out of the paint-stained jacket and settled her own long coat over her shoulders, buttoning the front to protect her from further embarrassment. Dana slipped her arm around her shoulders. "Come on, Claire. We're going home."

68

Jake sat on his leather couch, arm stretched across the back. His relaxed posture was a necessary ruse. Claire sat next to him, legs crossed, a blanket draped over her shoulders. She held a large bowl of popcorn in her lap.

The buttery smell mixed with the clean scent of her shampoo would've been comforting any other night. Tonight, however, his mind was consumed with thoughts of his impending deception. The sound of Dana tinkering in his kitchen made it impossible to think of anything else.

Claire picked at her popcorn, her gaze somewhere else entirely. Jake squeezed her shoulder. "You did good today, kid."

She glared at him over the rim of her cat-eye glasses. He'd grown used to the way she looked without the gobs of black eyeliner and dark lipstick she normally wore. He wasn't sure which look he preferred. Freshly showered and clean faced, she looked younger, more fragile than the tough-as-nails Smithsonian researcher he'd affectionately nicknamed Elvira.

"I'll do better tomorrow."

He'd heard about her wetting herself but knew better than to bring it up. Though it was nothing to be ashamed of. Jake had known many a good soldier who'd done the same in the face of action. Still, he'd wished Jenkins hadn't put Claire through that kind of scarring trauma.

Jenkins had obviously been trying to send a message, though it was unnecessary. He and Dana were too far down this path to turn back. Sighing, he pulled his arm from the back of the couch and grabbed some popcorn. "We'll all do better tomorrow."

Dana joined them in the living room, carrying a tray with three mugs of tea. She set it down on the coffee table and passed out the mugs.

Claire wrinkled her nose. "Tea?"

"We all need a good night of sleep," Dana replied.

Claire choked on a laugh. "Yeah. I think I'm gonna need something stronger than tea." At Dana's wide eyes, she added. "Kidding. Geeze. Tough room."

Dana sat down on Claire's other side. She held up her mug, her eyes burning with conviction. "Tomorrow, we end this."

Jake touched his mug to hers. "Tomorrow."

Claire joined them, echoing the sentiment. The three of them drank deeply. Jake set his mug down and picked up the remote. Dimming the lights, he began the movie queued up on his projection screen. Claire continued to sip her tea as cascading green numbers filled the screen. According to the dose Dana gave her, the girl would be asleep before Neo even discovered the Matrix.

Jake had his doubts, but sure enough Claire's head thumped against his shoulder before they got to his favorite scene: the red pill or the blue pill. Dana took Claire's empty mug and gave him a nod. Hearing her steady breathing, he stood and scooped her into his arms. Dana followed behind, taking over once he set Claire in his bed.

When Dana finally emerged, Jake was back in the kitchen, all traces of tea and popcorn erased. "This better work," he grumbled, drying the last mug.

She raised her brows. "I gave her the correct dose."

"I'm not talking about the tea."

Her lips twisted into a frown. "Did you get what I asked for?"

He opened the cabinet above the fridge and pulled out a paper bag.

Dana reached for it, but he didn't let go. "That last sim today ... I think Jenkins was aiming to rattle you."

"I know."

"What if she's right? What if there's some angle I didn't think of?"

"Then we'll face it together." Dana's hand closed over his. "Jake, we'll make this work. We have to, for Claire."

He nodded. "For Claire."

69

Jake was up before the watery sun rose to light the gray sky. Morning had arrived, whether he was ready for it or not. He cracked his bedroom door to check on the girls and found he wasn't the only early riser.

Dana sat in his dressing chair, watching Claire sleep.

"Hey," he greeted, pushing into the room.

She jumped. "Hey."

"Didn't mean to startle you. How's the patient?"

"Sleeping like a baby."

Jake crossed the room and sat on the edge of the bed. His finger sought out Claire's pulse despite the obvious rise and fall of her chest. Her vitals were strong, steady.

"Didn't believe me?" Dana asked.

He shrugged. "Old habit. You get any sleep?"

"Some. You?"

"Enough."

It was useless to delay the inevitable, but Jake allowed himself a few deep breaths, absorbing the calm around him. He'd need it to carry him through the day. Then he brushed a dark swath of hair from

Claire's forehead and pressed a kiss to her warm skin. When he stood, Dana was grinning. "What?"

"I'd like to see you try that when she's awake."

A smile cut his face "Elvira's all bark." He lifted his gaze to meet Dana's. "She loves you too, ya know?"

"Why do you think I'm doing this?"

The calm from earlier dissipated, giving way to thick tension. He hated thinking of Dana putting herself in harm's way, but there was no way around it.

When she'd first shared her plan with him, Jake had suggested using a female agent as a decoy, but Dana refused. She was adamant they not let anyone else in for fear it would get back to Vega thanks to Fuller's network of moles. He didn't disagree with her.

At least Jenkins knew their plan.

It was one small solace in the storm swirling around him as he stared into Dana's beautiful eyes, trying to memorize the pattern of gold flecks that made her irises glow like amber. The bruise on her jaw had begun to fade and her hair covered the tiny cut on her forehead, but her injured lip was harder to disguise. The swollenness of the delicate flesh drew him in.

He took a step toward her, unsure what he wanted to say, but she cleared her throat, backing away. "I'd better go get ready."

Jake nodded, letting another moment slip away. "I'll put on the coffee."

"How do I look?"

Jake turned his contemplative gaze from his windows at the sound of Dana's voice. He thought he knew what to expect, but the sight of her made him flinch.

"That bad?"

Jake knew he was staring at Dana, but it was Claire he saw in front of him. Or a future version of her, grown up and filled out in all the right places. Jake flinched again, uncomfortable with the part of his mind that kept seeking Dana's silhouette beneath Claire's clothes. "The wig is perfect. Just ... freaky."

Dana huffed a breath to clear the long, dark hair from her eyes. "I don't know how she deals with these bangs."

Jake moved closer, inspecting her with the sharpened eye of an agent. "You may have gone a little overboard with the makeup."

"Really?" Dana's eyes widened with alarm. "What part?"

"The eyes." No matter what Dana did, she'd never be able to disguise her beautiful brown eyes. Even with the colored contacts, her soulfulness shone through.

"Help me fix it! I'm not good with this kind of stuff."

Jake wet a napkin and pulled Dana over to the windows. The natural light made it easier to see her under all of Claire's trappings. With a steady hand, he leaned in, gently running the wet corner of the napkin beneath Dana's eyes. "Close them," he ordered.

She obliged, and he smudged some of the heavy strokes until they looked messy, the way Claire wore it. He was so close he could feel the warmth of Dana's breath against his neck. Closing his eyes too, he let himself savor the moment, knowing this was as close as he'd dare get. Today was too important for distractions. But if they made it through ...

The buzzing of his cellphone cut off his thoughts. He stepped back and answered the call. After a short conversation he turned back to Dana. "Claire's security detail is here."

"And they know what to do?"

"The only way someone is getting in here is over their dead bodies."

Dana nodded. "Good."

70

Tugging her black wool hat down further, Dana took one final look at herself in the mirror. The wig was spot on and the oversized coat and dark clothes helped disguise the natural curves Claire lacked. To complete the transformation, Dana borrowed Claire's cat-eye glasses. Thanks to the tea she'd dosed her with, she wouldn't be needing them anytime soon.

They were prescription, which would've been a problem if Jake hadn't thought of everything. He'd accounted for that when he'd precured Dana's corrective color lenses. Both prescriptions worked seamlessly together, though she had to admit there was a mildly dizzying effect if she moved too quickly or let the lenses slip far enough down her nose that she could see over the frames.

Pushing them properly into place, she pulled in a deep breath. This was the moment of truth. A team of agents waited outside to take her to the drop point. They hadn't been informed that Dana was now playing the role of "Claire."

It was risky to leave the team in the dark, but the fewer people who knew Claire was tucked away, safe and sound, the better. Jenkins and Jake knew, and Dana had faith they could smooth over any ripples if need be. She also took comfort in the weight of the small caliber handgun tucked into the ankle holster in her boot. If all went according to plan, she'd have no reason to use it, but she appreciated Jake's precaution for preparedness.

He knocked on the bathroom door. "The team is ready. You good?"

She opened the door. "Yep." This was it. If she could fool his team, it would bolster her confidence for fooling Vega.

Jake walked her to the door. He wouldn't be riding with her. Instead, he was joining Jenkins and the perimeter team who'd tapped into the DDOT's CCTV in order to keep eyes on the mission at all times.

"Remember," Jake said, before opening his front door. "I'll be with you the whole time."

He was referring to her earpiece. It gave her peace of mind knowing he'd be able to talk her through the whole thing once they were on site. She was also outfitted with a wire to record any conversation she might exchange with Vega.

If he shows. Dana blocked out the negative thought and grabbed Jake's hand. "I've got this."

"And if at any point you don't?"

"Tug on my left ear."

Satisfied, Jake opened the door and passed Dana off to the team waiting to whisk her to the scene. She held her breath for a few harrowing seconds, but when there were no objections or second glances, she released it, ready to meet her destiny.

71

With Dana en route Jake slipped into the mode he was most comfortable with: Army of one. He checked the magazine in his Sig Sauer before securing it in his hip holster. Today he was packing additional fire power. He strapped on his military issued Sig M17 and added enough magazines to his weapon belt to arm a small militia.

He refused to be caught off guard. There was too much at stake.

Boots laced, tactical vest in place, Jake grabbed his standard issued FBI field jacket and headed for the door. He gave the agents guarding his place a stern glare, a reminder that he'd make good on his threats if anything happened to Claire.

In his SUV, Jake checked the time displayed on his dash clock as he rolled out of his parking garage.

Right on schedule.

Gray skies crowded in overhead. A typical dreary D.C. winter day. He liked when things like weather cooperated. The averageness of the scenery soothed his nerves.

He turned right onto Constitution, following the prearranged route to rendezvous with Jenkin and the com team. The light ahead turned yellow, then red. Jake braked and rolled to a stop, his engine idling on the sleepy street. A countdown ticked in his head as he waited for the light to turn green.

Timing, predictability; it was the sweet spot of successful missions and something he thrived on. *Focus on the objective. Operate smoothly.* Dozens of Army catchphrases played through his mind on a loop. They'd been engrained so deeply, they were second nature now, but he didn't mind. Each one awoke the identity he'd left behind. A soldier with one purpose: success at all costs.

Vega was his. The sick bastard just didn't know it yet.

Jake's internal clock ticked down to zero, and the light turned green. He moved his foot to the gas and accelerated through the intersection. Less than two miles to the rendezvous point. Everything was going according to plan; until it wasn't.

By the time Jake saw the vehicle in his peripheral, it was too late. The blue Ford pickup barreled into his driver side door. For a moment Jake mistook the loud pop of the airbags as gunfire. Instinct had him reaching for his weapon, but the stench of burnt rubber and smoking fabric reminded him he was in D.C. not a war zone. Not yet anyway.

Adrenaline fueled his rage as he tore what was left of the burning airbag away from his face and unclipped his seatbelt. His SUV was still running, but it wasn't drivable. The blue pickup pinned him into another vehicle parked on the street.

Muttering a swear, Jake assessed his exit strategy. Deciding the shattered windshield was a sure bet, he slid over to the passenger seat and began kicking.

The emergency response system installed in his government vehicle crackled to life. "About time," Jake grumbled when the dispatcher's voice greeted him.

"9-1-1, what's your emergency?"

"This is Special Agent, Jake Shepard of the FBI." He rattled off his badge number and location, recounting the accident.

"I've dispatched the nearest patrol unit. Stay with your vehicle. Help is on the way."

"I don't have time for that. I'm en route to carry out active orders."

"Sir, please do not leave your vehicle."

Jake swore. This was the last thing he had time for. "I'm leaving. If you have a problem with that, contact Assistant Director Remi Jenkins with the FBI."

With a final kick, he finished clearing the windshield and climbed out of his vehicle. His boots had just hit pavement when the cavalry arrived, red and blues flashing. Jake walked toward the squad car, badge held high. If he could sweet talk the officers out of their ride, he had a chance of making it to his rendezvous point on time.

But the familiar face that stepped out of the squad car stole the last of Jake's hope. "What are the odds?" he muttered as he locked eyes with Officer Hartwell.

"Well, look what we've got here," Hartwell sang. "What happened, Shepard? Feds forget to check if you had a driver's license?"

"Hartwell, I don't have time for this. I'm in the middle of something. I need your car."

The officer laughed, and Jake felt his fists coil with the urge to punch him again. "It's not a request," Jake growled, shoving past the officer.

The smaller man unwisely got in his way. "Let me get this straight, you think you're gonna flee the scene of a crime in my squad car? You must be joking."

Jake looked across the hood of the black and white to where the other officer stood, his hand tense near his weapon. Taking them both out wasn't a problem. But shooting friendlies wasn't on his agenda. He'd be able to disable Hartwell easily enough, but not before his partner got a shot off, and Jake really didn't want to get shot at this early in the day.

He was going to have to sweet talk his way out of this one. "Hartwell, let's reschedule the pissing match for tomorrow. I've got a live op going down in ten minutes. If you're the reason I'm not there, you'll have to explain the body bags."

Hartwell glanced at his partner. "You aware the Feebs had a hustle going today?"

"Nope."

"It's covert," Jake muttered.

He could hear the ambulance sirens in the distance. He was running out of time. In a few minutes this would be a full-blown crime scene. He had two choices. Wait and hope to slip away in the chaos or keep pushing for an out with Hartwell.

Waiting wasn't really his style.

"Do you really want to invite this shitstorm into your life, Hartwell? The lives of sixteen federal agents, all decorated war heroes by the way, are in your hands right now. Make the right call." He could see he had him on the ropes, so he pushed. "Give me your car and you can write me any citation you want. I'll personally frame it for you."

Hartwell's face drew into a smirk, but the squeal of tires cut off his response. Hope filled Jake the instant he saw the dark tint and chipped navy paint job of the unmarked police vehicle. The shitty piece of transportation meant there was someone who outranked Hartwell behind the wheel. Jake just prayed he was more reasonable. He didn't make a habit of decking the boys in blue at crime scenes, so the odds were in his favor. But as soon as the driver's door swung open, Jake knew his luck had run out.

Mike Fuller stepped out of the car; a knowing grin already plastered on his face. "Agent Shepard. Fancy running into you here." His eyes roved from Jake to the blue pickup that caved in the side of his SUV. "My, it looks like you were in a hurry to get somewhere."

A tide of fear began to rise inside Jake. The traffic accident was no accident. He'd been set up from the beginning. His heart pounded as his mind raced into overdrive. If Fuller knew what Jake was up to, who else did? Had their operation been compromised?

Fuller walked slowly over to the two Metro officers. "What are you boys waiting for? Take Agent Shepard down to the station. I'd like him detained for questioning."

Jake's blood ran cold. "On what charges?"

"Manslaughter, of course."

"You haven't even checked on the other driver."

"I don't need to," Fuller said, his voice full of malice. "I make the rules around here. You'd do well to remember that. Cuff him."

Hartwell gladly complied, stuffing Jake into his squad car. "You'll never make this stick, Fuller."

The smug CIA agent leaned down, his oily grin back in place as he peered at Jake. "Don't worry. I'll be right along behind you." He paused. "On second thought, I might be a while. I gotta clean up your mess first."

As the squad car pulled away, siren blaring, Jake could only think of one play he had left. It was a gamble. But one he'd have to take.

72

Staring down at the ghost trains was unsettling, but Dana did her best not to let the empty cars speeding below add to her anxiety. In the simulation, they'd been full of people. This was more unnerving, but it meant the department of transportation had held up their end.

At least one thing was going according to plan.

Dana glanced at her watch again. It was five minutes past the time Vega had instructed, which meant she'd been standing in the freezing cold for almost thirty minutes.

Another cold burst of wind kicked up as a train rushed beneath making her skin stipple with goose flesh. The vibrations shook the rickety bridge and made her teeth clench. Dana watched as a second train flew by in the opposite direction. The breath of space between the passing cars made her stomach knot. It was wide enough for someone to stand with their hands extended but imagining doing so made her knees weak. Still, she couldn't look away.

Each time two trains passed like that she imagined falling through the gap in the rusted chain link and disappearing forever. She didn't know why. Delusions of grandeur weren't part of her repertoire. Neither were suicidal thoughts. Maybe the pressure was finally getting to her.

Was this how Vega intended to do her in? With sheer mental torture?

If so, it was working.

So far no one had questioned her appearance. Dana hoped it was because she looked convincingly like Claire, and not because the agents protecting her were the type who'd been trained to take orders without question. Or maybe now that they were on scene Jenkins had filled them in. Dana didn't know. She felt very much in the dark as she stood on the pedestrian bridge, the proverbial lamb, led to slaughter.

The other thing that was eating at her was the absence of Jake's voice in her ear. He'd told her he'd be with her. She could still feel the weight of his hand against her shoulder as he looked her in the eye before she left. *I'll be with you the whole time.*

When it came to Jake, that was as close to a promise as one could hope for.

So why isn't he here?

Dana couldn't answer that question. Nor could she silence the fears it evoked.

Something was wrong. She could feel it in her bones. Her mind spiraled down dark paths. Was this all just a trap to get to Jake? Or was it Claire who would pay the price?

She was at Jake's, drugged and defenseless. If something happened to her, Dana would have no one to blame but herself.

Fear lined her gut as the wind whipped around her. Her hair lashed her cheeks and her jacket danced making her feel as though she was controlled by a sadistic puppet master. The simulation seemed like child's play in comparison. The elements were one thing, but Dana's eyes fell to her watch again, wondering how long she'd be forced to endure the mental anguish of waiting.

Waiting to hear from Jake.

Waiting to see Vega.

Waiting for it to end.

The crackle of chatter in her ear made her heart leap with hope, but it wasn't Jake's voice who greeted her. "Tango approaching at three o'clock. All teams standby."

Dana whipped around, her heart in her throat as she faced the opposite bank of the Anacostia River. The cloud cover had burned off, forcing her to shield her eyes against the glare coming off the water. The silhouette moving toward her was male, maybe early fifties, wearing a dark suit and long tan jacket. He followed the path until he was on the pedestrian bridge with her.

When he came fully into view, Dana's breath whooshed from her body. "Fuller?"

She felt like she'd been sucker punched as a grin split his face. "Were you expecting someone else? Vega maybe?"

She took a shaking step backward, but that only goaded Fuller's elation. "We were expecting you, if that makes you feel any better, *Dr. Gray.*"

His emphasis of her name told Dana that her disguise fooled no one. "You knew all along, didn't you?"

"That you'd come in place of your junkie intern? Yes. Though I do have to say, I admire the lengths you've gone to trying to protect her. Jake was right, you really could've made a great Spook."

Dana stilled as Fuller recited Jake's words. Words he had spoken to her in private. *Shit! Jake's place was bugged. Fuller knew their entire plan!*

Had he done it himself or did he have an inside man?

Fuller had access to Jake's when he showed up to investigate the tarot card they'd found, but Jake had meticulously swept the place afterward. Still, dozens of agents and FBI personnel had access to his apartment over the past couple of days.

The sound of teams scrambling in her ear distracted her. There were arguments over whether or not to take the shot, but Dana hadn't given the signal. She'd been waiting for Vega. They hadn't rehearsed this scenario.

Fuller laughed. "They're all a little confused, aren't they?" he asked, pointing to her ear. "Don't worry, it'll all be cleared up soon."

"What will?"

"Our master plan."

"You mean yours and Vegas?"

"Ding. Ding. Ding. By the way, you can take that ridiculous wig off now. I've been waiting for this for a long time. When I fantasized about taking your life, you looked more like ... well, you."

Dana took another step back, but made no move for the wig, fearing it'd be interpreted as the signal to take the target out. Instead, she moved deliberately slowly, taking a step back. Her instinct told her to keep Fuller talking. Unsure whether it was morbid curiosity, or the desperate hope that Jake was somewhere out there, dialing his scope in on the back of Fuller's skull.

"I don't get it," she said. "You've spent your life serving your country. Why would you partner with a criminal?"

"That's the question, isn't it? If my country paid better, we wouldn't be in this situation."

"So that's it? This is all about money?"

"If you want to boil it down to brass tacks, but that's oversimplifying it in my opinion."

"Enlighten me," Dana challenged.

"Vega and I bonded over mutual interests long ago."

"Kaitlynn Ward?"

His grin was a slash of white. "Someone's been doing their homework."

"Vega killed her, and you helped him cover it up. Why?"

"You've got it backwards. I killed Kaitlynn. She wasn't my first, but she almost got me caught." He shrugged. "Vega took the heat. He was a minor so it wasn't a big deal. But he owned me after that."

"You're how he'd stayed one step ahead this whole time."

"I'm the angel on his shoulder. He's the devil on mine."

"Diablo?"

Pride filled Fuller's voice. "I was happy to play the part. Vega needed a few rivals out of his way to pave his return, something he paid handsomely for, I might add. I'd get to bag a few bad guys, look like a CIA hero, make some quick cash. It was a no brainer. But when he showed me his hit list, I knew it was fate. I immediately agreed, as long as he promised to leave you to me in the end."

"Why me? Why now? We haven't spoken in years."

"You really don't know?"

"This is because of Dante?"

His smile finally slipped. "It's so much more than what I did to Dante. You ruined my career. I had to leave the FBI because Cramer wouldn't stand for anyone hurting his precious pet." He choked on a bitter laugh. "Always knew he was a creep. His fall from grace softened my abrupt departure though. I didn't feel so bad about leaving an agency that had a serial killer living right under their nose. But still, my record was tarnished because of your inability to leave well enough alone. It followed me, even to the CIA."

"Rightfully, so," she hissed. "What happened to Dante? Just tell me. You killed him, didn't you?"

He grinned. "Let's just say Dante's untimely death is only the tip of the iceberg."

Her heart shuddered as she wondered who else Fuller had deemed disposable. "You're worse than Vega."

He sucked his teeth, clucking like he was schooling a toddler. "You wouldn't say that if you knew what he had planned for the rest of your friends."

"Claire?"

"The junkie that won't die?" Fuller laughed.

"She's not a junkie. I know you broke into my house and shot her up."

"I've got a badge, sweetheart. I don't have to break in anywhere. But yeah, that was me. I can admit it wasn't my finest work. It's why I usually pay people to take care of my dirty work. It doesn't matter though. Vega will take care of her. Right after he's finished with your boy scout."

Jake. Dana's heart flatlined. She knew something was wrong. Jake would never hang her out to dry. Not while there was breath left in his body. "What did you do to him?"

"I haven't done anything. But he won't be coming to your rescue if that's what you're counting on. No, I made sure he got a one-way ticket to county lockup. It's frightening what can happen to a Fed in jail."

73

The minutes ticked by, each one shredding the gears of his internal clock. Jake's mission had derailed before it even began.

Not since Ghazni had he failed so spectacularly. Jake pushed Ramirez's face from his mind. He couldn't go there. Not when it was Dana and Claire who would pay the price this time.

Fuller was on to them. The bastard must've smuggled a bug into his place. That or one of Jake's own had betrayed him. He would split heads when he found out who it was. That was if he ever got out of here.

He had no idea if his phone call had gone through.

On the ride to the station, he'd slipped his phone out of his pocket and dialed the only number stored under favorites. Dropping the phone to the floorboard, he'd began berating Hartwell in detail. He ranted about Fuller being a crooked CIA agent putting a sanctioned FBI mission at stake by locking him up. In a last-ditch effort, Jake named the station number as the squad car pulled around back to book him.

That had been almost thirty minutes ago. He had no way of knowing if his distress signal was received. Even if it had gone through there was no guarantee help would come. Jake was staking lives on a Hail Mary pass, but at this point, he was out of options.

The cuffs bit into his wrist as he was perp-walked to processing. "I get a phone call," he demanded for the hundredth time. Again he was ignored as the clerk busied himself cataloging his weapons.

All doubt that Fuller and Vega were working together vanished. There was no telling how deep their reach went. Which was why Jake needed his gamble to pay off before Vega's deep pockets paid for a clerical error that locked him in with Gen. Pop.

A Fed getting shanked? It would be chalked up to dumb luck.

An officer moved Jake down the line, where he was handed his DOC jumpsuit. The jail issued khakis were the last stop in this charade. If he walked through those doors to strip, he wasn't coming back out the other side. He could feel it.

The doors buzzed open, and Jake was escorted into the room that would seal his fate. The officer seated at the metal table didn't even look up as he pulled on a pair of latex gloves. "Strip."

Jake was about to argue when the doors behind him buzzed again. DA Stone Walsh walked through, an expression of fury carved into his hard features. He waved a sheet of paper, rattling off penal code proclamations. "You're to remand this man into my custody."

The seated officer stood, his expression no longer bored. "Come again?"

"Son, do you know who I am?"

He nodded emphatically. "DA Walsh."

"That's right. Trust me when I tell you this is above your pay grade. Do the smart thing and play along. Unless you want me to charge you with the misimprisonment of a federal agent?"

Minutes later Jake was standing on the sidewalk, his hand outstretched. "Thanks. You saved my ass in there. I wasn't sure Jo got my call."

The fuming DA glared down his nose at Jake, ignoring his gesture of gratitude. "Do not mistake this as an act of goodwill. I'm here at the behest of my daughter. If it were up to me, I'd have let you rot in there."

"Good to know."

"I don't know what she saw in you, but you're not good enough for her."

"That's something we can agree on."

"Then I trust I won't have to warn you not to call her again. She has a promising career ahead of her, and I don't want her dragged into whatever this is."

Jake looked at the BMW idling at the curb. He turned back to Jo's father. "One last favor and she'll never hear from me again."

"Name it."

"I need to borrow your car."

74

Frantic chatter exploded in Dana's ear. She winced, yanking the earpiece out before her eardrum ruptured. Not having the com in her ear left her in the dark, but the explosion of gunfire in the distance told her everything she needed to know. Fuller grinned. "See, I told you I'd clear up their confusion."

Dana looked frantically around the empty Metro line for any signs of life. It was eerily still.

"You didn't think I came here alone, did you?" He made the infuriating tsking sound again. "I know better than that. And since you were kind enough to share your plans, I knew exactly where to find your men. All. Of. Them."

Shit! Shit! Shit! Dana tried to calm her racing pulse. Fuller had gotten to everyone. Jenkins. Jake. Her. That meant when he was finished here, Claire would be next, if he and Vega hadn't orchestrated it already.

She tamped down on the panic coursing through her. She couldn't get ahead of herself. She had to survive Fuller first.

Jake's Special Ops matra flashed like a flare in her mind. *Place the mask over your own mouth and nose before assisting others.*

It was strangely fitting and filled her with determination. Men like Jake and the agents who'd volunteered to protect her faced monsters every day. She could handle one over-weight creep. Or at least she would die trying.

She was on her own, but that didn't scare her. Instead, she let the familiar feeling settle her. Being alone was nothing new. It'd been her role in life from the moment her parents died. She knew the feeling well, and that gave her the confidence she needed to see herself through. She'd done it for years. What was one more day?

"What are you waiting for, Fuller? Applause? Because you're not going to get any from me. You're a traitor, and your sins are going to catch up with you."

"Yeah, but not today. Take the wig off," he growled, pulling his gun. "I won't ask again."

Dana's hands moved slowly to her head. She knew there was no one left to see her signal and take the shot, but that didn't mean she couldn't. She could feel the cold steel, heavy against her ankle. With each step she took, the weapon reminded her it was there, ready should she need it.

Dana had never needed anything more.

If she was lucky, she would get one shot off, but that's all she needed. Her marksmanship had come a long way since Jake crashed into her life. Now was the moment to put it to use.

Her fingers nimbly removed her hat, then the clips securing the wig to her head. She kept each movement slow and deliberate as she steeled her nerves. Then, when she could wait no longer, she tore off the wig and dropped to a crouch, her hand finding her gun with deadly speed. But she wasn't fast enough. A single gunshot rang out, piercing its target, but it hadn't come from Dana's gun.

The steel was still cold in her hands, safety on. Eyes wide, she drew a breath, then another, surprised when each one wasn't her last. But then she saw it, the crimson stain blossoming on Fuller's chest. His gun fell from his outstretched hand, and he took one staggering step forward before he dropped face first, revealing a sight even more terrifying.

Even from a distance, Dana knew it was him, but she didn't want to believe it. She'd defeated one monster only to face another.

Terrance Vega stared at her, his expression pure hatred.

75

Gravel crunched under the tires as Jake skidded into the parking lot. He was out of the car and running before it came to a full stop. Finger pressed to his ear, he tried to reach Jenkins again. "Gamma Team, come in, over."

Nothing. Just more silence.

That wasn't a good sign. Especially now that he was within range. He could see the warehouse fifty yards ahead. Inside was the mobile command center they'd set up to run the mission. Beyond it, blocked by the view of the rundown brick buildings in the Navy Yard, was the pedestrian bridge. And Dana.

His legs pumped faster, driven by that sixth sense that hadn't failed him yet. It told him he wasn't too late, but he was running out of time. The crisp stillness of the yard sparked with the tension of what was yet to come. He wasn't sure what that was yet, but when he saw it, the hair on his arms stood.

Gun drawn, Jake dropped to an aggressive crouch. He took stock of his surroundings before moving forward in a tactical manner. His gaze returned to the warehouse. Particularly the quickzip lock, baring the door. Black singes marred the metal door jamb in three distinct locations. Jake knew a ballistic breach when he saw one.

Someone had beat him here, and they were pros. It would've worried him more if he hadn't handpicked the team for this mission. They knew how to watch their backs. But then who was watching Dana's?

Checking to make sure he was clear one more time, Jake covered the distance to the door. He unloaded two bullets into the quickzip, breaching the door. Inside, his eyes watered from the smoke. Flashbangs. The metallic scent was unmistakable. It took his eyes a moment to adjust to the darkness. He needed a moment more to recover from what he saw.

Three men lay dead on the floor, two more figures sat leaning against the wall, unmoving. He recognized one right away, her short blonde hair, stained with blood.

"Jenkins!"

Her eyes cracked open. "About time." Her voice sounded like gravel, but Jake had never been so happy to hear her griping.

"What happened?"

"Fuller. He had a team waiting for us. We didn't stand a chance. Get to Dana." Jenkins read his torn expression. "We'll be fine," she insisted, patting the leg of the motionless agent next to her.

From the pool of blood beneath him, he'd bled out almost immediately, but Jake could see the compression bandage on his stomach. No doubt the work of Jenkins. He didn't have the heart to tell her it hadn't made a difference.

Jake dialed dispatch and handed his phone to Jenkins. "Request backup. And a bus. I'm not letting you die on me."

Jake sprinted from the warehouse, the sound of Jenkins barking orders into his phone filling him with encouragement. It would take more than Fuller's lackeys to get the best of Remi Jenkins. The woman's will was made of steel. He hoped he could say the same for a certain librarian.

Covering ground quickly, the pedestrian bridge came into view as Jake rounded the last of the buildings. The first thing to catch his eye was the train whizzing below it. The next, stole his breath. Dana stood on the bridge, Vega in front of her, gun drawn.

76

ANOTHER OF THE GHOST TRAINS RUSHED BENEATH DANA, THE COLD AIR chilling her, but not as much as Vega's presence. He'd walked right up to her, stopping only a few feet away. He was almost close enough to touch. But with his gun drawn, the space between them vanished. What was distance when a bullet could swallow it?

When she'd first recognized him, she was too shocked to move. A voice inside her screamed. *Run! Run! Run!*

By the time her body caught up to her brain, it was too late. Vega was bearing down on her. Still she scrambled to her feet and ran, but the bullet that whizzed past her made her stop dead.

"The next one won't miss," he warned. "Drop the gun and turn around."

That's how she'd gotten here, unarmed and powerless as the man she'd been hunting, became the hunter.

Vega was the opposite of Fuller in every way. He stood there, silently appraising her like she was his next meal. Finally, he spoke, his voice low and hard. "You know who I am?"

She nodded.

"Say it."

It wasn't a request, but she knew the minute he got what he wanted, he'd pull the trigger. For men like him, it was all about control. Which he had at the moment, but if Dana was going to die, she was going to do it on her own terms. That meant not bowing down to the human trafficking psychopath who'd destroyed the life of her best friend and so many others.

"I'm not a patient man, Dr. Gray."

"Patient enough to plot this killing spree. Patient enough to decapitate people. Patient enough to lure Meredith Kincaid into your twisted game with the Priory of Bones."

His dead eyes stared back at her, empty and free of remorse. "Meredith was special."

"*Is* special," Dana shot back.

"No. Everything you loved about her is gone. I broke it. That's how I make them mine. I break them from the inside out, feasting on everything that once made them strong and desirable. I taught Senator Scott that. He and Meredith were valuable jewels in my treasure chest. Your interference cost me greatly."

"What about Fuller? Were you grooming him to be one of your minions, too?"

"He served his purpose." Vega stepped closer still, the butt of his gun pressing into her chest. "Though I do see why he was so taken by you." Dana swallowed her revulsion as Vega licked his lips. "Maybe I should take the time to get to know you? I bet I'd enjoy breaking you. If not, there's always room in the landfill."

The bridge vibrated as a train rushed beneath them. She could see the lights of another approaching. Empty trains on an ice cold day. Would that be her final memory?

It might have to be. There was no way she was letting Vega take her alive. She'd rather jump than give him the satisfaction. Madame Blanche's words echoed through her one more time. *Two roads converge, a path to be chosen. Heartbreak or happiness. You must look inward for the answers you seek.*

Dana had looked inward, but this hadn't been the crossroad she'd envisioned. She thought she was supposed to choose between pursuing Jake or letting him go. But she'd been wrong. The only thing that truly had power over her life was death. It was time to face it. Not like she did in books or from the safety of her research, but head on.

She didn't want to fear it anymore. Death wouldn't erase her. It would expose everything she tried to keep hidden. That vulnerability was what she feared. But no more.

She pictured the tarot card Vega had used to lure her here. Two figures toppling to their deaths. This was her Tower. It was time to stop fighting her fate.

"You're forgetting one thing, Vega."

"What's that?"

"I'm not one of your helpless victims. And I'm done letting you hurt the people I love." Then she lunged.

77

Jake saw it happen, the image seared into his mind, but he still couldn't quite believe it. One minute, Dana was standing on the bridge, Vega's gun pointed at her chest. The next, she was in motion. He watched both figures tumble off the bridge, Dana on top of Vega as they disappeared between the section of missing chain link.

The sound of Vega's gun firing was muffled by the screaming of the train below. A fall from that height wouldn't kill them, but the speeding trains would. Jake ran, shouting over the sound of the screeching rails. There was no way around. No way through. Crouching, he tried to see through the gaps as the trains blurred by. There was nothing he could do but wait in excruciating torment.

78

THE UNFORGIVING GRAVEL BROKE THEIR FALL, BITING INTO EVERY INCH OF Dana's exposed skin. But it was nothing compared to the fate they would've met if she'd hit the trains like she'd planned. She was aiming to end this once and for all. She'd come to the decision the moment she saw Jake come into view.

There was no way she was letting Vega get to him.

Her life was a small sacrifice if it meant no one else would die at the hands of this monster. But Dana hadn't calculated how quickly Vega's weight would drag her down.

They landed between the Metro lines. The fall was over before she had a chance to gasp. The ground had rushed up to meet her. Pain erupted in her side, making her wheeze so hard she couldn't find the breath to scream. But she had no time for pain or breath, only fear, as Vega staggered to his knees, crawling for his weapon.

It discharged when she tackled him. Her momentum skewed his aim, though the blood soaking through her side told her not enough. The bullet grazed her ribs. At least that's all she hoped it'd done, but if she didn't beat him to his gun, she'd never find out.

She wasn't foolish enough to wish for another miracle. Two in the span of minutes was more than she could hope for. Today, death had brushed against her, but she shoved back.

Walking side by side with the unliving had its perks. Dana's own mortality never entered her mind as she scrambled to her knees, launching herself onto Vega's back. The only thing that mattered was stopping him. Fate snipped the string of life, not Terrance Vega.

Dana gouged her nails into his eyes. He tried to buck her off like a feral beast but she held tight. The rush of the trains howling by kicked up debris and wind, static energy crackled through the air. She was lost in a cyclone of fury as they both took cheap shots; kicking, biting, punching, laying it all on the line. But in the end only one of them was victorious.

Vega may have dealt her the Tower card, but she refused to let him control her. This was her crossroad. She decided who came with her to the other side.

With the last of her strength she lunged for his discarded weapon, but Vega was faster. His hands wrapped around the gun first and suddenly the struggle was over. Dana panted on her hands and knees, wanting to collapse. She tasted blood, but it didn't matter. It would be over soon.

Instinct made her want to shut her eyes, but she was too stubborn. She'd fought tooth and nail for every moment of her life. She wasn't going to stop now.

Vega staggered to his feet, leveling the gun at her head. That's when she saw it. A sliver of hope granted by her stubbornness. If she'd closed her eyes she might've missed it.

She'd been wrong about the space between the rushing trains. It wasn't that big after all.

Vega took a step back to steady himself. He just needed to take one more. She clawed at the ground beneath her and hurled a spray of dirt and gravel at his face. That was all it took. His hands flew up reflexively, and he stepped back. The train did the rest.

79

THEY WERE GONE. WHEN THE TRAINS FINALLY CLEARED, THE SPOT WHERE Dana and Vega should've been was empty; like the ground had just opened up and swallowed them whole. The soldier in Jake knew better, already scanning the surrounding area.

Spotted more than fifty yards from where he'd expected to find them were two silhouettes. One standing. One not. Jake's heart leapt when he was sure who was who.

"Dana!" He shouted her name, but she didn't look up. "Dana!" He ran toward her, weapon drawn, though it didn't look like she needed his help.

She stood over Vega's mangled body, his gun in her hand. Vega twitched beneath her coughing blood.

What the Christ had happened? It was a damn miracle Dana was still standing, let alone standing over the monster he'd been hunting his entire career.

The lone thought running through Jake's mind was that he intended to keep her alive.

Pumping his legs, he quickly reached them. Vega was worse off than he'd thought, his arm bent at an unnatural angle, his words rasping with pain, but he was still spitting hate. "Do it. Come on. You know you want to."

Dana cocked the hammer.

"Don't!" Jake shouted.

She heard him. She had to. Jake was only feet away from her, but Dana refused to take her eyes off the man in her sights.

"That's it," Vega coaxed. "Pull the trigger. Be the hero."

"Dana, don't do it," Jake warned.

"Shut up!" she yelled; at him or Vega, Jake wasn't sure, but her hands began to shake.

Jake dared another step closer. "Dana, look at me. Don't do this. You'll be giving him what he wants. This is our chance to get real justice for what he did."

Her eyes flicked up, finally catching his. He saw the pain there, and he couldn't look away. "This feels like justice to me."

He shook his head. "It's not. Trust me. There's a price for pulling that trigger." Jake knew it all too well.

"You don't think I know that?" she whispered.

"This is different," he warned. "Self-defense is one thing, but this … If you pull that trigger it'll leave a stain on your soul. One you will feel every day of your life." He didn't want her to pay that toll. "You've already lost so much, Dana." Her parents, Dante, Meredith. Jake hedged another step toward her. "Don't let Vega take another piece."

Vega panted beneath her, his chest spasming as he gasped for air. Jake wanted him to see true justice, the kind only a courtroom could dole out, but by the looks of him, Dana might get her wish anyway. Jake holstered his weapon, determined to talk her down and get Vega medical attention before Death could steal the justice he deserved. "Dana, this isn't you."

Her eyes met his again. "What he did to Meredith … to all those women. The bodies in the landfill, working with Senator Scott, Fuller … he admitted it, Jake. Vega's poison will never stop. Not unless we make it."

"You already have. Look around you. It's over." He'd seen Fuller's lifeless body on the bridge and Vega was halfway there. "We won this time. But if you let Vega make you pull that trigger, you'll always have one foot in the grave with him."

JAKE'S WORDS broke through Dana's fog like the sun burning through the clouds. He was right. If she let her hate rule, she was no better than Vega. Pulling the trigger would rip away another thread of her humanity, unraveling her until there was nothing left.

The harsh reality made the gun heavy in her hands. She didn't want to be the girl in the grave anymore. That stigma had followed Dana her whole life. It was time for a new one. It was time to claw herself back to the living. All the way this time.

Dana lowered the gun, sliding the safety on. In an instant Jake was there, pulling her back from Vega and away from the tracks. She could already hear the sirens. Sagging against Jake's chest, she let his warmth zap the rest of the energy she had left. "Thank you," she whispered.

"For what?" he teased. "You had things under control."

She knew he liked to make jokes when things got real, but this time she wouldn't let him. She'd had one too many brushes with death today. This was her first step climbing back into the light. "Thank you for always showing up." Then she tipped her head up and pressed her bruised lips against his.

80

Dana walked down the courthouse stairs, reveling in the warmth of the sun on her face. Her cuts and bruises had faded away. All but the most stubborn scars were gone, but inside that courtroom each one had been torn open again. A small price to pay considering the verdict: life imprisonment.

Terrance Vega would die where he belonged, behind bars. Dana only wished Claire was here to enjoy the victory.

Jake walked out the double doors, Jenkins by his side. The assistant director still wore a sling on her arm, but the injury had done nothing to tarnish her fiery spirit. Dana waved, grateful for the instrumental role she played in pushing for the harshest sentencing. The agents she lost deserved nothing less.

Jenkins gave Dana a subtle nod, releasing Jake, who jogged down the steps two at a time to get to her. "There she is. Our star witness."

Dana frowned. "I don't know about that."

"Gray, you did good. Enjoy the win for a change."

"You're right." She exhaled a shallow breath. "It just doesn't feel real without her here."

"I know. Claire would've loved to see Vega get what he deserved. But she'll be back before we know it."

"Can we save the celebrating till then?"

"How much longer is she in rehab? Another three weeks?"

Dana nodded. She'd circled the date on her calendar, not that she'd forget. She let Jake put his arm around her shoulders and steer her down the stairs. "Do you think Claire will ever forgive us?"

He huffed. "You're paying for her rehab. I'd say you're further ahead than I am."

It wasn't true, but Dana didn't argue. Claire and Jake had an easier relationship. And his betrayal was smaller. He'd been in on the plan to keep her safe, but Dana had been the one who dosed her tea.

She'd do it again in a heartbeat. It was the reason Claire was still alive. Not just because they'd kept her safe from Vega, but they'd given her the time she needed to heal in the aftermath.

Being the target of a serial killer would be hard for anyone to process. That, coupled with having watched her friend die, proved too much. A few days after the case wrapped, Claire came clean to Jake about just how much she and Sadie had partied at the Grave. That led them to the difficult decision that Claire needed professional help.

"She's tougher than she looks," Jake said, opening the passenger side door for Dana. "She's gonna be okay. We're here to make sure of it."

"I know." Before climbing into the vehicle, she paused to put a hand on Jake's cheek, letting herself steal an intimate moment. There'd been no time for them in the busy weeks following what went down at the Navy Yard. Dana could feel that familiar tension building between them. They both wanted more but were tiptoeing around the how and when. "Claire's going to need to lean on us for support when she gets back."

Jake grinned. "Wouldn't have it any other way."

"I know, it's just that the timing of it ... of us ..." She gently let her hand slip down to his chest. "It might make things harder for her."

"How would us being together make things harder for Claire?"

"I don't know, but departures from the norm make recovery more difficult."

"So you're saying the timing isn't right?"

"I'm saying I don't know. We just need to take things one day at a time."

She felt Jake's chest rise and fall under her touch, his blue eyes searching. She expected anger, but it never came. Instead, he nodded. "I can live with that."

JAKE JOGGED around to the driver's side and slipped behind the wheel.

"Do you still want to come with me to see Meredith today?" Dana asked, glancing at her watch. "Her doctor says visiting hours don't apply to me."

He grinned. "Perk of being a genius witch doctor, huh?"

"Genius librarian," she corrected.

He threw her a wink and started the engine. "I'm glad she's making progress."

"Me too. I think all the time I've been spending there is helping."

"I know it is." He reached over and squeezed Dana's hand. "Do you mind if we make a stop first?"

JAKE STOOD in front of the small white tombstone. This had been a long time coming. It might've taken the strength of having Dana by his side, but the important thing was he was here. It was time to make his peace.

"I never know what to say," Jake muttered.

"Just talk to him, like he's here."

But Danny wasn't here. He hadn't even been in the pine box the Army had flown back from Ghazni. He was nowhere. Gone. Erased. The only part of him that remained was in the blood-soaked sands still blowing across that godforsaken spit of desert.

Jake stared at the name chiseled into the stone. *Daniel Martín Ramirez.*

It made him smile. Danny would've hated that. He could hear him clear as day. *Shit! Not even my mother says my full name!*

Jake's throat tightened. He put his hand to his chest, feeling the dog tags beneath his shirt. He reached for the chain and pulled them out, his fingers pressing into the familiar pattern of stamped letters and braille worn smooth by years of use. The tags had been all over the world with Danny and Jake. They'd collected the same dust, weathered the same storms.

Their tags were a symbol of survival: of who they'd been and how far they'd journeyed to fight their way back. Jake's sat at home in a box, locked up like he wished his pain was. Maybe returning Danny's tag would be the first step in letting some of his agony go.

He undid the clip and slid Danny's tag off the chain before securing the other two back around his neck. Kneeling, Jake pushed the tag into the damp earth in front of the tombstone. "I held on to this for you, brother. I wanted to make sure I didn't forget. But I could never forget." He paused, his throat rolling as he struggled for words. "Every day I try to make it right. Nothing will make it right. But I'm never gonna stop trying." He paused again, collecting himself. "You can have this back now." Jake pushed the dog tag deeper into the earth. "I don't need it anymore."

Standing, Jake reached for Dana's hand, turning back the way they'd come, but she pulled him back. "Would it be okay if I said hello?"

He looked from her to the tombstone in surprise. She wanted to talk to a dead man she'd never met? Curiosity had him bobbing his head.

Dana walked right up, putting her hand atop the stone like she expected to shake Danny's hand. "Hi, Danny. It's nice to finally meet you. Jake talks about you. Not a lot, but maybe we can change that. I bet you've got some great stories about him." She smiled, her fingers running across the etchings in the stone. "I'll look out for him for you."

Then, like it was the most normal thing in the world, she pressed her fingers to her lips before touching a kiss to his tombstone.

The laugh that escaped Jake surprised him.

"What?" Dana asked, slipping her hand into his when she got to his side.

"Nothing." But it wasn't nothing. Jake was standing at his best friend's graveside, fighting the urge to laugh. It shouldn't be possible, but with Dana by his side, it was. "Danny woulda loved you."

He also would've told Jake to stop dragging his feet. He could see Danny's crooked grin. *I'm gonna take her home if you don't.*

Jake shook his head and pulled Dana into his arms. "Screw timing."

He lifted her off her feet, losing himself in her lips. And for once in his life, he didn't hold back.

DID you enjoy reading **Girl in the Grave**? We would love to hear about it! Please consider leaving a review here:

https://www.amazon.com/gp/product/B09DW5MNLR

ALSO BY C.J. CROSS

Dana Gray Mysteries
Girl Left Behind

Girl on the Hill

Girl in the Grave

Stay up to date with C.J. Cross's new releases and download her **free** Dana Gray Prequel, *Girl Awakened* by heading to the link:

Find more C.J. Cross books and follow her on Amazon today!

ALSO BY WITHOUT WARRANT

More Thriller Series from Without Warrant Authors

Dana Gray Mysteries by C.J. Cross

Girl Left Behind

Girl on the Hill

Girl in the Grave

The Kenzie Gilmore Series by Biba Pearce

Afterburn

Dead Heat

Heatwave

Burnout

Deep Heat

Fever Pitch

Storm Surge (Coming Soon)

Willow Grace FBI Thrillers by Anya Mora

Shadow of Grace

Condition of Grace (Coming Soon)

ABOUT THE AUTHOR

CJ Cross grew up in a snowy little Northeast town, cutting her teeth on true crime novels to stave her love of all things mysterious. The writing bug bit her early and she found her way into the publishing world, writing 50+ books under various top secret pen names over the years.

Now relocated to a place where she can safely trade in her snowshoes for flip flops, she's found a reason to dust off her old Criminal Justice degree and she's turned an old passion into a new flame, writing compelling thrillers novels.

When she's not writing you can usually find her drinking bourbon with fellow authors or spoiling her rescue pup.

Sign up for C.J.'s newsletter and download her free **Dana Gray Prequel,** *Girl Awakened***:**

https://liquidmind.media/cj-cross-sign-up-1-prequel-download

Made in United States
Orlando, FL
16 June 2023